The fantasy effect

A NOVEL

PAIGE FIELDSTED

The Fantasy Effect

ISBN Print: 978-0-9985469-1-9
ISBN Digital: 978-0-9985469-0-2

Interior Book Design: Bob Houston eBook Formatting
Cover Design: Judi Perkins of Concierge Literary Designs & Photography, LLC.
Editing: Madison Seidler (www.madisonseidler.com)
Proofing: Chelsea Kuhel

For Mrs. Janet Oman.
The first of many to nurture and encourage my writing, and the best English teacher I ever had. I only wish you were here to see this accomplishment come to fruition.

1

A million thoughts raced through my mind. The tequila made it hard to focus on just one; images of naked skin flashed through my mind like a slideshow stuck on repeat. The thoughts brought a dirty smile to my face as music drummed around me. I was so lost in my own world I hadn't noticed Carson return to the table.

“Chloe!" he yelled over the music, bringing me out of my naughty daydream. I looked up into his eyes, the blue eyes I had just been thinking about, into the face of the man who was the star of all my dirtiest fantasies. Every time I saw him, it was like someone lit my sexuality on fire, taking it from robust and healthy, to an out of control urge that needed to be satisfied immediately.

"Let's dance!" He grinned.

"Where's Quinn?" I asked. Quinn, my husband of four years, best friend of the man who was currently grinning at me devilishly, and the one who received all the benefits of the spark Carson lit inside me.

"Who cares? I think he went outside to smoke."

I shrugged and drained my drink. Carson grabbed my hand and pulled me through the crowd to the center of the dance floor. I closed my eyes and let the music take over, moving my hips in rhythm with the beat. When I opened my eyes and saw Carson, I burst out laughing. He was doing some sort of barbershop quartet move that wasn't in tune with the music, at all. He moved closer and yelled in my ear so I could hear him.

"You don't like my dancing?"

"I love it … it's just a little unconventional." I laughed. He leaned back down and whispered in my ear.

"I save all my best moves for the bedroom."

He pulled back and winked at me, his words sending a new wave of naked images through my mind, causing all the muscles below my belly button to clench. Someone bumped into me, pushing me forward into Carson's arms, his hand accidentally brushing my breast as he caught me, the unintentional touch sending another shockwave through my nether regions. My face pressed into his chest, and I breathed in his cologne as he helped me stand up straight.

"Are you okay?" he asked, his hands still holding my waist.

"Yeah, I'm fine." I looked up into his eyes, which were normally playful, but were now full of fire, desire, and anger rolled into one. For the third time in seconds, my body tensed. God, I needed to get away from this man before I did something I seriously regretted.

But Carson didn't let go of my waist; instead, he starting dancing, more in tune with the music this time. Following his lead, I moved my hips again, his hands guiding my movements. I put my arms on his shoulders and let his body lead mine as we danced, his eyes never leaving my face. I blushed as I watched his eyes travel down my body, taking in my curves before returning to my face with a smile, never breaking the rhythm of the dance.

"You look hot tonight," he yelled over the music. I looked at him intently.

"If I didn't know any better, I'd think you were trying to get in my pants."

"Don't be so sure I'm not." He winked again. I didn't respond, not trusting my alcohol-fueled words to say anything appropriate.

Carson moved his hands from my waist, down the back of my shorts, grabbed my ass, and pulled me close to him. He tucked his hands in my back pockets and held me close, our hips still swaying in unison. I could feel the hardness of his cock pushing against my belly, and I raised an eyebrow at him. He just smiled and kept dancing, the intensity and passion in his eyes growing with every sway of our bodies. I was so wet, an aching need growing between my legs.

I wanted to fuck Carson—had wanted to for years. Quinn's and my spectacular sex life was oftentimes fueled by the fantasies I created and played out in my head—fantasies of the man who was currently grinding on me on the dance floor. My body begged me to take him somewhere quiet and finally do what I had been imagining for years.

The song ended and Carson untangled his body from mine, ran a hand through his hair, blew out a breath, and adjusted his jeans to hide his erection.

"I need some air." He turned and weaved his way through the crowd to the front door, leaving me on the dance floor alone.

I glanced over to our table. Quinn still wasn't there, so I followed Carson outside. Carson avoided my gaze as I joined them. I took Quinn's cigarette and inhaled deeply, hoping it would help clear my mind a little.

"Hey babe," Quinn said, putting his arm around my waist and pulling me close to his side.

Carson watched us awkwardly, and when our eyes met, I noticed the same desire from inside still burning behind the pools of blue.

Quinn ran his fingers under the hem of my shirt; the soft caress on my skin increased the wetness between my legs. I needed one of these men to fuck me now. Or maybe both. The thought took hold in my mind and grew before I could stop it. I had wanted to have a threesome for a long time but Quinn brushed off the idea whenever I brought it up. I had no idea if he would even consider it, especially with Carson, but I was feeling a little reckless, the burning need for sexual release—plus tequila—in complete control of my thoughts and actions.

I leaned up and whispered the idea in Quinn's ear.

"I think we should have a threesome … with Carson … tonight."

He looked down at me, shocked.

"Are you serious?"

"Dead serious … what do you think?" I bit my lip and gave him my sexiest look, not that it mattered to him, he knew he'd get laid tonight, regardless of his answer.

"Do you think that's a good idea?" He lowered his voice. "Carson? I don't know, babe. Is it going to be weird?" He took a long drag of his cigarette and glanced at his best friend.

"I think it'll be awesome," I said, hoping it wasn't a lie.

"You really want to?" he asked again, blowing out the smoke.

"More than anything," I said. Quinn looked at me seriously. I met his gaze, wanting him to know I meant it and wasn't too drunk to be making decisions. Out of the corner of my eye I could see Carson watching our exchange with interest. "Please," I said softly. Quinn knew I wanted to have a threesome, even though the conversation had never gotten far enough to discuss the who or when. I had made my desire very clear in the past, telling him how excited the idea made me. I was hoping that was what he was thinking about as he took another long drag on his cigarette and blew it out slowly, his eyes never leaving mine.

"Okay, I'll do it if he will, but you have to ask him," he finally said. I wanted to jump up and down and clap excitedly, but I kept my composure.

"Thank you." I kissed him on the cheek, turned, and walked over to Carson. He was taller than Quinn, and I had to stand on my tiptoes to whisper in his ear.

"I want you to have sex with us. Quinn and me. A threesome," I whispered. I wanted to make it very clear what I was asking for. Quinn was watching us closely when a guy from the bar asked to bum a cigarette, and the two struck up a conversation. Carson looked down at me, his face only inches from mine.

"I only want you," He lowered his voice to make sure Quinn couldn't hear him.

"You can't have me without him," I whispered back. "Not now at least," I added, unsure what I meant by those words. Carson stared at me, his brow furrowed as his eyes searched my face.

"Please," I whispered again, and before I could stop myself, added, "I've wanted you for so long." The dark passion from dancing returned to Carson's eyes.

"Just think about it for a minute," I said. I ran my hand down his arm suggestively before I turned and walked back to where Quinn was standing. Quinn wrapped his arm around my waist again, tucking a hand in my back pocket.

"So what did he say?" Quinn asked, ending his conversation with the stranger.

"He's thinking about it." I watched as Quinn and Carson looked at each other, having an entire conversation without ever saying anything. The wordless exchange seemed to drag on forever, as my eyes flickered between the two of them. I wanted desperately to be a part of the silent conversation.

"All right, I'm in," Carson said, looking at me again. I let out my breath, unaware I had been holding it, and smiled excitedly.

"Are we going now?" Quinn asked.

"Nah, let's have a few more drinks first," Carson answered before I could respond.

"I'm going to stay out here for a minute," I said. Quinn kissed me before walking back inside with Carson. They waited until they were out of earshot before saying anything to one another—no doubt talking about me and what was about to happen. Carson looked back over his shoulder and smiled at me as they went inside.

I sat down on a bench, the metal cold against my bare legs. I took several deep breaths and looked up into the night sky, any stars dwarfed by the city lights. I smiled into the darkness. Excited, and somehow even more turned on, I thought about Quinn and Carson both touching me, kissing me, fucking me. I closed my eyes and leaned back on the bench, letting my imagination run wild with ideas about how the next several hours might go. I stayed outside until the breeze picked up and I couldn't sit in the chilly night air any longer.

Two hours later, I was soaking wet and nearly shaking with anticipation. The slow buildup of the last few hours had been brutal, my desire growing every minute I spent thinking about what was coming.

We had another drink or two at the bar, Quinn and Carson talking about baseball and soccer, both giving me sideways glances every few minutes. I sat on my bar stool, trying to keep my composure until, finally, Quinn paid our tab and said we could go.

Now back at Carson's apartment, after an awkwardly silent Uber ride, I wondered if I was making a mistake. How would this impact Quinn's and my relationship, or his and Carson's? Would our relationships survive the next few hours? Would I wake up in the morning without tequila and desire coursing through my veins, and in the light of day regret it all?

I stood in the bathroom, staring at myself in the mirror. I had come in here several minutes before, leaving Quinn and Carson with instructions to figure out the logistics while I got ready; I didn't want any awkward fumbling or false expectations to ruin my fantasy. I was still fully clothed when Quinn knocked on the door.

"Babe, are you ready? Are you sure you want to do this?" he said. I heard Carson from somewhere farther away, trying to whisper but clearly failing.

"Don't try and talk her out of it. Come on, man." His words were husky and full of need, the same need I was still feeling. His voice swept away any doubts I had. I definitely wanted to do this.

"Yeah, I'm coming," I called through the door. I pulled my shirt off over my head and shimmied out of my shorts. I ran my hands through my hair, pushed my boobs up a little in my bra, flipped off the light, and opened the door.

The only light on in the room was a bedside lamp, and it looked like Carson had picked up a little since I went in the bathroom. Carson had taken off his shirt and was now just in his jeans, while Quinn was still fully dressed.

I studied Carson. He was slimmer than Quinn, his toned abs begging me to run my fingers over them. His jeans sat low on his hips, the waistband of his boxer briefs sticking out the top, a trail of hair running from his belly button and disappearing into the top of his jeans. I wanted to run my tongue along that trail, wrap my hand and then my mouth around his cock. I bit my lip, a moan almost escaping me at thought. Carson swore under his breath as he looked me up and down.

I was still standing in the doorway to the bathroom when Quinn took my hand and led me into the room. He pulled me close, ran a hand down my back, and squeezed my ass.

"You are so fucking hot," he said. I unbuttoned his shirt, as he trailed kisses down my neck and collarbone and back up again. He whispered in my ear, "There are no rules tonight. We talked about it, and I want this to be enjoyable for you. If it ever gets to be too much, just say stop and we will."

"Okay, thank you," I whispered back, glad they had actually talked about it. I wasn't sure they would.

I finished with his shirt and pushed it off his shoulders, running my hands down his muscular arms as I did. When I looked back up into his brown eyes, I saw a fire I'd never seen before. Then he kissed me, and all that fire came through his kiss. I closed my eyes and ran my hands through his hair, kissing him back with just as much passion.

I felt Carson move behind me; Quinn's kiss had almost made me forget he was here. He moved my hair off my back, kissed my shoulders and the back of my neck, before he unhooked my bra. Quinn broke our kiss and pushed the lace-covered fabric to the floor. He cupped both of my breasts, and ran his thumbs over my nipples. I moaned, the touch sending a wave of pleasure through my body, and my knees nearly buckled.

Quinn grabbed my shoulders, spun me around, and pulled me close to him. I could feel his erection pressing into my back. He reached around and continued playing with my nipples, rolling them between his fingers, tugging on them gently. I leaned back into him, rested my head on his shoulder, and closed my eyes.

Carson stepped closer and ran his fingers softly down my stomach. I opened my eyes and looked at him, his eyes dark with desire and passion, his fingers trailing down the front of my panties and between my legs. I groaned, my body begging for his touch, needing the sexual release that had been building for hours. He kneeled in front of me and pulled off my panties. He ran a hand up my inner thigh, his thumb brushing lightly over my clit, and I thought I was going to fall. I leaned even harder on Quinn, who hadn't stopped playing with my nipples. I closed my eyes again, taking in all the incredible sensations. Then Carson's mouth was on me, his tongue flicking over my clit.

“Holy shit,” I moaned, as he slipped a finger inside me. Quinn kissed my neck, and I thought I might explode. Two mouths and two sets of hands on my body was better than I could have ever imagined. My body tensed, and I could feel my orgasm begin to build.

"Oh my God, yes," I moaned, my breath coming in short gasps.

"Fuck, babe, come for us," Quinn whispered in my ear. "This is so fucking hot."

I moaned again, unable to form words. My mind couldn't focus on anything but the sensation building between my legs. Carson swirled his tongue around my clit, as a second finger dipped inside me. I looked down, Carson's eyes never leaving mine as he teased me with his tongue and fucked me with his fingers. I ran a hand through his hair, so close to the edge. Then it hit me, my mind and body exploding as my orgasm ripped through me. Both Quinn and Carson continued as my whole body shook with pleasure.

Quinn gave my nipples one more long tug before letting them go and resting his hands on my shoulders. Carson sat back on his heels and grinned at me as he put the two fingers that had just been inside me in his mouth and sucked on them gently. God, that was hot. I let my breathing slow, before I moved from my relaxed position against Quinn's chest.

I stood up straight and stepped out of my panties that were still around my ankles. I turned and kissed Quinn softly on the lips.

"You have too many clothes on," I purred and unbuckled his belt. "Take your pants off." I nibbled on his ear. "Both of you." I looked at Carson over my shoulder.

Quinn unbuttoned his jeans and pushed them to the floor. I kissed down his neck, pecs, and stomach as I sunk to my knees on the rough carpet. I pulled his boxers off as I ran my hands down his sides and over his muscular thighs. Keeping both hands on his thighs, I leaned forward and took him in my mouth. Quinn moaned as I moved up and down his shaft. Pulling my mouth back slowly, I took him in my hand and looked over at Carson. He stood a few feet away from us, his boxer briefs and jeans around his ankles, stroking himself as he watched. Our eyes met, and I smiled at him.

"Come over here." I motioned him closer with my finger. Carson stepped out of his jeans, leaving them in a pile on the floor. He closed the few feet between us in a couple steps. I looked up into his eyes and wrapped my other hand around his dick; his head fell back, and he let out a groan. I took Quinn back in my mouth, my hand and mouth moving up and down his shaft in unison.

"Fucking hell, Chloe, that's amazing," Quinn said in a low groan. After a few minutes, I pulled away, still stroking him slowly with my hand. I turned my head in Carson's direction and licked him slowly from the base of his cock to the tip, before I pulled him into my mouth. I felt his body tense as his cock grew harder in my mouth. Carson muttered something incoherent under his breath as he ran a hand through my hair.

I smiled to myself, being in control of not one, but two men, was hot and powerful. I pulled away from Carson, dragging my teeth gently along his shaft as I did so, eliciting a deep growl of pleasure from him.

"Get up." Quinn grabbed my arm and pulled me to my feet. He whispered in my ear, "Get on the bed. I want to you to blow me while I watch him fuck you."

I pulled back in surprise, the grin on his face and lust behind his eyes was something I'd never seen before. Even though he'd been hesitant, he was enjoying this. I kissed him hard and ran my fingers through his short hair. When I pulled away, Quinn roughly pushed me on the bed.

I'd never seen this side of Quinn before, and I loved it. Our sex life was great, but we'd never done anything close to this before. I had been worried about how Quinn would handle this, but now I wondered if maybe this was the beginning of a new, sexy chapter in our lives.

Carson's touch brought me back to the present. I was on my hands and knees on the bed, Quinn in front of me, Carson behind me. Carson's fingers trailed down my spine, across the pucker of my ass and to the pool of wetness between my legs. My breath quickened, and I gasped. I closed my eyes and dropped my head for a minute, before looking up into Quinn's eyes. I took his cock in my mouth, pushing the full length to the back of my throat. Quinn's hand moved to the back of my head, gripping my hair in a fist.

"Oh God, yes," Quinn moaned.

I heard Carson mutter something, but couldn't understand the words. I looked up at Quinn, and he mouthed, "Condoms?" Oh, for the love, this was something they probably should have figured out before this started.

It was Quinn's decision to make. I was on birth control and assumed Carson was clean. Looking at Quinn, I tried to convey my question without actually saying anything, and hoped he got the message. Was he okay with Carson not using a condom? Because I was. Quinn seemed to understand and nodded yes. I wrapped my hand around his cock and began stroking him.

I turned my head back to Carson and nodded. He didn't need further confirmation. He smiled as he gripped my hips with both hands and plunged into me.

"Oh God!" I cried out at the sudden fullness. Carson groaned as he moved slowly in and out of me. This was what I had fantasized about for years, and it was fucking amazing—better than I had ever dreamed.

"Jesus Christ, you feel so good," he grunted. I smiled to myself and pulled Quinn back into my mouth. His groans joined Carson's as his hand once again gripped the back of my head. I reached up and cupped Quinn's balls. He mumbled something, and his head rolled back.

Carson let go of my hips and reached around my body with one hand and circled my clit with two fingers as he fucked me harder. It felt amazing, my whole body clenching, and I could feel another orgasm starting to build. Quinn's cock dropped out of my mouth as I moaned and lowered my head.

"Oh my God, yes, don't stop," I said. Quinn lifted my chin, his eyes meeting mine.

"Look at me, babe … I want to watch you come," he said as he started stroking himself. *Who is this man? And what did he do with …* All rational thought ceased to exist as I my orgasm hit me, and I shattered into a million pieces. My eyes rolled back in my head and closed as Carson continued fucking me, never moving his fingers from my clit, drawing out every ounce of pleasure from my body.

"You're so hot when you come," Quinn whispered, bringing me out of my post-orgasm daze. *Seriously, where has he been the last eight years?*

Quinn nodded at Carson, another wordless exchange happening between them, before they both moved, suddenly leaving me empty and wanting more.

Quinn laid down on the bed and pulled me on top of him. He grunted and grabbed my hips, pushing me up and then pulling me down, his body arched, meeting mine with each thrust.

Carson stood next to me on the bed. I wrapped my hand around his cock, pulled him closer, and took him in my mouth. I could taste myself on him. He closed his eyes and gripped the back of my head, pushing himself so deep, I gagged.

Quinn ran his hand lightly across my body until he reached my ass. He trailed his fingers over the pucker there, before pressing gently with his thumb. I moaned, my mouth never leaving Carson's dick. Carson reached down, his fingertips brushing across my nipples. Quinn's thumb pressed inside me, and I felt like my body was going to explode; there were so many different sensations, it was almost overwhelming, but felt delicious.

I used my free hand to rub my clit, every part of me now stimulated. My body responded almost instantly, and I could feel another orgasm coming on. I closed my eyes and let the sensations wash over me, taking it all in—Carson's cock in my mouth, Quinn's inside me, hands everywhere.

My mind went completely blank as the strongest orgasm I'd ever had hit me, and I cried out in ecstasy. As the waves of pleasure subsided, Quinn moved both hands back to my hips, driving in and out of me faster. I swirled my tongue around the tip of Carson's dick before sucking him back in my mouth. I wrapped a hand around the base of his cock, my mouth and hand moving in unison. He ran a hand through my hair, and I felt his body tense.

"Oh my God, Chloe, I'm gonna come," Carson groaned. His head rolled back as he came, filling my mouth and throat with warm liquid. "Holy fuck," he said, as I pulled my mouth off him, and he stepped off the bed.

Quinn was close, too—I could tell by his breathing—so I clenched around him and swirled my hips, his fingers digging into me as he lost control.

"Oh fuck, yes, babe," he yelled as he came. I continued moving up and down, milking every last drop out of him. Quinn held me in place, his dick still twitching inside me.

"Shit, that was good," he mumbled, when he finally released me.

I rolled off Quinn, my muscles like liquid. My eyes closed as I let my breathing even out. I heard the bedroom door open and close and assumed Carson left. I felt Quinn get off the bed, and heard the bathroom door shut. And then I was asleep.

2

Light streamed through the windows, and I was tangled in the sheets, still naked. Quinn was asleep next to me, his arm draped over my stomach. I blinked several times, trying to wake up and take in my unfamiliar surroundings. We had fallen asleep in Carson's bed. I gently moved Quinn's arm and sat up. I noticed the guys' jeans on the floor beside the bed, and the memories of last night came flooding back. My pussy clenched involuntarily at the flashback, and I smiled. *That was fucking hot,* I thought to myself as I carefully got out of bed.

I found my panties and put them on, grabbed a T-shirt off the floor, and pulled it over my head. I freshened up in the bathroom and tiptoed out of the room. It was still early, and I didn't want to wake anyone, but I needed water. The tequila from the night before left me with a headache and dry mouth.

Carson was asleep on the couch, in only his boxers, a throw blanket covering part of his bare chest. I smiled again, thinking of last night. I filled a glass with water and gulped it down before filling it again. I was halfway through my second glass when Carson whispered in my ear, "Good morning." I spun around, sloshing water on the floor.

"You scared the shit out of me." I hit his arm playfully. "I thought you were asleep."

"Nah, I've been awake for a while. I saw you checking me out." He winked, and I tried not to blush.

"I wasn't checking you out," I said indignantly.

"Uh-huh, sure." Carson looked me up and down. "You're wearing my shirt."

Damn it. Of course it was his shirt I picked up.

"Sorry." I shrugged. "Do you have any coffee?"

"I'll make you coffee if you give me back my shirt." He winked again.

"I don't think so … I can make my own coffee."

"Come on, it's a little cold in here." He rubbed his hands up and down his arms.

"You have plenty of other shirts … put one of them on."

"They're all in my bedroom, and I don't want to wake up Quinn."

"Well, you're not getting this one, so you'll just have to be cold."

"I can think of another way you can warm me up," Carson said seductively, his deep voice sending shivers down my spine. I busied myself with making coffee, trying not to look at Carson. I had thought that last night would help rid my desire, but I was wrong. I wanted him just as badly as ever—maybe even more. I bent over to put the old coffee grounds in the garbage, and then reached up on my tiptoes to get a new filter out of the cupboard. With every move I made, his shirt rose.

"You know you're killing me, right?" Carson said from behind me. He was leaning against the kitchen counter, watching me closely.

"What do you mean?" I played dumb. I reached up into the cupboard again to get two mugs, Carson's shirt rising to reveal my lace panties as I did so. When I set down the mugs, Carson was right behind me. He put his hands on the counter on either side of me, his breath hot in my ear, his erection pressing into my back.

"Do you feel what you do to me?" He pressed himself even harder into my back and ran a hand up the inside of my shirt, his fingers tracing the underside of my breast before he ran them over my nipple. It hardened under his touch, and I let out a moan. I leaned into him as he kissed from my ear, down my neck, and back again. His other hand glided down my stomach and into my panties, and I moaned even louder when he used two fingers to rub circles around my clit.

I heard a door click closed behind us and ducked under Carson's arm, moving to the other side of the kitchen just before Quinn appeared in the doorway, in only his boxers. He rubbed his face and yawned as he walked over to me.

"Good morning babe," Quinn said, kissing me on the cheek. Carson hadn't moved, but he watched me out of the corner of his eye.

"Good morning," I replied, trying to keep my breathing steady. I avoided eye contact with Carson and made us all coffee. When it was ready, I took my mug and headed back toward the bedroom.

"I'm going to take a shower," I said, needing distance. I closed the bedroom door behind me and leaned against it, taking a few deep breaths, to calm my racing heart.

"Shit, that was close," I muttered to myself. I turned the water on as hot as I could stand it and let it run over my face and body, until my heart rate returned to normal. I had just finished washing my hair and was about to turn off the shower when the bathroom door opened and Quinn stepped in, naked and hard. He didn't say a word, but kissed me like his life depended on it. My body melted into his, as he pulled me close, the water running over both of us.

"I fucking love you, Chloe," he said. Then proceeded to show me just how much.

Ten minutes later, I got out of the shower, leaving Quinn to finish up. I towel dried my hair, put on my clothes from last night, and went back out into the living room. Carson had found shorts and a T-shirt while I was gone, and was sitting on the couch with his arms crossed. He didn't look at me when I entered the room.

"Did you just fuck him in my shower?" he spat, the words like venom.

"What?" He couldn't possibly be asking me what I thought he was.

"You heard me," he said, almost glaring at me. "You and Quinn just fucked in my shower." It wasn't a question.

"Are you shitting me right now? In case you forgot in the last twenty minutes, Quinn is my husband; he's the one I'm supposed to be fucking, not you."

Carson finally looked at me. He looked angry, and hurt, and confused all rolled into one.

"What about last night? I thought you 'wanted me so bad,'" Carson said in a mock girly voice.

"You're an asshole. I was drunk and horny."

"You're a liar. You come in here this morning half-naked, practically begging me to fuck you, and now you're going to try and tell me it was nothing."

"Do you hear yourself? Did you hit your head this morning? Did you forget that I'm married to your best friend?"

"So that's it?"

"What the hell do you want from me? What am I supposed to do?" I was asking Carson as much as I was asking myself. This was exactly what I had been afraid of, although I expected the possessiveness from Quinn, not Carson.

I'd known Carson for a just about as long as I'd known Quinn and we'd become friends almost instantly. Not the fake friendship you have with your boyfriend's friends just to keep the peace— a genuine friendship. Our friendship had only grown once his girlfriend dumped him for her CrossFit instructor, and he moved back to Portland.

There had been years of innocent flirting, but I had always thought Carson flirted with me just to mess with Quinn. There had been nothing to suggest Carson had feelings for me, nothing—until now—that had suggested my dirty fantasies were reciprocated. Hell, I was practically one of the guys with those two; the idiots talked about nothing but sports, beer, and vaginas when I was around.

"Unbelievable," Carson muttered under his breath, bringing my attention back to him. He looked hot as fuck when he was mad. I wanted to cross the room, run my hand through his messy blond hair, and kiss him with everything I had. But that wasn't an option right now.

"Fuck you. I'm leaving," I said. I grabbed my purse off the floor and my phone off the kitchen counter and left. I was glad Carson and Quinn had already been together when I'd gotten off work last night. I had been annoyed about having to drive to Carson's to meet them then, but now I was glad I had a way to escape.

I texted Quinn on my way out.

Me: Hey I'm going home. Call me if you need a ride later.

Quinn: Is everything all right?

Me: I'm fine, just have a headache.

Quinn: Are you sure? I can come with you. Just give me a few minutes.

Me: No, I'm really okay. I just want to take a nap.

I needed to get away.

Quinn: Okay, don't worry about me. I'll get a ride from Carson.

Great, more of Carson. I threw my phone on the seat of my car and pulled out of the parking lot, pushing the Bluetooth button on my steering wheel.

"Call Dani," I said. The phone rang for what seemed like an eternity. "Come on, come on, come on, please pick-up," I whispered. Just before I was ready to hang up, Dani answered.

"There better be a damn good reason you're calling me before ten on a Saturday," she said.

"Hello to you, too."

"Seriously, what time is it?" she asked through a yawn.

"It's almost nine … it's not *that* early." I glanced at the clock on my dashboard as I navigated the streets of Portland. "Get up I'll pick you up for breakfast."

"I'm going to hang up now." She yawned again.

"No, please don't," I begged. "I really need to talk to you." The desperation in my voice perked her up.

"What happened?"

"I'm not talking about it over the phone. Get dressed. I'll be there in fifteen minutes."

"Fine, but this better good."

"Trust me, it is," I said before disconnecting the call.

Dani was waiting on the curb when I pulled up, her blonde hair in a messy bun on top of her head. She was wearing yoga pants, flip-flops, dark sunglasses, and a T-shirt with the words "Bite Me" on the front. I couldn't help but smile at the sight of my best friend.

We had met at a dual-college sorority volunteer project freshman year. Dani had been at Oregon, and I was in the fashion design program at Oregon State. We had been paired together to pull weeds at the house we were fixing up. We'd bonded instantly over our hatred for weeds, ditching the project and using our fake IDs to get into a dive bar down the street, spending the rest of the afternoon getting drunk on $3 beers. We'd been friends ever since.

"Good morning," I said a little too cheerily. Dani wasn't a morning person and I could feel her death stare, even through her aviators. She didn't say anything, just pointed to her shirt. I laughed and pulled back out onto the street and headed to our favorite breakfast spot a few miles away.

"Spill the beans," she said five minutes later, the first words she'd spoken since she got in the car. I bit my lip and looked sideways at her. "Come on … out with it. I didn't get up before nine to have to drag information out of you."

"All right, all right." I pulled up to the diner, surprised there was anywhere to park. I turned to face Dani. She sipped on the water bottle she always had with her.

"I had a threesome, with Quinn and Carson." I just ripped off the Band-Aid. Dani coughed and spit her water all over me. "Come on!" I glared at her as I wiped water off my arms.

Dani finally regained her composure, took off her sunglasses, and stared at me, her blue eyes boring into me like lasers.

"Are you fucking serious? Wait, don't answer that, I know you are. Jesus, Chloe, when you said it was going to be good, I didn't think it would be this good. How did it happen? How was it? Oh my God, what happened this morning?" Dani rambled off the million questions I had known she would ask, getting more excited by the second. I'd talked to Dani more about having a threesome than I ever had with Quinn. She knew all about my secret crush on Carson, and all my dirty fantasies.

"Can we get some coffee and food?" I asked. "I promise I'll tell you all the details."

"Fine," she said, getting out of the car. When we were seated in a booth, coffee in front of us, orders taken, she turned and looked at me, a huge grin spread across her face.

"What?" I said.

"I didn't think you had it in you. I mean, you've been fantasizing about Carson for how long now? I didn't think you were ever going to do anything about it."

"Well, I did, and now everything is fucked up."

"Oh, come on, it can't be that bad."

"It's pretty bad."

"Tell me about the sex first. I don't want to be depressed before I even have breakfast."

I smiled as I remembered last night. Carson's mouth on me, two sets of hands on my skin, two cocks in my mouth, three amazing orgasms.

"Earth to Chloe." Dani snapped her fingers in front of my face. "That good, huh?"

"It was fucking amazing. Like, *ohmygod* incredible." A shiver ran down my spine at the memories.

"How many times did you come?"

"Dani!"

"What? It's a legitimate question. And I want to know." When I didn't say anything, she badgered me. "Tell me now, or we can't be friends anymore."

"Three."

She squealed with delight, and I laughed. "Well," she said a few minutes later, her mouth full of breakfast burrito.

"Well, what?" I said, taking a bite of biscuits and gravy.

"Details woman! I need details!" She pounded her fist on the table, and a couple a few tables away looked up at us cautiously.

"Fine." There was no point in arguing with her; I knew she'd win … she always won. She would know if I was leaving something out and would pester me until I finally gave up the details. "First orgasm, Carson went down on me. Second one, he was fucking me from behind, while I sucked Quinn off." A piece of burrito fell out of her mouth as she gaped at me, for once in her life speechless. "Third was with Quinn, me on top, while I gave Carson a blow job."

Of course, the waitress chose that exact moment to walk up to our table. She turned a deep shade of red and stared at me like I had three heads. She held a coffee pot in her hand, but was too stunned to speak. I lifted my cup so she could fill it, and then she was gone, practically running away from our table. Dani burst out laughing, but I was less amused.

"This was definitely worth getting up for," she laughed. I didn't say anything, just watched her over my mug. "What else?"

"What do you mean what else? What else can you possibly need to know?"

"Who initiated it? How did this even happen? Where, when, and how did they come?"

"Oh my God, okay, I get it." I put my hands up in surrender. "You want ALL the details."

"I initiated it. Well sort of..." I relayed the dance with Carson and conversation that followed.

"Damn girl, you've got some balls."

"I didn't think Quinn was going to agree, we've never really had a serious conversation about it and even then, I didn't think Carson would be on board. I still can't believe it actually happened." I leaned back in the booth and let out a sigh. It was something I was always going to remember.

"You didn't answer the last question," Dani said a few minutes later as we got back into my car. I gave her a look that said do-you-really-need-me-to-answer-that, but she just nodded. "Yes, I want all the details."

"Quinn, inside me. Carson, in my mouth. There … happy? You know all the dirty details now."

"Well, I wouldn't say I'm unhappy." She leaned back in the seat, a smug look on her face as I shifted into drive and headed for her house.

"So what happened this morning?" she asked. I sighed again, this time the sound more frustrated than content.

I launched into the story of this morning, leaving no details out this time, this part being where I needed the most help—the entire reason I'd called Dani. We pulled up outside her house before I finished, and Dani turned to face me as I shifted into park.

"Well, you're fucked," she said, matter-of-factly.

"Help me," I pleaded.

"Come inside. We can make some mimosas and figure out this giant mess you got yourself into." I groaned and buried my face in my hands.

Three hours and a bottle of champagne later, we were no closer to figuring out what I should do. Dani had asked a lot of uncomfortable questions, like best friends did. *Was I happy with Quinn? Was this thing with Carson just about sex? Was I going to tell Quinn about what had happened that morning? What did I want?* I'd rattled off the answers in my head: "*yes, maybe, no, I don't know.*"

The truth was, I was happy with Quinn. We'd been together for eight years and had just celebrated our fourth wedding anniversary in May. My love for him had grown and changed over time, so it wasn't the young, stupid, we're invincible kind of love we'd had early on, but it was still there, and felt stronger than ever. I couldn't imagine having a relationship with anyone else. But Carson made me feel things I'd never felt before, got me excited in ways I'd never imagined, and made my heart race and my head spin without even touching me.

"What are you thinking about?" Dani asked when I'd been quiet for several minutes.

"Why I'm never drinking tequila again," I responded dryly.

"Let's be real … this had nothing to do with alcohol. You saw an opportunity to bring a fantasy to life, and you took it." I leaned my head against the back of her couch and groaned. I knew she was right. There was no one to blame but myself.

"And don't sit there and pretend like you regret it either, because you and I both know you'd do it again if you had the chance. I don't really even see what the big deal is here … Quinn isn't the one freaking out. He's the one you should be worried about, seeing as you're married to him. Who gives a shit what Carson wants? He's the other dude, so he doesn't get a say. Tell him to fuck off. He'll get over it."

"Or he won't."

"So what? Then you three don't hang out together anymore, no big deal."

"I like hanging out with them," I said. "I like Carson. I've always liked Carson."

"Obviously…" Dani smirked. "But that's not the point. You might like Carson, but he's just your friend. If shit gets weird, you're going to have to see less of him. You're over-thinking this, Chloe, like you always do. This doesn't have to be the end of the world."

"What about this morning?"

"What about it?"

"Did you forget the part where I almost fucked Carson in the kitchen?"

"Eh." She shrugged. "Almost doesn't count. Call it an extension of last night." I rolled my eyes, but she was right. I didn't owe Carson an explanation. I didn't owe Carson anything.

"You're right," I sighed, admitting defeat.

"Of course I'm right." She smiled. "That's why you love me."

3

It was still early afternoon when I got home. Quinn wasn't there, but I had three text messages and a missed call from him. I text him back, letting him know I was fine, before I changed and went for a run. Forty-five minutes and five miles later, I felt better; running always helped clear my mind. I had taken Dani's advice to heart and was going to stop over-analyzing things. It happened, I couldn't change it, and I sure as hell didn't regret it, so I'd just remember it for what it was—a night of hot sex—and leave all the drama behind.

My plan worked until Quinn got home.

"Hey babe." He put his keys on the table by the door. "Is your head feeling better?"

"What?" I said, a little confused, before remembering my white lie from earlier. "Oh yeah, I took a nap and it feels a lot better."

Quinn came over and wrapped his arms around me, leaning over the couch and kissing my neck.

"I was a little sad when you left so quickly. I was hoping for a repeat," he said playfully.

"Really?" I turned sideways on the couch to face him and turned down the TV.

"Yeah. I'll admit I was pretty skeptical about the whole thing at first, but it was fucking awesome." He walked over to the refrigerator and pulled out a beer. "I think we should do it again."

"No," I said a little faster and harder than I meant to. Quinn looked at me suspiciously, his eyebrows raised.

"It looked like you were having a pretty good time," he shot back. "I thought you'd be all for it, since it was your idea in the first place."

"I did have a good time … a great time actually." I stood and walked around the couch, wrapping my arms around his neck and pressing my body against his. "But I also think it's pretty awesome just the two of us." I kissed him, hoping to distract him with the possibility of sex. He didn't go for it, instead pulling away and walking to the window.

"Carson already said he'd do it again."

"Really?" After the little tantrum he'd thrown, I was surprised he even wanted to see me again, let alone have another threesome.

"Yeah, he's in whenever we want."

"We'll see." I sat back down on the couch and turned the TV back up, signaling the end of our conversation. I didn't want to give Quinn any sort of mixed signals or say something he might misconstrue as a yes. Quinn took the hint and wandered down the hall into our room.

I couldn't believe Carson had agreed to do it again. Part of me wanted to call him right then and ask him what the fuck? Less than twelve hours ago he'd chastised me for fucking my husband, because he apparently thought he had some sort of claim on me, but now he was ready to do it all over again. It didn't make any sense.

I thought about texting Dani, but I knew what she'd say. I tried not to think about it but every time I closed my eyes, I saw Carson's mouth on me, his eyes burning with desire as he fucked me, the look on his face as he came in my mouth.

I bit my lip and leaned back on the couch, looking down the hall to see what Quinn was doing. The door to our bedroom was shut. I slouched down on the couch, spread my legs, pushed aside the fabric of my panties and shorts, and slid my fingers into the wetness. My head dropped back against the couch, and I let out a low moan as I used two fingers to circle my clit. All the memories of last night flooded back—the fire in Quinn's eyes, the way he'd talked dirty to me, the way he'd screamed my name. The feeling of being pleasured in every possible way, over and over again. My toes curled as I felt my orgasm start to build, and I closed my eyes and let my fingers work their magic. Seconds later, I came, biting my lip to keep from moaning.

The next week passed in a blur. As a radio sportscaster, Quinn was busy gearing up for college football season, and Oregon was slated to be one of the top teams in the country again, meaning he was constantly driving to Eugene to do interviews, watch team practice, and meet new players. When he wasn't going to Eugene, he was in Corvallis doing the same for Oregon State. I had barely seen him in the past five days, which was fine by me. Every time we talked, he dropped not-so-subtle hints about what, and who, he thought our weekend plans should involve. I tried my best to ignore him, but he was annoyingly persistent.

My week wasn't any less busy than Quinn's. As a designer for Nike, finalizing colors and patterns for the women's winter line was how I spent my week. I'd gotten home after Quinn was in bed more than once. He produced an early morning radio show, which meant he often went to bed before ten.

By Friday afternoon, I finally had a few minutes of spare time and decided to call my mom. Every time we talked, she tried to convince me to move home. As nice as sunny California sounded, I loved Oregon. It was where I'd met Quinn, and I'd fallen in love with Portland and its quirky neighborhoods, not to mention I loved my job.

"Chloe!" My mom beamed through the phone when she answered.

"Hi, Mom. How are you?"

"I'm a little lonely down here in San Diego without my only daughter."

"Oh … we're starting on the guilt trip early this time?" I teased.

"You hush … I just miss you, that's all. You haven't been home since Christmas."

"I know, Mom. Maybe once the new designs launch, I can come visit. Or you could come visit Quinn and me." In the ten years I'd lived in Oregon, my parents had only visited three times.

"It's cold and rainy there." I imagined her dismissively waving her hand through the air.

"Maybe you can come for Thanksgiving," I offered.

"Oh no, it's your brothers turn to spend Thanksgiving with us, the twins will be here!" Her voice lit up at the mention of her grandbabies. My brother Derek and his wife Adrienne had two-year old twin boys, Max and Dylan.

"Speaking of babies," She said. Oh lord, I rolled my eyes, knowing what was coming next.

"No mom, I'm still not pregnant, not even trying. I still have my IUD in so a baby won't be happening anytime soon."

"You know after you turn 30..."

"Mom, drop it. I didn't call so you could badger me about having babies."

"How is Quinn?"

"He's good—getting ready for football season. He's been so busy."

"Is he finally going to get on board with the rest of the family and support USC this year?"

"No way."

"He's not turning you into a Ducks fan, is he?"

"You know I couldn't care less about football, Mom."

"Are you happy, Chloe?" she asked suddenly. My mom was famous for abruptly changing the conversation and asking uncomfortable questions. The question threw me off, and I took a second longer than normal to answer.

"Yeah, Mom, of course I'm happy. Why would you ask that?"

"Oh, no reason. Just want to make sure my baby girl is taken care of."

"I can take care of myself, but yes, I'm happy," I said, then added, "Quinn and I are very happy." I said it to reassure her as much as to convince myself. All the doubt and emotion from last weekend came crashing back, and suddenly I was worried about the whole situation all over again. "I've got to go, Mom. I've got a work meeting to get to."

I needed to get off the phone before my mom, who I swear could've been an FBI interrogator in another life, caught on to the subtle change in my voice and started pestering me with questions.

"Okay, I love you. Take care of yourself."

"I will. Love you." I set my phone down on my desk, closed my eyes, and took several deep breaths. Just then, my phone pinged with a new text message.

Quinn: I love you babe. I'm sorry we haven't seen each other much this week. Can't wait to spend the weekend with you.

My heart melted a little. Just when I had begun worry that Quinn was mad and avoiding me, he reassured me, without even knowing my concern.

But I couldn't get Carson out of my head. I wanted to kiss him again, feel his hands and lips on my body … I wanted more of everything.

I shook my head to dispel the thoughts, and got back to work, excited to spend time with Quinn later.

I called Quinn from my car on the way home.

"Hey babe," he answered.

"Hey, I'm just leaving work. Do you want me to stop and get some Chinese on the way home?"

"No, it's all good. Carson is on his way over to watch the Marlins game. He said he'd bring pizza."

"Oh, Carson is coming?" I didn't try to hide the disappointment in my voice.

"Yeah, is that okay?"

"Well ... I was really looking forward to spending some time with just you, but I guess that's fine. I brought some work stuff home with me; I can work in the bedroom and let you guys watch the game."

"Okay, yeah, whatever you want," Quinn said and I could tell by his response he was more interested in whatever was on TV than what I was saying.

"Okay, well, I'll see you soon. I love you," I said.

"Love you too," Quinn mumbled. I hung up and swore under my breath. I was suddenly very irritated. What happened to him looking forward to spending the weekend with me? Jackass.

When I pulled into our apartment complex twenty minutes later, I noticed Carson's Jeep was already parked along the curb.

"Great ... this should be fun," I muttered to myself. With my head down, as I walked inside, replying to a work email on my phone, I almost bumped right into Carson, who was still waiting for the elevator, a pizza box in one hand. He grabbed my arm just before I crashed into him.

"Hey Chloe," he said nonchalantly.

"Oh, hey, sorry. Emailing my boss," I said. His fingers were still wrapped around my arm when I looked up into his eyes. Big mistake. While his voice was calm and smooth, there was a storm raging behind his eyes, one that intensified when they met mine.

The elevator dinged, announcing its arrival and cutting our little moment short. Carson released me, his fingers skimming lightly down my arm as he did so. My skin tingled underneath his touch, my breath caught in my throat, and my pussy clenched at the contact. He turned and walked into the elevator, but I just stood there. What the fuck was wrong with me? All he said was hello and I was ready fuck him right there.

"Are you coming?" he said, his arm holding the doors open.

"Oh … yeah." I stepped inside and leaned against the opposite wall, as far away from him as possible. Carson looked at me with an eyebrow raised. I bit my lip and turned away.

"You shouldn't do that," he said.

"Do what?" I responded without looking at him.

"Bite your lip like that." His voice was husky and dripping with sexuality. I wanted to reply with some smartass comment, but being that close to Carson made it impossible to form a functional thought. "It makes me want to push you up against the wall and kiss the fuck out of you."

That got my attention, but the connection between my brain and my mouth appeared to be broken. I opened my mouth, and then closed it again, and then out of habit bit my lip, then let it go when I remembered what Carson had just said.

He took a step toward me, before the elevator dinged again, letting us know we'd arrived on the fourth floor. Carson didn't say anything else; he just winked at me and walked off the elevator. I didn't move—couldn't move. I stood there long enough the elevator doors started to close, and I had to run to get off before it went back down.

"I am so fucked," I mumbled to myself as I walked down the hallway to our apartment. How was I supposed to spend the next three hours with him?

I had managed to regain my composure by the time I reached the door to our apartment, which had been left open by Carson.

"Hey babe," Quinn said. "Perfect timing, Carson just got here."

"Oh, hey Carson," I said, like we hadn't just seen each other. Carson raised his already open beer at me and smiled as he grabbed a slice of pizza. Quinn walked across the room and planted a kiss on my lips. He pulled me close, lengthening the kiss as he ran his hand down my back. I could see Carson over his shoulder, staring at us. I pulled away from Quinn. I needed to get away from them and this uncomfortable situation.

"Let me change into something more comfortable," I said and walked away. I closed the bedroom door behind me and stripped off my dress and heels. I put on some yoga pants and a T-shirt, and pulled my hair into a low knot, then took a few deep breaths and went back out into the kitchen.

In the few minutes I'd been gone, Quinn had turned the game on and both men were sitting on the couch, pizza and beer on the coffee table in front of them. Thank God … I wasn't up for any awkward conversation.

I grabbed two slices of pizza and a beer and sat down at the kitchen table and listened to them yell at the TV. When my pizza was gone, I took my beer and excused myself to do some work, not that either of them noticed, let alone cared.

Three hours later, I was still working when Quinn knocked on the doorframe to our bedroom.

"What's up?" I said, setting down the papers in my hands.

"Carson and I are going to grab some drinks at the Rusty Nail. Do you want to come?"

"Is the game over?" I hadn't realized I'd been working for so long.

"No, but it's a blowout and we're bored."

"I still have some work I need to get done before next week, so I'll stay here and keep going. That way I won't have to work tomorrow, and we can hang out."

"Are you sure?" he asked. I could hear the disappointment in his voice and didn't have to wonder what he was hoping would happen.

"Yeah, you guys go have fun."

"All right," he said, defeated. "I love you."

"I love you, too."

4

I awoke the next morning, tangled in the sheets and Quinn's arms. I tried to move, thinking I could get out of bed without waking him, but he tightened his arms around me and pulled me close.

"I'm already up," he whispered in my ear before he nibbled on it, pressing his erection into my back to let me know his words had a double meaning. He slid his hands under my tank top, cupping each of my breasts. He ran his fingers lightly over my nipples, and they hardened under his touch before he tugged gently. I moaned and rolled over to face him, taking his face in both my hands and kissing him like it was the last thing I'd ever do. I was determined to fuck the idea of another threesome out of him—remind him why we were enough, just the two of us. I ran a hand down his stomach toward his boxer shorts, but he grabbed my hand and stopped me.

"Not yet baby." He kissed me lightly and pulled my tank top over my head, leaving me in just my panties. "Lay back," he commanded. Quinn rarely told me what to do in bed, but it was hot as fuck when he did.

"Put your hands above your head," he said. I complied, stretching my body out along the bed. "Now, don't move."

Quinn hovered above me, kissing me lightly on the lips, my cheek, my neck, and down my collarbone, but when he reached the top of my breasts, I squirmed. He pulled back.

"I said don't move." He started again, working his way from my lips, down to my nipples. When he sucked one into his mouth, I squirmed again, arching my back off the bed and moaning. He pulled back again. "I'm gonna start over every time you move," he said, and when I made a pouty face, he added, "I've got all day."

He started again, and this time I held perfectly still. My breathing quickened, and my heart started to race as he moved farther down my body. By the time he reached the top of my panties, I thought I was going to explode, the wetness between my legs growing with every kiss.

Quinn looked up at me, his eyes meeting mine as he continued his descent, and when he nibbled my most sensitive spot, it took every ounce of control I had to hold still. The combination of my panties and Quinn's mouth created a delicious friction that drove me wild. He never took his eyes off mine as he pulled down my panties.

Then he resumed his slow torture, kissing from the inside of my knee up my inner thigh, skipping over the place that was screaming for his touch, and starting the same pattern on my other leg. When he reached my core, he licked lightly, and I lost it. My head rolled back, and I groaned. I reached down and ran a hand through his hair.

"Put your hands above your head or I'll stop," he said, slightly lifting his head.

"Please don't stop," I breathed, putting my hands back where he demanded. Then his mouth was on me again, his tongue slowly circling my clit. When his tongue dipped inside me, I cried out, "Oh my God, Quinn."

"I love how wet you get for me." His words were a warm tickle against my sensitive skin. It was seriously so hot when he talked dirty to me. I was ready. I needed him inside me so bad it almost hurt.

"Quinn, please," I whispered.

"Please what, Chloe?"

"Please fuck me."

"Not yet. I'm gonna make you come with my mouth first." He flicked his tongue over my clit, and my whole body shuddered. "You like that?"

"Oh my God, yes," I moaned. "Don't ever stop." He did it over and over again, my body climbing higher with each flick of his tongue. When he wrapped his lips around my clit and sucked, I lost it. I screamed his name as my orgasm washed over me, my back arching off the bed as he continued sucking, drawing my pleasure out until I collapsed on the sheets.

He kissed his way back up my stomach, over my breasts, leaving a trail of kisses along my collarbone and neck before gently kissing my lips again.

"Good morning." He smiled.

"That was one hell of a good morning," I said, still breathless.

"I'm just getting started." I screamed as he wrapped his arms around me and rolled over, so I was on top of him, the hard length of his cock resting against the crack of my ass.

"You're so beautiful," he said, his hands roaming over my body. Without warning, he lifted my hips and shifted so he was at my entrance. I tried to shift, move myself down, but he held me firmly in place, denying me the fullness I craved. He moved in an inch, then back out again. It was pure torture.

"Quinn," I begged. He ignored me and continued to tease me with just the tip of his cock. "Quinn, please." I tried and failed to get out of the death grip he had on my hips. He stopped moving altogether, holding completely still, and smiled up at me like he had won some sort of contest. Then he slid into me.

"Oh fuck yes," I cried out as he pulled out again. He released his grip on my hips, and I moaned as I sank back down on his cock, burying him inside me. He groaned when I did it again.

"You feel so good," he said, moving his hands from my hips to cup my breasts and rub my nipples with his thumbs. My head rolled back, and I closed my eyes.

"Oh my God, babe, that feels so good," I breathed. I shifted and picked up the pace, my breasts bouncing up and down in his hands.

He reached between our bodies and pressed his thumb against my clit. My body tensed involuntarily at the contact, as pleasure started to build in my core. I closed my eyes and let my orgasm wash over me. Quinn grabbed my hips again and continued thrusting, moaning my name as he followed me over the edge. When he finally stopped moving, I collapsed on his chest. I could feel his heart beating rapidly against mine. I rolled off him, my body sinking into our mattress.

When my breathing had returned to normal, I sat up on my elbows and looked at him, his brown hair getting long, sticking out every which way. I smiled and ran my hand through it, making it stick up even more. He opened one eye and looked at me.

"That was fucking amazing," I said.

"I know." He smirked. I hit him in the stomach with a pillow.

"What if I was faking it?" I raised an eyebrow at him.

"You weren't; you're not that good of an actress," he said.

"You're right. I forgot I was married to a sex god." My voice dripped with sarcasm as I got out of bed.

"Oooh, yeah, that's a good way to describe me." He stretched out and put his arms behind his head, his wide shoulders and muscular biceps flexing. He laid there, smiling, his naked body on full display. "Quinn, the god of sex, I like it."

"Of course you do." I laughed and rolled my eyes. "I'm getting in the shower. Try not to woo any unsuspecting women into our bed with your incredible sex powers while I'm gone." I could hear him laughing as I shut the door to the bathroom and turned on the water.

Quinn and I spent the day together, running errands, perusing local farmer's markets, and just hanging out. We talked about everything we'd missed all week.

With football season starting in three weeks, Quinn's Saturdays would soon be filled with pre-game analysis, game coverage, and post-game interviews. I was lucky if I saw him at all during the season; he often left before I was awake, and when the games started late, he wasn't home until well after I'd already gone to bed. I hated it when I didn't get to see him for days on end, but he loved his job, and college football was his favorite.

The August weather was warm and sunny as we strolled along the river, hand in hand.

"Are you excited for football season?" I asked, well aware I might be opening the door for a monologue about football.

"Yeah, it's going to be a good year..." He carried on excitedly about things I didn't understand, and I started daydreaming. "But ... I'm going to miss spending days like this with you." He lifted my hand and kissed it. "It's really too bad you don't like football; you could come to some of the games with me."

"I have much better things to do with my Saturdays than watch college dudes run each other over and throw a football around."

"Like what?"

"Oh, you know, binge watching *Keeping up with the Kardashians,* painting my fingernails, helping Dani scout for men ... girl stuff." I shrugged, and he laughed.

"Yeah ... I'll just stick to getting paid to watch football while you do all that."

"See, it works out perfectly then."

We fell into a comfortable silence as we walked. We got back to Quinn's Subaru a few minutes later and were halfway home before either of us spoke again.

"Soooo, I have a question to ask you," Quinn said, his voice full of nerves. I didn't like where this was going. Quinn was never nervous or shy; it was one of the things I liked most about him. "I know you already said no, but I was thinking—"

"The answer is still no," I interjected.

"Now wait, hear me out. You don't even know what I was going to ask."

"Quinn, I'm not dumb, but fine, I'll listen. Although, you should know my answer will probably still be no."

"Just listen," he said. I folded my arms across my chest and huffed out a breath. This was the last thing I wanted to talk about, especially after the amazing day we'd had so far.

"I always thought you were crazy for wanting to have a threesome, but now I know why people do it. It's hot."

"Is it not hot when it's just us?" I spat out.

"Don't try and twist this around … of course it is. But seriously, babe, it never hurts to spice things up a bit."

"No," I said angrily. "And just so you know, we-have-great-sex-but things-could-be-spicier, isn't a good argument."

"Chloe," he said matter-of-factly. "You loved it. I know you did. I didn't think I would, but I loved it too, so why not? Besides, Carson—"

"Why does it have to be Carson? Why couldn't it be someone else?"

"Just some random dude?"

"Or girl."

"You just want to pick someone up at a bar or what? How would you go about finding some random stranger who wants to have a threesome? Never mind, it doesn't matter, because we're not doing that. I don't want to bring someone we don't know into this. What if they're psycho?"

"You know people do this all the time, right? There are social media sites and clubs specifically for this purpose. It's called swinging."

"It's just easier with Carson. He's into it, I'm into it, and whether you try to deny it or not, you're into it too," he said, and I let out a groan. "What's your problem anyway? I don't get it."

Other than I want nothing more in the world than to be fucked completely senseless by your best friend, nothing. Everything is peachy, I thought to myself.

"Nothing," I huffed. "Can we just talk about something else?" I knew I was overreacting, but I didn't have a good reason for not wanting to do it again—not one I could tell Quinn anyway.

Quinn mumbled under his breath and turned up the music.

He didn't drop it, though. He was fucking relentless—every single day the same conversation. He brought it up, I told him no, we both got pissed. To help make his point, he'd refused my advances twice since our conversation on Saturday.

When I got home from work Friday night, Quinn had cooked dinner, set the table, and poured the wine. I was so impressed with his scallops and wild mushroom risotto I didn't even question his motives.

We made it all the way through dinner and dessert—ice cream from a shop down the street—and were sitting on the couch on our patio, my feet in Quinn's lap, before he brought it up.

"Chloe," he said, rubbing his thumbs in circles on the bottom of my foot. "Can we ... I ... please," he stumbled over the words. I rolled my eyes at him, he'd asked me the same question every night for a week, but now he suddenly couldn't get the words out?

"You're never going to drop this, are you?" I took a long sip of my wine.

"I probably would, eventually, but it might be a long, cold winter before that happens." He smiled and winked, like he thought it was funny he was withholding sex. It wasn't.

"You're an ass."

"Yeah, but you love me anyway."

"Right now I'm not so sure about that," I said. He didn't say anything, just looked at me, his big brown eyes begging me to say yes. "Fine." I glared at him. "But this is not going to be a regular thing."

"Whatever you say, babe," he said, grinning.

"I'm serious." I tried to sound annoyed, but secretly I was a little excited, too. Maybe this could work? We could just have threesomes with Carson—I'd get to keep my marriage, and have sex with the man of fantasies. It might all work out.

5

Quinn

I had always thought Chloe was crazy for wanting to have a threesome, but I was wrong. It was unbelievable, and now it was all I could think about. It made me hard just imagining the look on her face when she came. I loved watching her get so excited about it. I didn't understand why she was so against it now. For years, she'd been asking me to have a threesome, and now that we had, she was acting like it was the worst experience in her life. Which was bullshit, too. We had a great sex life, but I'd never seen her as turned on as she had been that night. I'd never seen her lose herself so completely in the moment.

Was it weird that it was my best friend who'd helped bring out that side of her? I shook my head. It wasn't weird; Chloe and Carson had always been close. It was probably amazing because of their comfortableness with one another. I loved that they were friends. I'd had friendships dissolve because of a girl before, and I was glad that hadn't happened with Carson and me.

Carson was the brother I'd never had. I was the youngest of four and the only boy. He was new at my junior high school, and I'd noticed he had an Oregon Ducks notebook. I'd instantly gone into sports mode and started talking all about the season.

When he'd confessed he didn't actually know anything about Oregon, but that his grandma had just bought him the notebook so he'd fit in, it only made me more eager to tell him everything I knew. From that moment on, we were inseparable. He spent more time at my house than he did his own. We had roomed together our freshman year in college, but then Carson transferred to business school in Portland.

When he'd moved to Chicago for fucking Jenna, it was the most time we'd spent apart since we were thirteen. I was glad he was back, although I wasn't happy he had to find out the hard way how big of a bitch Jenna really was. I'd told him it was a mistake to move with her, that she wasn't good for him. But he'd loved her and I couldn't argue with love. And when he'd moved back to Portland after catching Jenna fucking their CrossFit instructor, I'd let him crash on our couch for two weeks.

My mind floated back to Chloe. Maybe it was weird that we had included Carson in our sex life. But to find someone else, and go through all the logistical bullshit again—no thanks. It was easier with Carson, and he sure as hell didn't seem to mind. Something just wasn't right about Chloe refusing. She never did give me a good reason why. Maybe I shouldn't have pushed her. But I was too excited to back out now.

6

Halfway through my Sunday afternoon run, my headphones pinged in my ear with a text alert. I pulled my phone out of my sports bra and stopped running. What the hell? Carson never texted me.

Carson: Are we really going to do this again?

Apparently, the message about our threesome had been relayed.

Me: I thought you were on board? That's what Quinn told me.

Carson: I told him I'd do it if you agreed, but I didn't think you would.

Me: Well maybe one of us should have had the balls to tell him no.

Carson: What am I supposed to say? That I didn't enjoy it? Because I did. I loved every fucking second.

Before I could respond, Carson sent another message.

Carson: I want to taste you again, listen to you scream as you come, run my hands over every inch of your body.

Me: You have to stop. I'm married.

Carson: You started this. I was perfectly content, and then you had to go and bring me into your crazy sexual fantasy. Now I want more.

I wanted more, too, but that wasn't the point. We were playing a dangerous game here—one I wasn't sure anyone could win.

Me: Goddamn it, Carson! Can't we just drop it and go back to the way everything was before?

Carson: Sorry babe. That ship has sailed.

Me: Why can't we just enjoy it this way then?

Carson: Because I'm not Quinn. I don't like watching you get fucked by someone else. Not when I want you to myself.

His words shocked me. I stared at my phone for a long time before I decided I wasn't going to engage in that conversation with him.

Me: Then tell Quinn no … that'll solve all our problems.

Carson: Will it? It wouldn't change anything about how I feel.

Me: No one cares about your feelings, Carson. We're doing this one more time, and then that has to be the end. Of everything. We can't do what you're suggesting.

Carson: Whatever you have to say so you can sleep at night. See you Friday.

I screamed out loud in frustration, and a guy on the street skirted around me. Why did Carson suddenly want me? Why did he think he could have me?

In a handful of text messages, he managed to make me incredibly horny and very pissed off at the same time. I turned up my music and ran even faster, letting the frustration and anger fuel me for the next twenty minutes.

By the time I got back home, my top was plastered to my body with sweat, my hair was wet and matted against my head, and my lungs and muscles were screaming. But the only thing I'd accomplished was making my body sore—my mind still clouded with anger and sexual frustration. No matter what I tried to tell myself, Carson was right: this whole situation was my fault, and to make matters worse, it hadn't even satisfied my desire. I still wanted him just as much as ever. I got turned on at just the thought of him, my body refusing to listen to the voice in my head that kept telling me I should forget about Carson and move on.

For a long time, Carson and I had had a strange, flirtatious relationship. Quinn either never noticed or didn't care, but somewhere along the way the flirting had turned into full blown fantasies. Quinn often reaped the benefits without knowing that many times it was thoughts of his best friend that fueled my lust. But they had been just fantasies, some improbable idea I'd had in my head. Now everything felt different. It wasn't just an exciting idea anymore; I'd made it a reality, and I knew Carson felt the same way. And that changed everything.

And even after eight years, Quinn still gave me butterflies, but with Carson it was different. The sexual connection I felt with Carson, a connection I had thought was just in my head, was unlike anything I'd ever experienced before. It was a pull I wasn't sure I could resist. God knows I wanted more of Carson and more of everything that'd happened a few weeks ago. I was obsessed—now, more than ever—with ideas of what could happen.

I thought of Carson as I stripped off my running clothes, thought of what his hands, mouth, and cock could do to me as I touched myself in the shower; and that night, when Quinn made love to me, I imagined it was Carson.

7

As the week passed, my mind grew increasingly conflicted about our impending ménage a trois. I had good reason to be apprehensive. I couldn't ignore the fact that this could all blow up in my face.

I was supposed to meet Quinn for dinner after work on Friday, and then have drinks with Carson before the main event. But as the clock ticked closer to five, the pit in my stomach grew. I felt like I was going to be sick.

I was still sitting at my desk at 5:45, staring at my computer screen and the color schemes I'd been looking at for the last two hours, when my phone pinged with a new text message.

Quinn: Can't wait to see you soon.

Me: I'm running a little late. See you soon.

I ignored his response, knowing he'd be mad, and texted Dani instead.

Me: You free tonight? I need to hide out for a while.

Dani: What are you running from the cops or something? ;)

Me: Or something. I'll bring food and alcohol.

Dani: Sure, I'll be here.

Me: Thanks, I'll call you when I'm on my way.

I thought about texting Carson, telling him I couldn't do it, but I didn't need both him and Quinn blowing up my phone. I set an alarm on my phone for 7:30, put it on silent, and got back to work, finishing up the designs I'd been ignoring. When my alarm went off, I had four texts and three missed calls from Quinn.

I was just getting ready to call him back when my phone buzzed again, his face filling my screen.

"Hey," I answered.

"Where are you?"

"I'm sorry, this is a freaking nightmare. The color scheme we had picked for the winter line got rejected, now we have to go back to the drawing board. They want new mock-ups and colors by Monday." I was surprised how easily the lie rolled off my tongue.

"So you're not coming? At all?" Quinn blew out a frustrated breath, and I could tell he was pissed, but I didn't care.

"I don't know, I think it's going to be a pretty late night here. I'm really sorry," I lied again.

"We're not supposed to meet Carson until 10:30 … call me if you get done before then," he said, a tiny bit of hope in his voice.

"I will," I said, even though I had no intention of calling him. I hung up the phone, turned off my computer, and left work.

Half an hour later, I knocked on Dani's door, holding up the pizza box and six pack of beer when she answered. She grabbed the beer and held the door open for me, but waited until we were both sitting on her back deck before she said anything.

"So are you going to tell me what exactly you're hiding from?" she said, taking a huge bite of pizza.

"Quinn and Carson."

"Oh Jesus." She rolled her eyes at me.

"What?" I said through a mouth full of pizza.

"I thought we figured this all out ... how did you screw it up now?"

"Who said it's my fault?" I said. She just raised her eyebrow at me. "Fine, it's probably my fault. Quinn kept pestering me to have another threesome, and I agreed, but then when it was time to meet them tonight, I just couldn't do it." I sighed and took a long drag from my beer.

"Okay, so what is the real problem here?" She set down her food and turned to face me. "I don't understand. You and Carson have flirted for years, and it's never been a problem. This is what you wanted! How many times have we talked about you guys having a threesome? Like, a million, and now Quinn's on board, and you're being a pussy ... what gives?"

"I don't know," I whispered. Dani was the first person I'd ever told I wanted to have a threesome, and the only person I'd told about my crush on Carson. She was the one that first suggested I should just have a threesome with Carson and Quinn.

"Don't bullshit with me. I know you better than that. What the fuck, Chloe?" I looked at her sideways, hating and loving that she knew me so well. She folded her arms and waited for my answer.

"Carson has come onto me twice since last time. Not just flirting. It's like he all of the sudden doesn't give a shit that I'm married, and says whatever is on his mind, and let me tell you, what's on his mind is not just innocent flirting."

"Soooo ... what's the problem? Doesn't that make it hotter?" Dani asked.

"No! The problem is I'm afraid of what will happen if we keep doing this. I don't know if I can avoid his advances forever," I said, then added in a whisper, "I don't know if I want to."

"So let me see if I've got this right ... you're afraid if you have another threesome, it's going to lead to an affair with Carson? And you think you might want to have an affair with Carson?"

"Basically, yes." I sighed again. There it was, out in the open, the thoughts that had been rolling around in my head for over a week now. It sounded so much worse when she said it out loud. Did I want to have an affair with Carson? I dropped my head in my hands and took in a few deep breaths.

"So I guess you just ignored what I said about Carson not getting to dictate the rules?" Dani said.

"What? No, I didn't ignore you." My head snapped up, and I looked at her.

"But you didn't tell him this was on your terms or not at all?"

"Well ... no."

"Then this is definitely your fault."

"Thanks, that makes me feel much better," I said sarcastically.

She snorted.

"You shouldn't have come here if you wanted someone to make you feel better."

"You know how I feel about Carson. I've had a crush on him forever. I just don't know if this is a good idea."

"We're not in junior high, Chloe. We don't make decisions based on who we have *crushes* on. I probably have crushes on, like, five guys right now, but that doesn't mean I'm going to make irrational decisions based on some silly infatuation."

"So you think I should go do it?"

"I think you should stop being a little bitch and be the Chloe I know," she snapped. "Stop playing the victim here. Be the badass chick my best friend is. Do what you want, and fuck everyone else. Don't let Carson make the rules; don't be such a fucking pushover."

"Are you done?"

"No, I'm not done…" Then she paused. "Okay, yeah, I guess I'm done. The point is this..." she waved her hand up and down in my general direction, "is not the Chloe I've always known, and I kinda liked her."

I looked at my phone. I still had time to meet Quinn and Carson if I wanted. I stared out into the darkness. Is that what I wanted? An image flashed across my mind, me kneeling between Carson and Quinn. The power I had felt in that moment washed over me, and I snapped out of my daze.

"Okay, I've got to go." Energy surged through my veins as I set down my beer and stood up. Dani stood with me, and I wrapped my arms around her. "Thank you," I whispered in her ear.

"No problem. I'll always be here to kick your ass back into shape when you need it."

"I don't even know why I like you," I called over my shoulder on my way out. "I'll call you tomorrow."

"Can't wait," Dani said sarcastically. I jogged down her front steps and to my car.

I waited to call Quinn until I was headed in the direction of our apartment in Hillsdale. He didn't answer the first time, so I tried again. It rang five times before he picked up.

"Hello," he said flatly. He was still mad.

"Hi baby," I said sweetly, even though I wanted to snap at him. For all he knew, I really was at work, and he shouldn't be this mad, but getting in an argument wouldn't get us anywhere right now. "I'm sorry about dinner, I really am, but what about the rest of the night? Do you still want to?"

"Hold on a sec." I heard muffled voices through the line. He must've met Carson early when I bailed. I couldn't tell what they were saying, but it was taking forever, and I worried if they took too long to decide, my surge of confidence would disappear.

"Yeah, fine, we can still do it," Quinn came back on the line.

"Don't sound so excited about it," I snorted. "If you don't want to, it's fine."

It wasn't fine; I was already excited and ready for what was coming.

"No," he said, a little rough. "No, I still want to ... I—" Quinn's sentence was cut-off, and Carson's voice came on the line.

"I want to, too," Carson said, his voice thick with restraint. I didn't know what else he wanted to say, but I knew he couldn't say it in front of Quinn.

"You do?" The words popped out of my mouth before I could stop them.

"Yes."

I couldn't say anything else, the raw need in his voice left me speechless. Heat pooled in my core, and my nipples stood at attention. Just one word from him, and I was turned on.

"Chloe?" he said after a few moments of silence.

"Yeah, I'm still here," I said. "Okay, let me talk to Quinn."

Quinn's voice came back over the speakers in my car. "So, we're on?"

"Yes. Give me an hour, and then meet me at our apartment. I'll be ready."

An hour later, I had candles lit in every room in the apartment. I wasn't sure where the action would happen, so I had gone a little overboard with the candles. I had made the bed I'd neglected that morning, fluffed the throw pillows on the couch, and closed all the curtains.

I'd taken my dark brown hair out of the loose braid it had been in earlier, and it fell in pretty waves down my back. I'd changed into a pair of black lace panties and matching push-up bra, and was wearing a teal silk robe.

Even though I knew what to expect, I was nervous, and my stomach dropped when there was a knock on the door. I drained my second glass of wine, the red liquid warming my throat as it went down, but I didn't move from my spot in the kitchen.

Quinn opened the door a crack and peeked inside.

"Chloe? Are you ready?"

"Yes." His eyes narrowed when he saw me leaning against the kitchen counter, and he swallowed hard. His eyes traveled up my body before they met mine. I licked my lips and smiled. Quinn leaned his head back through the open door and said something I couldn't hear, before they both came inside.

Carson shut the door behind him, and I lifted my head at the click of the lock, my eyes meeting Carson's. His gaze was full of fire—lust, desire. Need burned behind his blue eyes. I stepped toward them and pulled the tie on my robe, the silky material falling open. Carson ran a hand through his blond hair as his eyes raked over my body, taking it all in. Quinn made a noise in his throat that was somewhere between a groan and growl.

I ran my hand through Carson's hair, and then down his cheek and across his chest before I pulled Quinn's head down for a kiss. I gave him just a taste before I pulled away and continued walking down the hallway. I let my robe slide off my shoulders, the cool fabric pooling around my ankles.

"Let's go to the bedroom," I said over my shoulder. When neither of them moved, I reached a hand behind my back and undid the clasp of my bra, letting it fall to the floor with my robe.

I looked over my shoulder again and smiled. "Coming, boys?"

Dull light was shining through the curtains when I woke up the next morning. I stretched and rolled over in bed, muscles I didn't know I had complaining loudly at my sudden movements. It was the good kind of sore, reminding me of the incredible night I'd had. I had expected to see Quinn still asleep next to me, but instead, found a note tucked under his pillow.

Went golfing with some guys from work. I'll be home before noon. Love you.

What time was it? I rolled back over and looked at my phone. 10:33. I didn't know what time it was when Carson had finally left last night. I leaned back onto my pillows and pulled the blankets around my naked body.

Last night had been even better than the first time; no awkward conversations about condoms or nerves to get in the way—just raw lust feeding the fire that burned between the three of us. Everyone knew their role and had played it well. If Carson had been uncomfortable, he certainly hadn't shown it, and Quinn had come even further out of his shell than before. I loved this new, sexual side of him.

My phone buzzed on my nightstand. I had fully expected the incoming text to be from Dani, wanting to know all the dirty details from last night. Butterflies formed in my stomach when I saw it was from Carson.

Carson: Meet me for coffee in the morning.

I stared at the screen for a long time, trying to formulate a response. Three little dots informed me that Carson was typing another message.

Carson: 9 a.m. at the Starbucks down the street from you.

Quinn didn't normally work on Sundays, but with college football season kicking off later in the week, his station was doing a big show the Sunday before, so he had to be there at seven AM, and probably wouldn't get home until late afternoon.

I swung my legs over the side of the bed and locked my phone. I wasn't going to respond. Anger washed over me as I turned on the shower. Who the fuck did Carson think he was? He didn't get to demand that I meet him. And why did he want to meet me anyway, when he knew Quinn would be at work? There was no way meeting Carson alone would end well.

"Fuck you, Carson," I mumbled under my breath. "I'm not playing this game." But there was a small part of me that came alive at the thought of meeting him; I knew the risk and wanted to see if the reward was worth it. I shook my head again … I wasn't going down that road. I'd done what Dani had said, and taken back the control, so I wasn't going to willingly hand it back over to Carson.

After my shower, I made myself a late breakfast. It was a gloomy day—dark and overcast—the clouds heavy, like any second they might open up and start pouring. Typical Portland.

I painted my toenails while I let my hair air dry, and then put on some light makeup. I was just pulling on my jeans when Quinn got home.

"Hey, beautiful." He came into the bedroom and gave me a kiss.

"How was golfing?" I pulled a tank top over my head and layered it with one of the dozens of Nike jackets I had.

"Shitty. It was cold, and I sucked at driving."

"Well," I walked closer to him, wrapped my arms around his neck, and kissed him again, "if it makes you feel any better, you definitely didn't suck last night." I pulled his head down for another kiss, this one deeper and full of passion.

"Oh really?" He rested his forehead against mine.

"Yeah, in fact, I'd say you were pretty awesome." My heart beat a little faster as the memory of last night washed over me.

"I am a sex god, remember?" He smirked and planted another short kiss on my lips before pulling away. I rolled my eyes.

"Oh jeez," I laughed.

"You said it first, not me." He collapsed on the bed and stretched his arms behind his head. "Let's take a nap." He winked.

"I just got up, like, an hour ago," I said, even though I knew he didn't actually want to sleep. "I'm going to go get some groceries for this week."

"All right, fine, I guess I'll just nap alone," he whined.

"You do that." I leaned down and kissed him before I left. "I'll be back later.

I sent Dani a text on my way down the elevator.

Me: You were right. Being in control is way more fun. Last night was awesome!

Dani: I'm always right, but you're welcome.

Me: Ha, I didn't say thank you!

Dani: Well, you should have, so you're welcome. :)

Me: Wanna go to a yoga class with me in the morning? There's a class at 9 just down the street from me.

I figured if I had plans, I wouldn't be tempted to give in and meet Carson for coffee. I started my car and waited for her response.

Dani: You want me to get out of bed at 9 a.m. on a Sunday? Haha, not going to happen.

Me: Come on, it's not that early.

Dani: I love you but no. A girl needs her beauty rest.

Me: You're plenty beautiful already.

Dani: Your attempts at flattery won't work, the answer is still no. Call me when you're done, and I'll get mimosas with you though.

Me: You're impossible.

Dani: Meeting my mom for lunch, gotta go.

Ugh. Yoga was still a good idea, even if Dani wasn't going to come with me—a welcome distraction, anything to occupy my mind for a while.

The grocery store was only a few miles away, and it didn't take me long to gather a few items for dinners that week. Quinn and I spent the rest of the day doing random chores around the house—laundry, dishes that had been neglected through the week, cleaning the bathroom, and dusting. Later that night, Quinn grilled brats and vegetables, and we ate on the patio. The clouds had finally broken up, and the sun was peeking through. I watched the clouds as they moved across the sky, completely lost in my own world. When I looked up, Quinn was staring at me intently.

"What?" I blushed.

"You're beautiful, and I love you. I got lucky, that's all."

"Nah," I replied. "I think I'm the lucky one."

"Let's just say we're both lucky."

"Deal." I smiled.

8

I woke to my alarm at eight and pulled on a pair of yoga capris, a workout top with a built-in bra, and a jacket. I slipped on a pair of Toms, pulled my hair into messy bun, and walked the three blocks to the yoga studio.

It had been too long since I'd been to a class. It was just what I needed. I felt the stress of work and everything else melt away as I flowed from pose to pose. I was a little out of practice and winded and sweating by the time the hour-long class was over. Before walking home, I stopped for a latte at the coffee shop near our apartment.

I had my headphones in and was scrolling through Facebook as I walked off the elevator, and toward our apartment at the end of the hall. When I lifted my head, I stopped walking so suddenly I almost dropped my coffee. Carson stood in front of our door, with his head down, and his hands on either side of the doorframe. He looked so hot in his white T-shirt and black jeans, a baseball cap covering his hair. Coffee leaked from the lid of my cup and onto my hand, the hot liquid burning my skin.

"Shit," I mumbled under my breath, licking the coffee off my hand. Carson lifted his head and looked at me, not moving his hands off the doorway. I pulled my headphones out of my ears but didn't move from my spot twenty feet away.

"What are you doing here?" I said coldly. I took a sip of my coffee and glared at him. Damn him. I had ignored him, had an excellent stress-relieving time at yoga, and now he was here, fucking everything up again.

"I thought we were meeting for coffee?" His blue eyes never left mine. Even from twenty feet away, I could see the storm raging behind them.

"I don't know what made you think that. I went to yoga."

"I can see that." He finally moved his hands and stood up straight, taking a few steps toward me. I held up my hand, needing the distance between us.

"Stop," I said harshly. "Really, Carson, why are you here?" I pleaded. "Why did you want to meet me for coffee?" He ignored my command to stop and cleared the space between us in just a few steps. He reached his arm out to touch my face, but I danced around him, careful not to spill my coffee as we traded places.

"I needed to see you." He took another step toward me. *Uh-oh.* I had nowhere to go but into our apartment, and I knew I couldn't unlock the door and get inside fast enough to avoid Carson. He saw my predicament and smirked.

"Why are you trying so hard to avoid me?"

"Because we can't do this. I'm married. Quinn is your best friend," I pleaded with him. He stepped closer, leaving only a few feet between us now. My mind was screaming at him to stop, to stay away, but my body wanted him closer, wanted every part of him touching me.

"You keep talking about *this*, but I just came to have coffee with a friend," he said, but the mischievous look on his face said coffee was the last thing on his mind.

I took a step backward, the hard wood of the door meeting my back. I tried to control my breathing, tried to calm my heart that threatened to beat out of my chest. I could smell his cologne, and the scent made desire pool in my core.

He grabbed my coffee and took a sip, his eyes never leaving my face. He took another step toward me, our bodies just inches apart, and I could feel the heat radiating off his body. It took every ounce of control I had to keep from raising my hands and running them up his arms and into his hair. Instead, I kept them pressed against the door behind me.

Carson put a hand above my head and leaned closer. He leaned his head back and took another sip of my latte.

"This is disgusting." His words were a whisper against my lips.

"Then quit drinking it," I replied sarcastically.

"But then I'd have to find something else to do with my mouth." His lips were dangerously close to mine. I dropped my head; I was out of smart ass comments. I put my hands on Carson's chest and tried to push him away, but he didn't budge. He laughed at my feeble attempt. "Aren't you going to invite me in?"

"What?" My head snapped up, and I looked up at him again. A strange combination of laughter and lust filled his eyes. Before I could blink, Carson's lips crushed against mine. Energy surged through my body, fire burning from my lips down through my core, like someone had lit a firework.

He pulled away long enough to put my coffee down on the floor, then his lips were on mine again, as he ran his fingers up my arms, leaving a trail of tingling heat on my skin before he cupped my face with both hands and deepened our kiss. He ran a hand down my neck, across my collarbone. His tongue followed the trail his fingers had made. Pulling the top of my workout tank down, exposing one of my breasts, his tongue skimmed across cleavage before circling my nipple. I moaned, and my back arched away from the door, suddenly realizing we were still in the hallway.

"Let's go inside," I said.

"Where are your keys? He breathed against my lips.

"I don't know." They had been in my hand when I had rounded the corner. Carson scooped them up from the ground and put the key in the lock. He pushed me inside, his hands grabbing my hips, and his lips meeting mine again as he kicked the door closed behind him.

The sound of the door shutting brought me back to reality, and I pulled my mouth away from his. But he didn't let me go—only rested his forehead against mine, both of us breathing hard.

"Carson."

"Don't talk. Don't think." It was impossible not to think; my mind was racing a hundred miles an hour.

"Carson please," I begged. Was I asking him to leave or keep going? Then Carson lowered his head and pulled my nipple back into his mouth, and all thoughts about anything but Carson and that moment ceased to exist. I moaned again. Carson tugged the other side of my top down and cupped my breast with his hand, rubbing his thumb over my nipple. Every touch was like fire on my skin, intensifying the need burning inside me.

I fumbled with his shirt as we stumbled to the couch, like two teenagers who couldn't get naked fast enough. He pulled my top off over my head and threw it to the side, his lips barely breaking contact with mine. Pushing me down onto the couch, he climbed on top of me.

Adrenaline coursed through my veins, my shaking fingers struggling to get his belt undone. Finally, I loosened the buckle, undid the button and zipper of his jeans, and pushed them to the floor, along with his boxers. His cock sprang free, hard and ready, a drop of pre-cum already glistening at his tip. I wanted to taste him, to take him in mouth and make him come all over me. I wrapped my hand around his cock, and he moaned, his grip on me finally relaxing. I slid down the couch and took him in my mouth.

"Fuck, Chloe," he said through gritted teeth as I moved my mouth up and down and cupped his balls in my hand. I felt his hand on the back of head, the pressure pushing me to take him deeper in my mouth. I pulled him in and sucked hard. "Chloe, oh my God, you have to stop," he gasped.

"Why'd you make me stop?" I pouted, reaching for him again. He pushed my hand away and flashed me a mischievous grin.

"Because I didn't come here for a blow job."

"Oh really? Why did you come here then?" I raised an eyebrow at him.

"To do something I've wanted to do for years."

Carson dropped to his knees in front of me and pulled down my pants. I wasn't wearing any panties and was left naked and exposed. He ran his hands up my calves, pushing my knees apart. His hands continued up my inner thighs, and when his fingers brushed over my clit, I moaned.

Carson slid a finger inside me, and I gasped.

"You're so fucking wet," he mumbled and pumped his finger inside me. My hands dug into the fabric of the couch, and my head dropped back, eyes closing in pleasure.

"Look at me," Carson demanded. My eyes popped open and met his. He didn't break eye contact as he pulled his finger out and put it in his mouth, sucking gently before he lowered his head.

"Oh my God, Carson," I moaned when his tongue dipped inside me. He gripped my hips, holding me in place while he fucked me with his tongue. When his tongue flicked over my clit, my eyes rolled back in my head and pleasure began to build at my center. I moaned Carson's name as he took my body higher and higher. "Yes ... please ... don't stop..." I gasped out. I was so close.

"Look at me. Let me see you come," he said. I forced my eyelids open and met Carson's gaze, but the eye contact was short lived. My head fell back, and my fingernails dug into the couch moments later when I came, a string of swear words tumbling out of my mouth. Carson finally pulled his mouth off me and wiped his face on the back of his hand, a giant grin plastered on his face.

"Stand up," he ordered.

"I don't think that's possible." My legs felt like Jell-O. Carson grabbed my wrist and pulled me up, kissing me roughly before spinning me around and pushing me against the couch, using one foot to spread my legs. He put a hand on the small of my back and inched his way into me. It felt perfect, like his body was made for mine. He moved out slowly and back in even slower; it was killing me.

"Carson," I whispered. His pace didn't change; every movement was deliberate and excruciatingly slow.

"Do you know how many times I've dreamed of this?" He slapped my ass, and I let out a yelp. "How many times I've gotten off while I imagined fucking you?" He slapped me again, and I let out a moan. "I've wanted to be inside you so many times." He pulled out and slammed back in. "And it's fucking amazing."

"Holy shit, yes," I whispered.

"Tell me how you like it," he commanded.

"Hard."

He slapped my ass again, and I let out another moan.

"You like that?"

"Yes," I breathed.

"Tell me you love it."

"I fucking love it."

"You're so fucking hot," he said, never breaking his rhythm. He grabbed both of my hips and fucked me like it was the last thing he was ever going to do. His fingers dug into my hips as he slid in and out of me.

He let go of one of my hips and reached around me, pressing two fingers on my clit and rubbing in circles.

“Oh fuck yes,” I moaned. Carson slapped me again, and my orgasm began to build.

“You’re fucking amazing, Chloe … Oh my God,” he grunted. I came moments later, screaming his name as he fucked me.

As my orgasm subsided, he pulled out and flipped me over. He stroked himself, his breathing hard and ragged as he moaned my name and came on my chest. He collapsed on the couch next to me. Neither of us said anything as we caught our breath.

When my muscles would finally cooperate, I grabbed my pants off the floor and used them to clean myself off before I pulled a blanket off the couch and wrapped it around me.

“I’m going to take a shower.” I turned away from Carson, unable to look at him right now. “You can show yourself out when you’re ready, but just be gone before I get out, please.” I picked his T-shirt up off the floor and threw it to him.

“Chloe,” he said. I stopped, but I didn’t turn around. I waited for whatever else he was going to say, but it never came. What was there to say?

“I think it’s better if we don’t talk.” I took a few more steps toward the bathroom. He didn’t say anything to stop me, so I kept walking. “Lock the door behind you.”

I turned on the shower, then sunk to the floor and cried. What had I done?

9

Carson

I knew it was wrong—knew I should be anywhere else—but I didn't care. I was thinking with the head between my legs instead of the one on my shoulders.

Chloe made me fucking crazy. I had been attracted to her since the moment I first saw her. As I got to know her, it only made me want her more. But she was Quinn's. I thought it was just like every other crush I'd ever had and it would fade, or some new, hot chick would eventually grab my attention.

Our instant flirting cooled briefly after I'd met Jenna, but picked right back up when I returned to Portland. I told myself it was normal to want to fuck my best friend's girl. And since she was hot, any straight guy would want to—anything to make myself feel like less of a douche bag.

I'd even followed Jenna halfway across the country when our relationship was already dead, just to get away from Chloe. I'd known it was a mistake, but I needed to get away. I had thought maybe Jenna would be the one to make me forget about my desires for Chloe, but I was wrong. It didn't do a damn bit of good. Not only did it not help with Chloe, but I had to catch that bitch in bed with Tom from our CrossFit gym.

When I'd moved back to Portland, it was like I'd never left, except my feelings had grown stronger. I'd tried to keep my distance, but Quinn was my best friend, and Chloe was always around. Who would've thought that was because she wanted me, too?

I'd almost said no to the threesome—almost told her and Quinn to find someone else to play in their twisted sex game, but curiosity had gotten the best of me, and when she had said 'please,' her lips pouting and her perfume in the air, I couldn't say no.

When she didn't respond to my text, I knew she probably wouldn't show up for coffee, but I had to try. I needed to get her alone, and this was my only chance. Her defenses were down, I'd seen the little cracks in her armor, and I was going to use that to my advantage.

It was supposed to be a one-time deal, but I'd gotten a taste, and now I was addicted. It didn't matter anymore that she was Quinn's.

My thoughts drifted to my best friend. In junior high, my mom had sent me to live with my grandma after I'd gotten caught smoking pot. She was a single mom and said she couldn't handle a delinquent. I'd moved in the middle of the school year, and everyone was assholes, except Quinn. He'd droned on for hours about sports, but I was just happy that someone was talking to me. He became my brother.

I tried not to think about what would happen if he ever found out about this. I knew it'd mean the end of our friendship, but fuck, was she worth it? The image of fucking her the other night flashed across my mind. I needed more, and sharing her in a threesome wasn't going to cut it.

I didn't know what I had expected, but being thrown out of her apartment wasn't it. All the irrational, possessive feelings from our first threesome came rushing back. I was ready to argue with her, fight her over this, but I wasn't leaving, not like this.

I looked around the apartment, trying to figure out where this was coming from. When my eyes fell on a picture of Chloe and Quinn from their wedding day, all the anger dissipated and the guilt from before returned. I was a fucking asshole. I wondered if Tom ever felt guilty about fucking Jenna. Probably not, the fucking prick. I couldn't compare myself to Tom anyway. Compared to me, Tom was a stand-up guy. Jenna and I were over … their affair had just made me face the truth. Quinn and Chloe weren't anywhere near over. As far as I could tell, they were in for the long haul. Until now.

I deserved to be thrown out on the street like some cheap hooker. After Chloe turned on the shower, I got dressed and helped myself to a beer. I didn't give a shit that it wasn't even eleven o'clock yet. I walked down the hall and stood outside the bathroom door. I heard a sniffle from inside and knew she was crying. I wanted to break down the door, wrap my arms around her, hold her tight, and tell her everything would be all right. But I was pretty sure that was a lie.

My cock started to get hard again at the thought of her on the other side of the door, naked and wet. I stood there longer than I should have, imagining us in the shower together, then the water stopped running. I flinched. Shit. She didn't want me here. I moved away from the bathroom door, drained my beer, and pulled the door open, taking one last glance at the bathroom door before I left.

10

I stood in front of the mirror and stared at myself for a long time before I got in the shower. My eyes were red and swollen from crying, matching my swollen lips from kissing Carson. I still looked like the same Chloe, but I felt like a totally different person. I had always imagined people who cheated on their spouses were in unhappy, sexless marriages. I was wrong. Here I was, with the marriage and relationship I'd always wanted, but had still cheated.

God, how did I let this happen? I was weak and pathetic for letting Carson just waltz right in here and do whatever he wanted. Somewhere in the back of my head, a little voice taunted me: *you wanted it too.* Damn it, I did. And I wanted it again and again and again. Fucking Carson was so different than Quinn; it was raw and animalistic, and unlike anything I'd ever experienced.

But it didn't matter … there could be no more threesomes, definitely no more cheating, and no more Carson. I stayed in the shower until the water was cold, wishing it could somehow wash away my sins.

When I finally opened the bathroom door and looked around, Carson was gone. *Thank God.* As I was changing, I noticed the big red mark on my ass from where Carson had slapped me, and I hoped it didn't leave a bruise. There was no way I would be able to explain that to Quinn.

As I was brushing my hair, my brother, Derek, called.

"Hey," I answered.

"Hey Chloe, how's it going?"

Just cheated on my husband, no big deal. "Work has been busy; we are getting the new winter women's line ready to launch in a week or so."

"Oh how exciting," I could tell even through the phone he was rolling his eyes. Derek and I were only 18 months apart and had always been really close.

"Hey we can't all be police officers out there saving people every day," I replied.

He laughed and told me his wife, Adrienne, was pregnant again and we talked about all the things that had happened since we last talked, while I picked up my discarded clothing off the floor and started a load of laundry. We talked about the boys and their latest shenanigans, before I congratulated him on the new baby and hung up.

I laid down on the couch and turned on reruns of *Sex and the City*, but it wasn't long before I dozed off.

A door closing somewhere in the distance jarred me from my sleep. I bolted upright to see where the sound had come from. Quinn was standing by the front door, sorting the mail with his back to me. I yawned and stretched.

"Hey babe," I said through my yawn.

"Oh hey." He turned around. "Sorry, I didn't mean to wake you."

"It's no big deal. I didn't actually mean to fall asleep." He walked over and kissed me.

"How was the show?" I asked.

"It was good. Everyone is pretty stoked for the season to get started. What have you been up to?"

"Oh, nothing much. I went to yoga this morning." *Fucked your best friend on our couch.* "Got caught up on some work emails, then fell asleep watching TV. Nothing exciting."

My mind flashed back to just a few hours ago, my ass still tender from Carson's hand. I clenched my thighs and shook my head as if that would help get rid of the memory. "What's wrong?" Quinn asked.

"Oh, nothing, I just got a chill," I lied. Quinn linked his fingers with mine and changed the channel to ESPN, and less than five minutes later, his eyes closed and his breathing evened out as he dozed off. I stared at him intently, studying the lines of his face, the muscular curve of his jaw, his slightly curly brown hair, his pouty pink lips, and felt incredibly sad. Part of me wanted to wake him up right now, tell him what had happened, and beg for forgiveness. Another part of me wanted to bury this secret so deep inside me no one would ever find it. I couldn't tell him. It would break his heart.

My phone pinged from the coffee table. I put it on silent before opening the text.

Dani: Hey, what happened to mimosas? I was serious about that!!

Me: I got busy and totally forgot, sorry!

Dani: Busy doing what? It's Sunday.

Damn it, she was nosy. I wasn't telling her either—couldn't drag her into this.

Me: Just catching up on some work stuff. Things I should have done last week.

I didn't need twenty questions from Dani right now, so before she could answer, I sent her another message.

Me: Wanna come over for dinner? I'm making chicken parm.

Dani: That sounds amazing. What time?

Me: 6:30?

Dani: Done. I'll bring some wine.

Me: Awesome, see you soon.

That was easy enough. I could always distract Dani with food. I decided to run down to the bakery and get some fresh bread to go with dinner while Quinn was napping. I left a note on the fridge and walked the few blocks there.

When I got back, Quinn was awake and watching *Conair* for the millionth time.

"How many times are you going to watch this?" I asked.

"It's a classic … you can't watch it too many times."

"If you say so," I said and started getting dinner ready.

Twenty minutes later, the kitchen smelled like fresh baked bread, garlic, and spaghetti sauce. Just before I pulled the bread out of the oven, the doorbell rang, and Quinn looked around, almost startled by the sound.

"It's just Dani." I wiped my hands on a towel and opened the door for her.

"Hey," she said, holding up two bottles of wine.

"Make yourself at home, dinner is almost ready."

"You should have told me Dani was coming; I would've invited Carson too," Quinn said without looking up from the TV.

"Oh, I didn't think about it," I said, my voice sounding weird and nervous. Dani raised her eyebrow at me, like she knew something had happened without me even telling her. I just shrugged.

She plopped down on the couch beside Quinn and started pestering him with football questions.

"So, who is Oregon's new quarterback? Why won't they just tell us already?"

Dani was more into football than any other girl I'd ever met, and the Ducks were her team. Poor Quinn, she was going to badger him until he gave up any information he had.

Quinn just laughed.

"You know I don't know either. They don't tell that stuff to the media weeks in advance and expect us to keep it a secret. When I know, you'll know," he said.

She rolled her eyes. "Riiigghhtt, and they haven't dropped any subtle clues about who it might be?"

"Not that I've picked up on." Quinn's smile revealed he actually did know something but wasn't going to say. I shook my head and turned back to dinner. Those two could talk football all night long.

"Dinner is ready," I announced five minutes later.

"Chloe, will you please go to a game with me this year?" Dani begged as she loaded pasta, chicken, and sauce onto her plate.

"Why do you ask me every year when you already know the answer?"

"Please! There are tons of cute guys there. I need a wingman." The last thing Dani needed was a wingman; she was a smoking hot blonde who knew more about football than most guys I knew. Any man in his right mind would want her.

"I will be worse than useless as wingman at a football game." I snorted. "I'd probably make you look bad by yelling at the wrong player or something."

"You're probably right, but still, I don't want to go alone, *and* I already have tickets," she said, like it was a done deal. "Plus, you've got to know something about the Oregon account with Nike … people are into that stuff."

"If by people you mean girls whose boyfriends or husbands or crazy best friends have dragged them to football games against their will, then you are right." I laughed. "Guys don't give a shit about what color combination the uniforms are going to be this week."

"That's not true," Quinn piped in. "The ones that are all forest green are terrible." Dani tilted her head in Quinn's direction as if to say, *see I told you so.* "I personally like the ones that look like they have duck wings on the shoulder pads."

"You know that is almost all of them, right?" I said. Quinn shrugged and Dani laughed.

"I have a better idea … we'll go to bar, and I'll help you pick up a guy, and then you can take him to the game instead," I said, as we sat down at the table on the patio.

"How about this? I'll go out with you, and if we don't find me a date for the game, then you have to go with me," Dani said. "Deal?"

"Deal, but you have to actually try to meet a guy."

"Yeah, sure … whatever," she said noncommittally and stuffed her mouth full of chicken and pasta so she couldn't talk anymore. Quinn laughed.

"What?" I asked him.

"Nothing," he said. "You two are just funny." It had taken Quinn a while to warm up to Dani when we'd met. He told me more than once that he thought she was a bitch, but that was just Dani. She told it how it was, and sometimes that came across as bitchy, but she was the best friend I'd ever had. I had even told her when I'd started dating Quinn that'd I'd break up with him if they couldn't be friends too.

"You can't even say anything," I said. "You and Carson are a thousand times worse than we will ever be." My pussy clenched involuntarily at the mention of Carson. *Jesus Christ, Chloe get a grip.* I wanted to slap myself for letting him have such an effect on me.

"Touché," Quinn said, raising his fork.

"This is amazing, Chloe," Dani interjected. "You should cook me dinner more often."

"You know you're welcome anytime … and thank you."

"You guys want more wine?" Quinn asked. Dani and I both nodded as he picked up his empty plate and went inside to get the second bottle. Dani leaned over the table, double checking that Quinn had shut the door.

"Sooo, how was it the other night?" she whispered excitedly.

"Unbelievable."

"Better than the first?"

"Way better. No nerves, no bullshit. Everyone knew what they were doing … it was awesome."

"Did you DP?"

"Oh my God!!" I whisper-yelled and turned bright red. "No! What is wrong with you? How big of a slut do you think I am?" The truth was I'd thought about it, wanted to try it, but we weren't there yet—probably never would be given the current situation. She held up her hands in surrender and nodded her head toward the door to let me know Quinn was coming.

"I had to ask." She laughed, and then whispered, "And I know you're a pretty big slut."

"Gee, thanks." We both laughed.

"What's so funny?" Quinn said, returning to the table with the other bottle of wine and a plate full of mini chocolate éclairs he'd gotten out of the freezer.

"Nothing you'd understand," I said.

"Girls and their inside jokes." He shook his head and poured everyone more wine.

"It's better for there to be mystery," Dani said. "If you knew all our secrets, what fun would that be?"

"It'd be a lot easier than guessing what is going on in your crazy heads," Quinn responded.

He definitely didn't want to know what was going on in my head. Guilt and lust wrestled through me. I went back and forth between feeling guilty and wanting to do it again.

"Earth to Chloe." Dani snapped her fingers in front of my face.

"Hmmm ... what?" I said, looking up at her.

"While you were off in La-la Land, I asked you eight million questions about work." Her voice was all breathy and exasperated like she'd gone out of her way to talk about my job, and then got all butt hurt when I didn't respond. "What were you daydreaming about anyway?"

"No daydreaming, just thinking about work actually," I lied.

"Uh-huh, sure." It was almost dark on the patio now, and Dani checked her phone for the time. "Oh, I better get going, I've got the early shift at the office in the morning." Dani was an ultrasound tech and especially loved the shifts when she worked at the OB's office and got to tell all the pregnant mamas if they were having a boy or a girl.

"I'll walk you out," I said as we both stood. Quinn told Dani goodbye and lit a cigarette as we went inside.

"What is wrong with you?" she asked when we were in the hallway.

"What are you talking about?"

"I've never seen you so distracted before. And you nearly jumped at any mention of Carson. Don't think I didn't notice … I'm a ninja." She pointed at me. I laughed, but on the inside I was scrambling. I didn't know what on Earth I was going to tell her.

"Oh, just thinking about the other night," I said in what had to be the most unconvincing voice ever.

"Lady, when are you going to learn you can't lie to me?" She pressed the down button to call the elevator.

"I'm not lying," I said more convincingly this time. Telling her about cheating on Quinn wasn't an option, so I had to make her believe me. "Between all the threesome drama and shit at work, I've got a lot on my mind. I'll be more attentive next time, I promise." She looked at me suspiciously, but then the elevator dinged, announcing its arrival.

"I still don't believe you."

I started to get on the elevator with her, and she waved me off. “I’m a big girl; I can walk to my car by myself.”

“Well, all right then.” I stepped back off the elevator. “See you Friday.”

“See you later, slut,” she said as the elevator doors started to close. I saw her crack up laughing just as the doors slid together.

“Bitch,” I murmured under my breath, with a smile, as I walked back to our apartment.

11

I had barely sat down on Monday morning, when my boss's 19-year-old intern came to my desk. She just stood there awkwardly, her hands clasped behind her back.

"Can I help you, Chelsy?" I asked, without looking up from my computer.

"Sean wants to see you," she said. Oh, this couldn't be good. Sean was the head of the entire design department. He'd been part of the hiring committee that had interviewed me, but I had barely spoken to or worked directly with him in the six years I'd been here. The only other time I could recall him wanting to talk to me personally was when I'd been taken off a project my first year here. I'd thought for sure I was getting fired, but luckily had been placed on a new project, and a few months later was promoted to the women's team.

"Do you know what he wants? I asked nervously as I stood and smoothed out my skirt.

"He didn't say." We walked in silence down the hall to his office. Chelsy stuck her head in the door.

"Chloe is here to see you, Mr. Jackson."

"Thank you, Chelsy. Chloe, please come in." He stood from his desk and gestured to a seat in front of it.

"Chelsy, shut the door behind you," he said as he sat back down. I tried not to look worried, but my breakfast shifted uncomfortably in my stomach.

"Chloe, how are you?"

"I'm good, everything is great, the winter line is almost ready," I rambled.

"I'm aware." He shifted papers around on his desk. "But I didn't call you in here to talk about the winter line." My stomach dropped, and I seriously thought I might vomit on my shoes. "You may have heard Jackie will be leaving at the end of the year," he said.

"I have heard rumors, but nothing official," I responded, perking up a little.

"She gave me her official notice a few weeks ago. She won't be back after the new year. Which means we are going to need to replace her." My heart skipped a beat; he couldn't really be offering me this job, could he?

"I've spoken with other members of the leadership team, and we'd like you to apply," he said. Of course, he wasn't offering me the job … who did I think I was? "We'll be opening up the job, but only by invitation to a select handful of people."

"All from within the organization?" I asked.

"No, a few from other companies that we've had our eye on as well. But the field will be small, less than ten."

"And you want me to apply?" The question tumbled out of my mouth skeptically.

"Yes. I've been overseeing your work for quite some time, Chloe, and I'm impressed. You've come a long way, and I think you have real potential to do amazing things here."

"Thank you, sir."

"Please, call me Sean," he said. "Don't share this news with anyone here at work, as we'd like to keep the applicant pool tight and the job search low profile."

"I can do that," I forced my voice to remain calm and even. I was so excited I wanted to run out of his office and call Quinn right now.

"Chelsy, will send you all the details about what the application will entail, but it will be quite rigorous. I hope you're up for it."

"I am, I promise."

"That's it," he said. That was my cue I was being excused. I thanked Sean one more time and left. I walked quickly to my desk, grabbed my phone out of my drawer and nearly sprinted outside to call Quinn.

"Hey, what's up?" he answered on the first ring.

"On my God, you'll never believe it. Jackie really is leaving, and they want me to apply for the head of the women's design team!"

"That's amazing!" Even through the phone, I could tell he was smiling.

"I can't believe it!"

"I'm so fucking proud of you, babe. You've worked really hard for this."

"Well, I didn't get it yet. I still have to apply, and Sean said the application process will be intense. And Jackie isn't leaving until December."

"But still it's awesome, and we should celebrate tonight." My phone dinged in my ear—a reminder, for a meeting starting in five minutes.

"Shit, I've got to go, but we'll definitely talk more tonight. I love you."

"I love you too. Go kick some more ass."

I ran back inside, trying to catch my breath while I gathered a few things off my desk and made my way to the conference room.

The rest of the day passed in a blur of meetings. I checked my email eight million times, waiting for details from Chelsy so I could start planning, but they never came.

I was doodling a new design on my notepad when my stomach growled loudly. I looked up and realized the office was mostly deserted, as it was nearly six. I gathered my things and headed to my car, texting Quinn on the way.

Me: I'm on my way, sorry I lost track of time.

Twenty minutes later, I opened the apartment door and was greeted by the most amazing smell. Quinn had on music and was dancing around the kitchen while he cooked.

"What are you making? It smells delicious," I said as I walked over and kissed Quinn on the cheek.

"Fajitas and margaritas. We are celebrating." He stirred the onions and peppers, and then spun around, pulled me in close, and gave me a kiss. "I'm seriously so proud of you."

"Nothing is official. I still have to apply."

"Yeah, but you'll crush it. I know you will."

"Thanks, I hope so. Is dinner almost ready? I'm starving."

"Yeah, it'll be done in five minutes."

"Awesome, I'm going to change."

When I came back out of the bedroom in shorts and a tank top, Quinn had the steak fajitas and all the fixings on the table and was mixing up a pitcher of margaritas.

"Cheers. To you and the amazing places you're going." Quinn lifted his margarita glass when we both sat down.

"Thank you. I'm really excited," I said.

Three margaritas later, I was full of fajitas and more than a little tipsy. I leaned back in my chair and studied Quinn. His brown hair was getting long; the ends were starting to curl around his neck and ears. I loved it when his hair was long, loved running my fingers through it. He was scrolling through his phone and laughed at something he saw on Facebook. His face lit up as he laughed, the joy reaching his dark brown eyes. I could get lost in his eyes, so deep and serious, but full of light and laughter when he smiled. Quinn looked up and caught me staring at him.

"What?" he asked.

"Oh nothing," I blushed. "Just admiring my super-hot husband."

"Super-hot?" He smirked. "Is that so?"

"It is. A super-hot sex god, if I'm not mistaken."

He threw his head back and laughed again. When his gaze returned to me, his eyes were dark, promises of passion and sex swirling behind them. The look he gave me shot straight to my core. I bit my lip and gave him my sexiest look in return.

"Those are some pretty big shoes to fill." He stood up and walked around the table.

"I think you're up for the job," I said. He leaned down, his hands resting on the arms of my chair.

"Oh you do?" he whispered against my ear.

"Definitely," I whimpered, moisture gathering between my legs.

"Are you sure all the margaritas aren't clouding your judgment?"

"Nah, I'm smarter when I drink tequila," I smirked. Quinn laughed so hard he let go of my chair and leaned over the table, clutching his stomach.

"Way to ruin the moment," he snorted, when he finally regained his composure.

"Oh, we were having a moment?" I teased.

"You, Chloe Louise Parker, are impossible." He leaned back over my chair.

"Oooh, using the middle and maiden names, I must be in trouble." I laughed, and he rolled his eyes at me.

"I don't know what to do with you sometimes." He kissed me gently before he pulled away. "But I love you anyway."

His lips crashed down on mine, nothing gentle about it this time. I ran my fingers through his hair and pulled him closer. I moaned against his mouth when he slipped one hand under my tank top and ran his thumb over my nipple. I needed him closer, wanted to feel his body against mine, to make me forget how Carson had made me feel. I wrapped my legs around his waist and pulled him closer to me, and his hands slid under me as he lifted me up. Our lips never parted, our mouths devouring each other as he carried me down the hall toward our bedroom.

When he laid me down on our bed, the mood changed. His kisses went from feverish and uncontrolled to slow and gentle.

"Get comfortable, baby." Quinn smiled as he stood and pulled his shirt over his head. "I'm going to spend the rest of the night showing you just how much I love you."

And then he made love to me. Nothing about it was rushed; there was no fucking, no urgency, just love being poured from his body into mine.

It was beautiful and amazing, and for a few hours I forgot there was a crack in our relationship. A crack I had created, a crack that threatened to break open and swallow me whole.

12

Carson: I need to see you.

The text came through during Wednesday afternoon's staff meeting. My phone vibrated in my lap, and I read the message under the table in the conference room.

Me: No.

I had nothing else to say to him. I couldn't see him. I knew what would happen if I did. I was weak, and he knew it. No matter how hard I tried to forget, my body wouldn't let the memory of Carson fade. It craved more of his touch. I felt my phone vibrate three more times, but kept it locked and out of sight until I was back at my desk.

Carson: Chloe, please.

Carson: I promise I'll keep my hands to myself this time.

Carson: I need to explain.

He was delusional.

Me: Explain what?

Carson: How I feel.

Me: I don't care how you feel, Carson.

Carson: Are you going to make me beg?

Me: You can beg all you want, the answer is still no.

Carson: I need you.

Me: I'm married. To Quinn. Fucking drop it.

I didn't get a response, but I knew it wasn't over. I had unveiled a connection I didn't know existed—stronger than anything I'd ever felt. If Carson didn't keep his distance, I wasn't just going to fall into the crack … I was going to jump in willingly.

My Friday girls' night with Dani took forever to arrive. With the winter line approved and in the manufacturing process, and no news on the application process, work was slow. I organized my desk, twice, went through old files looking for possible portfolio pieces, in case that was needed for the application, and finished several sketches that had been sitting on my desk for weeks.

When it was finally five o'clock on Friday, I practically sprinted out of the office.

When I got home, Quinn was sitting on the couch, beer in hand, watching ESPN.

"Hey babe," he said I as shut the door.

"Hi."

"How was work?"

"A little slow; I'm dying to know what the application process is, but still haven't heard anything from Chelsy."

"Don't stress about it. I'm sure you'll get all the details soon," Quinn said.

"What are doing tonight?" I asked.

"I'm just gonna hang here. Carson might come over, but he wasn't sure. What are you and Dani doing?"

"We're going to do dinner, drinks, dancing. I'm going to find Dani a date to the football game if it takes me all night."

"You know it wouldn't kill you to just go to the game with her."

"You're supposed to be on my side!"

"I'm on the side of football." He laughed. "We both love it; you could probably at least tolerate it for one game."

"Did Dani call you? Are you guys ganging up on me on purpose?"

"I'm innocent, I swear." He put his hands up in mock surrender.

"Fine, I'll forgive you this time. But I still hate football," I called over my shoulder as I went in the bedroom and shut the door.

I emerged thirty minutes later wearing dark jeans, a red off-the-shoulder top, and gray ankle boots. My hair was straight and hung past my shoulders. I'd touched up my make-up a little and put on silver dangly earrings.

"Damn, are you sure you're not the one trying to pick up a guy?" Quinn said as I walked into the living room. "You look gorgeous."

"Thank you, baby." I walked over to the couch and leaned down to give him a goodbye kiss. Quinn grabbed my waist and pulled me down on top of him. He put his hands in the back pockets of my jeans to hold me in place.

"Are you sure you don't want to stay home tonight? I'd make it worth your while." Quinn smirked.

"I'm sure you would, but I've got to go … I promised Dani."

"All right, fine," he pouted. I leaned down and gave him a kiss before he let me go.

Dani waited until I was three drinks in, and she was no closer to finding a date, before she brought it up.

"So are you going to tell me why you were being all weird on Sunday?" she asked.

"I don't know what you're talking about." Just then, the waitress appeared with two tequila shots I didn't know Dani had ordered.

"Here, drink this, and then stop being a pussy and tell me," she said, handing me the glass. I downed my shot. And then, because I knew she wouldn't leave me alone until I told her, and I couldn't lie to her, I just spit it out.

"I slept with Carson. Alone." Dani hadn't finished her shot and coughed violently as she swallowed the rest of it.

"What? Please tell me you're kidding."

"I'm not … it happened Sunday morning, after yoga. I told you this is what I was afraid of."

Dani groaned.

"Fuck, Chloe, I didn't want to know about this!"

"Well, you shouldn't have asked then."

"How did it happen?"

"You need all the dirty details about this, too?"

"No! Just how did it get to this point?"

"He wanted to meet for coffee after the second threesome, and I told him no, but when I got home from yoga, he was there. He was fucking standing in front of our apartment door, looking hot as shit."

"And you just jumped his bones?"

"No, Jesus. I do have some restraint."

"Sorry." She shrugged.

"He wouldn't leave, we argued, and then he kissed me, and … well, I don't need to spell it out for you."

"Now what?"

"What do you mean now what?" I snapped.

"What are you going to do? Are you going to tell Quinn? Are you going to do it again? What if Quinn wants to have another threesome?"

"No, no, and I'll tell him no." I answered her questions in order, holding back the urge to make some smart-ass comment about all the questions.

"I can't see him again, Dani. He does something to me, something I've never felt. Sex with Quinn has always been great; I always thought we had a great connection, but this..." I blew out a breath. "This takes it to a whole other level."

"You know that makes it sound like you're trying to justify what you did, right?"

"I literally hate you sometimes." I glared at her.

"What? Am I supposed to sit here and be all supportive of the fact that you cheated on your husband? Because I'm not. I love you, but that doesn't make what you did any less shitty."

"You think I don't know it was wrong? I know, but..." I trailed off. Dani wouldn't understand. Hell, I didn't understand.

"But what?" She glared back at me. "You want to do it again, don't you?"

"You don't understand."

"What is there to understand? Please enlighten me."

"It's a connection I can't explain—something stronger than me."

She snorted.

"That's bullshit and you know it. Don't try and justify your shitty actions with some deep philosophy garbage. I was supportive of your threesome fantasy—go get it, girl—but I would have never thought you were capable of having a full-blown affair."

"I'm not having a full-blown affair. It was one time, and it's over. It's not happening again," I snapped.

"But you want it to?"

"Enough with the goddamn questions. I'm done talking about it. I never should have told you anything." I glared at a girl walking past, who had the nerve to look me in the eye in that moment.

"Okay, jeez, fucking relax," Dani said.

"I need some air. Find yourself a man already, so I don't have to go to the fucking football game with you. I'll be back in a few minutes." I weaved my way through the crowd to the front door.

What had I expected? Dani's parents had split when she was thirteen, after her dad cheated on her mom. I knew she wouldn't approve, but I had underestimated how intense her reaction would be.

I stepped outside and shivered. It was August, but fall was already in the air. I walked a few blocks down the street and sat on the steps outside a cute little house—the kind I'd always hoped I'd buy with Quinn, to grow old in.

"Fuck you and your questions, Dani," I muttered to no one. Did I want to sleep with Carson again? All the muscles below my waist tensed at the thought, and I had my answer. What the hell was wrong with me? How could I want something so bad when it meant throwing away everything I already had?

No one has to know, a devilish little voice in the back of my head chimed in. I shook my head to dispel the thought.

"No, I love Quinn. I want to be with him. That's it. I'm happy. I'm not doing this."

"It sounds like you're trying to convince yourself of something you're not sure of." I jumped and looked up. A homeless man was standing on the sidewalk in front of me. I wondered how long he had been standing there, listening to me talk to myself.

"Life's too short to be questioning yourself, princess," he said.

"What if you want the wrong thing?" I asked.

"I just follow the wind, lady … I don't got all the answers," he mumbled and shuffled on down the sidewalk. I laughed and shook my head. Had I had really expected to get answers to all my life's questions from a bum? I pushed myself up from the step and walked back to the bar.

Dani was still alone at our table when I returned, two drinks in front of her.

"I wasn't sure you were coming back," she said as I approached.

"We've still got to find you a date. I couldn't leave yet."

"I'm not sorry for what I said—you know how I feel about cheating—but know that I'll always love you. I don't want to hear about your affair though. Leave me out of it."

"I'm not having an affair." She raised her eyebrow at me like she wasn't sure she believed me. I wasn't sure I believed me. It should've been easy to just walk away and never see Carson again, but every time I thought about it, the urge to be with Carson again grew stronger, right alongside the guilt I had for betraying Quinn.

"Good, I don't want to have to beat the shit out of you," she said finally. I laughed.

"Like you could," I taunted.

"Oh, I definitely could." She stretched up so she was a little taller, but even in her super high heels she was still a couple inches shorter than me. At five-foot-seven, I made Dani look like a shrimp.

"I actually believe you." I took a sip of the drink Dani had ordered me— gin and tonic, one of our favorites.

"So did you talk to any guys while I was gone?" I asked, even though I already knew the answer.

"All the guys here are douches."

"How do you know that if you don't talk to them?"

"I just know."

"Come on, you said you'd try!"

"I put on a dress and heels. What else do you expect from me?"

"I mean, you look hot, but you might actually have to talk to someone if you are going to take them to a football game. It is a four-hour event where you are going to have to do at least some talking."

"I'd rather take you. I don't have to be all fake and stupid with you; you like me even when I'm a moody bitch."

"You're right, maybe you shouldn't talk to guys … you might scare them all away."

She just rolled her eyes and took a sip of her drink.

"If I go to the game, will you leave me alone about it?" I asked. "For the next five years."

"Two," she countered.

"Three."

"Two, and I'll buy all the snacks and beer at the game," she said. I thought about it for a second, and then stuck out my hand.

"Deal." I'd had worse dates in my life; spending a few hours with Dani at a football game couldn't be that bad. She didn't shake my hand, but instead jumped up and down—an impressive feat in her heels—and then came around the table to hug me.

"Yay! I'm seriously so excited. I'm going to teach you some of the rules this year, and then you'll actually like it."

"Don't make me change my mind. I've been groomed to "like" football since I was a toddler; if it hasn't happened already, it's not going to happen."

"Okay, got it, no rules."

We fell into a rare, awkward silence, full of unspoken words about my actions and how Dani felt about them. I twirled the ice around in my now empty glass, the cubes clinking together. I popped a half-melted cube in my mouth and crunched down on it. Dani winced.

I lifted my glass to get another cube, but Dani reached over and pushed my hand back down to the table.

"Stop, that is so bad for your teeth." Dani grabbed my empty glass and shook it in the waiter's direction, letting him know we needed refills. "I'm sorry … I didn't mean to ruin our night out."

"You didn't ruin it," I sighed. "I did."

"You know we'll always be friends, right? No matter what you do, I'll always love you."

"You sound like my mom."

"Who cares? Your mom is awesome. Chicks who like football have to stick together."

"Did you just call my mom a chick?" Our eyes met, and we burst out laughing. And just like that, all the tension left, and we were just two best friends having a good time out on the town. I finally stopped laughing and wiped the tears from my eyes.

"Thank you," I said.

"For what?"

"Being you and putting up with all my shit."

"The feeling is mutual, lady." She raised her glass, and we toasted to our friendship. We spent the rest of the night talking and laughing about nothing. It was almost three AM when I stumbled into the apartment and dropped my keys on the floor. I swore and hoped the loud crash didn't wake up Quinn. I pulled off my clothes and crawled in bed. I wrapped my arms around Quinn and snuggled my head into his back. I breathed him in; the faint smell of his body wash filled my nose, and a tear rolled down my cheek.

"I love you, Quinn," I whispered and hoped I hadn't ruined everything.

13

I awoke to someone pounding on the door. At first I thought it was in my dream. I rolled over and tried to go back to sleep, but whoever was at the door was fucking persistent. I looked at my phone—9:15.

"Fuck..." I mumbled to myself and stumbled out of bed. I grabbed one of Quinn's T-shirts off the floor and pulled it on. Louder, more relentless pounding came from the door.

"I'm coming, I'm coming," I yelled.

I undid the lock and yawned as I pulled open the door. Carson's frame filled the doorway. The image of him standing there snapped me out of my sleepy haze. I slammed the door as fast as I could and locked it again.

Carson pounded on the door again.

"Chloe! Damn it. Let me in."

"Go away!" I yelled back. He pounded again.

"I'm not leaving until you let me in."

"I'm not letting you in. Go the fuck away." He alternated between yelling my name loudly and banging on the door with his fist.

"I'm sure your neighbors love this," he said, continuing his racket. I let out a frustrated cry as I undid the lock and yanked the door back open.

"Stop yelling, you fucking crazy person."

"Are you going to let me in?"

"No, what the hell do you want?"

"I told you I wanted to talk to you."

"Do you not understand what *no* means?"

"I'm used to getting what I want … not very many girls tell me no." He smirked and pushed the door the rest of the way open, before shoving his way inside. He stood in the kitchen and ran a hand through his hair, his basketball shorts hanging off his hips, and a black T-shirt tight across his muscular arms and chest. I shook my head to clear my thoughts, but my body was already responding to the sight of Carson.

"You can't just come here and force your way into my apartment," I said. "I don't want to see you; I don't know how to make that any clearer."

Carson just stared at me.

"Hello?" I snapped my fingers. He lifted his head, and his eyes met mine.

"You should probably go put some clothes on," he said. I looked down at myself. I had forgotten I only had on Quinn's T-shirt and my thong from last night.

"Why don't you just leave instead?"

"I'm not leaving until we talk. I already told you that."

"There is nothing to talk about!" I yelled.

"Fuck, Chloe," Carson growled. "I don't have enough self-control to stand here and argue with you while you're half-naked."

"You're the one who came here, pounded on my door, woke me up, and demanded that I let you in. If you don't like what I'm wearing, too fucking bad. You can leave or deal with it." I knew my words were dangerous, a threat I wasn't sure I was prepared to back up. My mind screamed at me to run to the bedroom, lock the door, and not come out until Carson left, but my body pulled me the opposite direction.

"Don't say I didn't warn you," Carson huffed out and took a step toward me. I put up my hand to stop him.

"Stay over there. Tell me whatever it is you must tell me, and then leave. I want to go back to bed."

Carson looked at me intently. A storm raged behind his eyes, like he was seriously struggling to keep his composure. He ran a hand through his hair again and blew out a frustrated breath.

"Well? I'm waiting. What was so important?" I was stalling. I didn't really believe Carson had come here just to talk, and I had no defenses against him.

"Can you please put some pants on?" Carson said, his eyes traveling up and down my body. When his eyes met mine again, I bit my lip, and he let out a groan. "Are you trying to kill me?" He adjusted his shorts, and I knew he was hard. "I didn't come here to fuck you, but you are testing every ounce of my self-control right now."

"Really? Why did you come here then? Because I can only see this ending one way."

"I wanted to tell you I was sorry, for what happened before. I shouldn't have come here and definitely shouldn't have..." he trailed off.

"Yet here you are again, on a day when you knew damn good and well Quinn would be gone."

"Okay, fine, maybe my intentions weren't entirely honorable." Carson smirked.

"Carson, this isn't a fucking game. This is my marriage we are talking about ruining here."

"I can't get you out of my head. I had to see you."

"You are infuriating," I yelled again and threw my hands in the air.

"Yeah, you definitely should have put some more clothes on," Carson said, closing the few feet between us in two easy steps. He ran a finger down my cheek and tucked a stray strand of hair behind my ear.

A piece of my heart broke for Quinn as I realized what I was doing, what I was going to do. My heart and body had battled, and my body had won; it wanted Carson, so Carson was what I was going to have. I didn't try and fight him anymore. I gave in easily, diving head first off the deep end. I bit my lip again and looked him straight in the eyes.

His body collided with mine as he kissed me, and we stumbled backward into the kitchen, until my back pressed into the counter. He kissed me hard, his hands roaming over my body, and then picked me up and set me on the counter top.

I wrapped my legs around his waist and pulled him closer to me. When his erection brushed between my legs, I moaned against his mouth.

"Carson," I whispered, not even sure what else I had to say, but there was no turning back now.

"Shhh, don't talk, just kiss me." He cupped my face with both hands and kissed me deeply as he ground his pelvis into mine. Pulling my shirt over my head, he rubbed his palms across my nipples as he did so, sending a shockwave through my body. I didn't know it was possible for everything to feel so wrong but so right at the same time. All I knew was I needed more.

"Fuck me," I breathed against his mouth.

"I thought you'd never ask," he said, his breath ragged in my ear.

His hands dropped from my face to pull down his shorts. He grabbed my hips and pulled me to the edge of the counter, fumbling for a moment, trying to pull off my thong, before he gave up and ripped the thin fabric off my body.

He lowered his head and kissed my neck as he thrust into me. He ran his hands down my back, and dug his fingers into my ass as he moved in and out of me, slow and deliberate. I ran my nails down his back, grabbed his ass, and pulled him in deeper.

"Holy shit, Chloe," Carson groaned.

"Oh my God, yes," I whispered as he picked up speed. When he nibbled on my ear and kissed my neck, I moaned even louder.

"Fuck, Chloe, I'm close. Touch yourself for me." I looked up, startled by his words. It was a command I'd never heard before, but it was hot as hell, and there was no way I was refusing. I reached a hand in between our bodies and pressed two fingers against my clit, moving them in light circles. Carson's thrusts did the rest. It didn't take long before my body clenched around him as my orgasm tore through me. Moments later, Carson grunted and followed me over the edge.

It was quick, and dirty, and amazing.

Carson stilled, his dick still inside me, and rested his forehead against mine, both of us breathing hard. After a few minutes, he picked me up and lowered me to floor, sinking down beside me. We sat there, leaning against the kitchen cupboards for a long time. Neither of us said anything … neither of us looked at the other.

I reached for the T-shirt I'd had on, but Carson used his foot to push it out of my reach.

"Leave it off, I like looking at you naked."

Just then, there was a knock on the door, and I swore my heart stopped beating. I didn't move for a full minute, and whoever was outside knocked again. I stood up quickly, grabbed the T-shirt off the floor, and pulled it over my head as I tiptoed toward the door.

I pulled the door open a crack and poked my head out. Our neighbor, Sarah, stood in the hallway.

"Hi Sarah, how is everything?" I said, hoping I sounded nonchalant.

"I'm good," she said. "I just heard a lot of banging and yelling earlier, so I wanted to make sure everything was okay?" *It's been twenty minutes since there was banging and yelling … if something was wrong, I'd be dead by now,* I thought.

"Oh no, everything's fine. Quinn just forgot his keys and got locked out. I was still asleep, and he had to knock pretty loudly to wake me up," I lied.

"Oh okay," she said, sounding deflated, like she had been expecting to hear something exciting.

"Thanks for checking, though," I said and started to shut the door.

"Of course. Have a good day."

"You too." I closed the door and locked it. While I was at the door, Carson had put his shorts back on and was standing by the kitchen sink, leaning against the counter top.

"Way to go, you disturbed my neighbors."

"Eh." He shrugged. "It was worth it."

"Until they get suspicious and start asking more questions," I said, annoyed.

"Nah, your lie was totally believable."

"See what you've done? You've made me a liar and a cheater."

Carson just shrugged again. I wanted to punch him in the face. How could he be so nonchalant about this? I wasn't innocent here, but I was freaking out, and he seemed to be so cool and unaffected. I shook my head.

"I'm going to take a shower, and then go back to bed. Show yourself out."

"I don't think so," Carson said. "If you're taking a shower, I'm coming with you. I stood outside your bathroom last time and got blue balls just thinking about you wet and naked."

"God, you are creepy. And no, you aren't showering with me. You're going home."

"What if I don't want to go home?"

"I don't really care where you go, so long as it's not here."

"I'm not done with you yet this morning, Chloe." Carson pushed himself off the counter and walked toward me. He stopped a few inches in front of me, cupped my face gently, and kissed me. I pulled free from his grasp and tried to push him away; he couldn't be tender and loving. This was passion and fucking, and couldn't be anything else. My heart couldn't handle anything else.

"Why do you even try fighting?" He smiled. "You know I'll win." He grabbed me and kissed me harder this time. When he pulled away, I was breathless again.

He took my hand and led me to the bathroom. He closed and locked the door, turned on the shower, and pulled my T-shirt off.

"Get in," he said and slapped my ass. I let out a yelp and stepped under the hot spray, the water washing over my face. I felt Carson step in behind me and heard the shower curtain close.

"Turn around, let me see you," he said. When I did, Carson ran a hand through his hair again. It was even hotter when he was wet, and he made a noise that sounded like a growl.

"Fuck, you naked and wet is even better than I imagined." His eyes trailed down my body.

"You do that a lot," I said.

"Do what?" His head snapped up from staring at me.

"Run your hand through your hair."

"It's just a habit. I do it when I'm nervous or frustrated or…" He stopped.

"Turned on," I finished for him.

"That's what you want to talk about right now?"

"I don't really want to talk at all." I smiled and winked.

"Well, that can be arranged, baby." He grabbed my hips and turned me back around, entering me from behind in one swift motion.

"Oh God," I cried out. Water pounded down on my back, dripping over my face as Carson drove in and out of me.

"Holy shit, Chloe," he groaned. Carson grabbed a fistful of my wet hair and pulled my head back, arching my back and pushing himself even deeper inside me. The new angle hit just the right spot. My moans got lost in the spray of the water.

"I could fuck you all day long," he said. I clenched my pussy around him in response. "Jesus, that feels so good. You feel so good."

Carson never broke the rhythm, each thrust hitting my g-spot and bringing me closer to the edge. He pulled my hair even harder as he picked up the pace. What would've been painful in any other situation only intensified the pleasure I was feeling. I reached between my legs and rubbed my clit. The added sensation was all I needed.

"Oh yes, don't stop," I cried. "Don't stop." I had to brace myself on the shower wall as my orgasm hit me; my knees buckled, and I felt like the only thing holding me up was Carson's grip on my hair. Carson groaned as my body convulsed around him.

"Oh, fuck yes," he yelled as he buried himself inside me and came. His grip on my hair finally relaxed as he grabbed both my hips and pushed himself as deep as he could go for a few final thrusts. I stood up straight and leaned against the shower wall, while Carson washed himself off under the hot spray.

"I'll let you finish your shower now." Carson grinned and disappeared behind the shower curtain.

"I'm going to hell," I said out loud to myself when I heard the bathroom door shut. I took my time washing my hair, trying not to think about where this was going. By the time I was done, the water was starting to get cold.

I got out and wrapped one towel around my head and another around my body. I had every intention of crawling back in bed and sleeping for a few more hours.

"I don't know how Quinn ever leaves you."

I jumped and spun around. I hadn't expected Carson to still be here. He was fully dressed again, leaning against the kitchen counter, drinking a beer.

"Don't," I snapped, taking a few steps into the kitchen.

"Don't what?"

"Talk about Quinn, compare yourself to Quinn." I closed my eyes and rubbed the bridge of my nose. If he talked about Quinn, then I would have to think about him. And if I thought about him, all the guilt would come rushing back.

"Okay, sorry, just making a statement."

"Well, don't. It's bad enough that you're here, that we're doing ... whatever the fuck this is. But don't make it worse by talking about him like he's some piece of shit boyfriend I shouldn't be with."

"Oh, so this is a thing now?" he said with an eyebrow raised. It pissed me off that he thought this was some sort of joke.

"Get out." I glared at him.

"What?"

"You heard me—leave. I'm done with your bullshit this morning."

"Fine, I won't talk about Quinn, I get it."

"Carson, just go," I pleaded. "If you thought we were going to snuggle on the couch and chit chat, you were wrong; that's not what this is."

"You keep talking about *this*, like it's something that is going to keep happening." I didn't understand why he couldn't just leave; why did he insist on talking about it?

"It's not an isolated incident anymore. It's not just a one-time mistake." I closed my eyes and rubbed my nose again. When I opened my eyes, Carson was standing right in front of me.

"Is that what this is to you? A mistake?" His words were cold as ice.

"I don't know, Carson, what did you expect? I'm married, remember? This isn't just hot, unattached sex. What we're doing has consequences."

"Fuck the consequences," Carson mumbled.

"What about Quinn?" I asked.

Suddenly, it was like there wasn't enough air in the room. I thought of Quinn, of the look in his eyes last night before I left with Dani, a look of total adoration and love, and I couldn't breathe.

"You have to leave," I choked out. "Please."

"Fine, I'll go, but just know whatever *this* is, it is not a mistake for me." With that, he turned and left, the door slamming shut behind him. I stared at the door for a long time wondering what on Earth he meant by that, but my brain was too tired to think. I locked the door and went to the bedroom. I dropped both towels on the floor and crawled under the covers. I was asleep almost as soon as my head hit the pillow.

My dreams were full of more hot sex with Carson. Except in my dream, Quinn was cheating too, with Dani. I guess my subconscious thought it was a good idea to share some of the guilt. I woke up an hour and a half later, my stomach growling.

I threw on some clothes and rummaged through the kitchen in search of food. I found half a pepperoni pizza that Quinn must've had for dinner last night. I pulled two slices out of the fridge and ate them cold, standing in the middle of the kitchen.

I checked my phone to see an email from work. It was from Sean. Subject line: Women's Design Team Lead Position Opening

"Oh my God!" I yelled excitedly, when I'd finished reading the email. "This can't be real." I read the email three times and double checked that it was really from Sean, not some coworker trying pulling a prank on me. When I was sure it was real, I jumped up and down and danced around the kitchen. I started to call Quinn, but then looked at the time. He'd probably be right in the middle of the pregame show. I sent him a quick text instead.

Me: I've got the best news! I can't wait to tell you. I hope you're having the best day. I love you.

I was so excited; I went to my closet and picked outfits for both Monday and Tuesday. After that, I pulled out my old portfolios and started making a checklist of items I wanted to include in my job application. Within hours, I had sketches strewn across the bed and the floor, with several piles of items I definitely wanted to include, possible options, and absolute no's. I laid back on the bed and closed my eyes. I had only planned to rest for a few minutes, but I woke to Quinn knocking softly on the doorway to the bedroom.

"Hi," I yawned. "What are you doing home?"

"What do you mean? It's two AM, where else am I supposed to be?" he asked, confused. I had been asleep for hours.

"Oh, I must've fallen asleep," I said. Quinn laughed.

"Clearly, but what were you doing before that? There are so many sketches on the floor I can't even get in the door over here." I scanned the room. It looked like a bomb had gone off.

"Oh!" I jumped up and stood on the bed, trying not to disturb my piles as I picked my way over to Quinn. "Oh my God, Sean emailed me, Jackie is leaving next week. He wants me to be interim team lead until they can hire someone permanent, which is hopefully me! I was trying to get my portfolio ready."

"That's amazing!" Quinn kissed me gently on the lips. "I'm so proud of you, babe."

"I'm so excited! He said it could be like a trial run. He also said he expects my portfolio to be amazing … hence the mess. I'm sorry, you must be exhausted, and I've got sketches all over the bed."

"It's okay, I'll help you pick up. I didn't think you'd still be awake, so it's good to see you." He planted another kiss on my forehead, and then started to pick up piles of paper.

"Wait! Don't mix them up … I have a system!" He raised an eyebrow at me and scanned the room; his look made it clear he was doubtful there was any sort of organization to my mess. "I promise there is."

Quinn spent the next thirty minutes trying to help me pick-up, but mostly getting yelled at for putting the wrong sketches together. Eventually, he gave up and laid on the bed, while I finished.

"I'm sorry that took so long; it was supposed to be put away before you got home."

Quinn yawned and put an arm around me, pulling me close.

"Don't worry about it. I love seeing how excited you get about it. You run around like the Energizer Bunny on Red Bull. It's fun to watch." He yawned again. I let my excitement get the best of me and launched into a monologue about all the ideas I had for my portfolio and for my meeting with Sean.

"Do you think they'll give me any real responsibility as interim team lead?" Quinn didn't respond. I lifted my head off his chest; he was sound asleep. I turned off the light and then snuggled back down next to Quinn, and was asleep within minutes.

Sunlight was streaming through the windows when I woke up. I snuck out of bed without disturbing Quinn and went to the kitchen to make him breakfast.

While the coffee brewed, I cooked bacon, sausage, and waffles. Twenty-minutes later, I was just getting ready to fry some eggs when the bedroom door opened and Quinn emerged. His hair was a mess, and he was shirtless.

"Good morning, sexy," I said.

"What's all this?" Quinn rubbed his face and yawned.

"Breakfast." He looked skeptical.

"I can see that, but what did I do to deserve a spread like this?"

"Nothing ... I just know you had a long day yesterday and wanted to cook you breakfast." *I'm having an affair with your best friend and feel guilty about it. This is guilt bacon.* Quinn didn't look convinced.

"No, really, what do you want?"

"What? A girl can't make her husband breakfast for no reason?" I poured him coffee and added cream and sugar, just how he liked it. He took the mug, but still looked at me like he was waiting for me to give him some bad news. My stomach growled; I hadn't eaten anything since the pizza yesterday afternoon.

"Come on, quit interrogating me about breakfast and let's eat ... I'm starving."

"Fine, but I still think you're up to something," he said. *You have no idea.*

"I'm not, I swear." *Dirty liar.* I dished us up plates, and we went outside to eat on the patio; it was one of the last warmish days before fall really hit.

"How was the first game day of the season?" I asked when we'd finished eating.

"It was great. Oregon and Oregon State both won, all the shows went off without a hitch, and yours truly was a hit as always."

I'd listened to him do interviews before; he asked thoughtful questions and established real relationships with players and coaches, and got great insight and stories because of it. His boss had even been talking about letting Quinn have a weekly show, where he could do live interviews and tell the stories that got lost in the usual pre-game, post-game shuffle.

"How do you know you were a hit?" I teased. Any show Quinn was on always got good ratings, which was why he was so busy during football season. A lot of fans tuned in just for him.

"Oh, I just know," he said confidently.

"I'm sure you were great … you always are." I got up and started to clear our plates. "Have you heard any more about getting your own show?" Quinn followed me inside and helped me clean up my cooking mess.

"No, not yet. The corporate office is dragging their feet. Some bullshit about funding and advertising, even though Rick says we've already got advertisers on a waitlist for the show."

Rick was Quinn's boss. He'd been on the radio for years, but now just managed all the other talent, schedules, and shows.

"Well, if Rick says so..." I laughed. Rick was notorious for exaggerating the facts, something Quinn was well aware of. He just laughed and shook his head. I put down my dish towel and walked over to Quinn, wrapping my arms around his neck. "Don't stress about it, babe. I know it'll happen. They'd be idiots not to give you your own show."

"This coming from the girl who doesn't even know what a first down is."

"Hey! My football knowledge is irrelevant here. I've listened to you on the radio before, and you're pretty damn good, even if I don't always know what you're talking about." Quinn just laughed and kissed my forehead.

"Oh, Chloe, I love you."

14

Work was absolute chaos, from 6:45 AM, until well after 7 PM, every single night. Sean had me attend as many meetings as I possibly could with Jackie to get a feel for what I would be doing, and then Jackie kept me late most nights, going over things she thought I should know.

Most of the team seemed genuinely happy for me, though there were a few who were quite bitter.

The week after Jackie left was just as busy, if not more so. There were so many meetings, it was unbelievable. I had to stay late almost every night just to find time for the projects I was supposed to be working on but hadn't had time for because of my new responsibilities. For now, I was expected to keep up with my old duties, as well as take on Jackie's tasks. It was more than a little tiring.

On top of that, Chelsy had finally sent the requirements for the application. The timeline had been extended a little, but they wanted all applications in by the end of September, which only gave me three weeks, and Sean hadn't been lying … it was rigorous.

Between football games, late practices, and my crazy schedule at work, I had barely seen Quinn. And had even less time to think about Carson. I hadn't talked to him since our last hook up, but every night, in one way or another, Carson made his way into my dreams. One night, the dream of him was so real and intense, I was awakened in the middle of a real-life orgasm.

"Hmmm, what's wrong babe?" Quinn had asked when my movements woke him up. I had snuggled up close to him, my bare breasts brushing up against his chest.

"Oh, nothing … just a really, really good dream," I whispered. Quinn slipped a hand down my panties.

"How good of a dream?" he asked, then groaned when he felt how wet I was. I bit my lip and moaned as he dipped a finger inside me. "You got that wet just from a dream?" He breathed in my ear.

"Mmmhmm."

"It must've been one hell of a dream."

"It was, now shut up and kiss me." I had two more orgasms that night.

Two weeks passed, and I had so far survived being in charge of the women's design team. My application for the official position was due next week, but was practically done, and I had finally gotten a handle on all the meetings and new tasks.

I felt like I could breathe again. I was done with meetings, and pressing deadlines, so at 1:30 on a Friday, I decided to take the rest of the afternoon off.

I picked up a couple bottles of wine and headed home, with every intention of taking a nap, before spending the evening drinking wine and hanging out with Quinn.

As I turned down the hallway off the elevator, I could hear voices and laughter coming from our apartment, which was strange since I didn't know Quinn had the afternoon off as well. Quinn and Carson were sitting on the couch playing Mario Kart, several beer bottles on the coffee table in front of them.

My heart sunk into my stomach, and I almost dropped the wine.

"Fucking Peach, get out of the way!" Carson yelled.

"It's too late, man, you'll never catch me!" Quinn chided. He stood up and cheered, his arms in the air, when he crossed the finish line only seconds later.

"Damn it! I was going to win that time." Carson tossed his controller down onto the couch.

"Sure you were," Quinn laughed. "Have you ever beat me at Mario Kart?"

"Shut up, man."

Neither of them had noticed I was standing there watching their entire exchange.

"You guys having a good time?" I said, finally letting the door close behind me. They both visibly jumped and turned around to look at me. I laughed and shook my head at them.

"Chloe, what are you doing here?" Quinn said. Carson didn't say anything; he just stared at me with his mouth open.

"I could probably ask you two the same thing." The voice that came out of me didn't sound like my own. I was trying so hard to keep my emotions in check, but seeing Quinn and Carson in the same room made my head reel and brought so many feelings to the surface that they all threatened to bubble over and make a giant mess. "I decided to take the afternoon off; it's been so crazy lately, I figured I deserved it."

"Same thing here," Quinn said. "With another double-game day tomorrow, Rick let me leave at noon." That didn't explain what the hell Carson was doing here, considering he should also be at work right now.

"I'm just playing hooky," Carson said, as if he could read my mind. "Quinn called and asked what I was doing this afternoon, so I left work, got some beer, and here we are."

"Awesome, I'm going to go for a run," I said. Suddenly, napping was the furthest thing from my mind.

"Why don't you play with us?" Carson said.

"Yeah, you can be Peach," Quinn piped in.

"You guys don't really want a girl ruining the giant bro-fest you've got going on here, do you?" I took off my heels and walked toward the bedroom to change. "Besides, you wouldn't want to end up embarrassed."

"Oh, come on, you can't talk shit like that, and then not play!" Carson called after me.

"Don't worry, she'll play," I heard Quinn say. "And she'll probably kick your ass." They started arguing again about who was better at Mario Kart as I closed the door to the bedroom and changed out of my work clothes.

When I went back out in the living room, Quinn was in the kitchen making onion dip, and Carson was on the couch drinking a beer. I had put on running shorts and a tank top, even though I really had no intention of going running. I plopped down on the end of the couch, as far away from Carson as possible.

"Hey, will you bring me a beer?" I said to Quinn.

"I thought you were going running?" Carson asked, looking at me skeptically.

"And miss the look on your face when I beat you at Mario Kart? Nah, this will be way more fun."

"I'm not losing to a girl," he said all huffy.

"Don't be so sure about that," Quinn said, returning to the couch and handing me a beer. "She's pretty damn good."

"You probably just let her win so you can get laid," Carson snorted.

"You know I'd never do that. I'm way too competitive," Quinn replied.

"Are we going to sit here and chit chat, or are we going to play? I interrupted.

"Let's play," Carson said.

We spent the next two hours playing Mario Kart, and, true to my word, I kicked their asses. Quinn did win once, but only because Carson had crashed into me on purpose. Carson never even got close.

"I'm fucking done with this stupid game," Carson fumed after I beat them both, again. Quinn got up and went to the bathroom.

"I told you I was good," I said arrogantly. I leaned back on the couch and put my arms behind my head.

"I already knew you were good," Carson said quietly, his eyes narrowed. I swallowed hard. God damn it, why? "But I didn't know you were a Mario Kart prodigy." Carson's tone returned to its normal playfulness as Quinn came back in the living room.

"Derek and I used to play for hours," I explained.

"Don't feel bad, dude, she beats everybody." Quinn patted Carson on the head like a little kid, and I laughed so hard I snorted.

Carson just sat on the couch and sulked, which made me laugh even harder. Quinn's phone rang, interrupting my fit of laughter.

"Oh, hey Rick," he answered and went down the hall into the bedroom.

"Wanna play again?" I said.

"I don't think my ego can handle it," Carson said dryly and ran a hand through his hair.

"I think your ego will be just fine."

"Fine, one more game, but I swear to God I'm winning this time." Carson scooted over on the couch so we were right next to each other; his hand brushed against my bare thigh and my heart skipped a beat. He smiled and ran his hand up the inside of my thigh under the edge of my shorts, and I inhaled sharply.

"Ready, let's play." Carson pushed the start button while my mind was still reeling from his touch.

"What? Come on, that's not fair."

"Life's not fair, baby," He laughed.

"Fucking cheater," I mumbled as I navigated Peach out from behind Mario and Donkey Kong. Carson was Luigi, and was winning because he had cheated. I was gaining on him, but not fast enough.

"Come on, you stupid bitch, go faster!" I yelled.

"Easy there." Carson laughed. "It's just a game."

"Bite me."

Luigi crossed the finish line half a second before Peach, and Carson erupted into cheers. You would've thought he won a gold medal at the fucking Olympics. He danced around, rubbing it in my face.

"You beat her?" Quinn asked from behind us.

"Only because he cheated," I sneered.

"Hey, a win's a win." Carson shrugged.

"I beat you like fifty times."

"Yeah, but I beat you the last time, so that makes me the winner," Carson taunted. I rolled my eyes and glared at him. His eyes met mine and neither of us moved. There was no playfulness in them now—all fire and desire. We stood there staring at each other for too long. Long enough that I was sure Quinn was going to notice the air between us had changed. It was no longer light and playful but thick and full of sexual tension.

"Carson, are you staying for dinner?" Quinn asked, opening the fridge.

"What?" Carson snapped out of his stare and looked over at Quinn.

"Dinner?" Quinn repeated.

"No, I've got to get going," Carson replied. Thank God. I felt like I deserved a gold medal for keeping my composure for the last three hours. "I should probably go do some of the work I skipped out on this afternoon."

Carson grabbed his jacket and headed toward the door. Quinn didn't seem to question his abrupt exit, but I knew the reason behind Carson's sudden need to leave. He was struggling just as much as I was.

"See you guys later," Carson said, letting the door slam behind him.

"That was fun," Quinn said. "I'm glad you got the afternoon off, too."

"It was fun," I said. I walked over and wrapped my arms around Quinn's body as he stood and stared into the fridge. I didn't realize I had missed hanging out with Quinn and Carson as just friends, but our afternoon of childish games had reminded me why I used to like hanging out with them in the first place. It was impossible not to think about how it would all end if Quinn knew.

"What did Rick want?" I asked Quinn, suddenly remembering his phone call.

"Oh, we're leaving a little earlier than planned tomorrow. The weather in Corvallis is supposed to be shitty, so we want to get there early and get all the equipment unloaded and set up before it starts to rain."

"Oh. That's going to be a long day."

"Tell me about it. You and Dani are coming to Eugene, right?"

"Oh damn it! I totally forgot! That's probably why she tried to call me yesterday. What time is the game?"

"Not 'til 8:30."

"Fuck … I better call Dani," I said. "There is nothing in this fridge. Do you want to order us some Chinese?"

"Yeah, that sounds good," Quinn said, finally shutting the fridge door.

I picked up my phone and walked down the hall to the bedroom. Dani answered on the first ring.

"I thought you were ignoring me in hopes I would forgot about taking you to the game," she said.

"Normally I would say that's the truth, but I actually really just forgot about it. It has been crazy busy at work."

"Aah, I'm so glad you're coming with me!"

"Quinn said it's supposed to rain."

"This is Oregon … it rains every day."

"Dani! I already don't like football; I'm going to hate it even more in the rain."

"It's only going to rain in the morning. We'll be fine, I promise. You can't bail on me now; I'd never find anyone else to go. And we had a deal!"

"Fine, what time are we leaving?"

"I'll pick you up at 4:30, then we can get dinner in Eugene before the game."

"You're going to owe me more than dinner."

"Love you!" Dani said and hung up before I could say anything else.

I groaned and collapsed on the bed. Quinn laughed from the doorway.

"I take it you're still going to the game?"

"Yes, why do you and Dani insist on trying to make me like football?"

"We just like torturing you," he said. I threw a pillow at him. "It should be a pretty good game; Utah is supposed to be good this year."

"Maybe I'll wear red."

"You wouldn't," Quinn gasped dramatically.

"Anything is better than Oregon green."

"I'm going to pretend you didn't say that."

"I think I *will* wear red." I stood up and started to dig around in my closet. I pulled out two red hoodies and watched Quinn's look of horror, before I pulled out the white Oregon hoodie he'd given me our first Christmas together. It had a big green "O" on it, but it was wearable.

"You about gave me a heart attack. I seriously thought you were going to wear red for a minute."

"I guess you'll just have to see what I'm wearing tomorrow," I laughed.

"If you show up in red, I may never speak to you again," Quinn said, his face serious but his eyes full of laughter.

"Of course you would … you love me," I laughed. I let out a yelp as Quinn tackled me on the bed and tickled me.

"Stop, stop," I squealed through my laughter. "I won't wear red, I promise!" Quinn stopped tickling me, but didn't move from on top of me. He held my hands above my head and looked at me intently.

"I do love you, Chloe," he said before he leaned down and kissed me deeply. His lips were on my neck when the doorbell rang, letting us know the delivery boy was downstairs with our food. Quinn groaned as he rolled off me and went to get our food.

We enjoyed egg rolls, beef and broccoli, and sweet and sour chicken while we watched *The Big Bang Theory*.

"This was seriously just the day I needed," Quinn said after we had cleaned up dinner. "I'm glad you came home early." He leaned in and kissed me.

"Me too." I yawned. I hadn't gotten my nap, though, and was still exhausted. "Wanna watch a movie in bed?"

"That sounds amazing." Even though it was only 8:30, we both got ready for bed. Quinn turned on *Gone Girl* and turned off the lights. We both fell asleep before Amazing Amy disappeared.

It was gray and gloomy outside when I woke up. I seriously doubted it would clear up before the game and made a mental note to take a rain jacket with me. I sent Quinn a text telling him to have a good day, since he'd left hours before I'd woken, and another to Dani just to make sure she hadn't changed her mind about me going to the game. She hadn't.

I was just about to get in the shower when I got a text from Carson.

Carson: Spending all afternoon with you and not being able to touch you was fucking torture.

Me: It's about time you learned some patience.

Carson: I've never been patient. Wanna come over?

Me: I shouldn't.

Carson: That wasn't the question.

Me: Yes, but just because I want to doesn't mean I should do it.

Carson: Yes it does. Come over, bring me some coffee.

Me: You're demanding.

Carson: You love it when I tell you what to do. Especially when I tell you to touch yourself.

The message sent a shiver down my spine. He knew exactly what to say to turn me on.

Me: I'll be there in half an hour.

Carson: That was easy ;)

Me: Don't make me change my mind.

Carson: Please don't change your mind. I'm hard just thinking about you.

Quinn had never been much for sexting, so I decided to have a little fun with Carson while I got dressed.

Me: It makes me so wet when you talk dirty to me.

Carson: I love how wet you get for me. I love touching it, tasting it.

I threw on a pair of jeans and a Nike jacket with nothing underneath, slipped my feet into a pair of Toms, and headed out the door. I replied to Carson on my way down the elevator.

Me: I'm so turned on right now. I don't know if I can wait until I get there.

Carson: Get your ass over here before I come in my pants like a teenage boy.

Me: I thought you wanted coffee?

Carson: Fuck coffee. I need you.

I got in my car and headed north toward Carson's. My phone vibrated every few seconds with a new text. I read them at a stoplight.

Carson: I need to see you naked, on my bed.

Carson: I need to run my tongue over every inch of your body.

Carson: I need to taste you.

The texts didn't stop the entire twenty-five minute drive to Alberta.

Carson: I need to be inside you.

Carson: I need to see the look in your eyes when you come.

Carson: I need you to scream my name over and over again.

Carson: I need to fuck you until you fall apart in my arms.

By the time I parked outside Carson's apartment building, it felt like fire was coursing through my veins instead of blood, and the need growing between my legs was so intense it almost hurt. I took the stairs, two at a time; I couldn't wait for the elevator.

Carson opened the door, wearing only his boxers. His hair was a mess, like he had just gotten out of bed.

"It's about damn time," he said. "I thought maybe you changed your mind."

"Traffic was a bitch." I stepped inside. Carson's lips were on mine before the door clicked shut. He pushed me back against the closed door, his mouth devouring mine. I ran a hand through his hair and pulled him even closer. Carson dragged the zipper of my jacket down and smiled when he realized I wasn't wearing anything under it.

"I think you missed some pieces when you were getting dressed," he said, his words a hot whisper in my ear.

"What's the point of putting on clothes if you were going to take them off anyway?"

"Touché," he said. He undid the button of my jeans and pulled the zipper down. I wasn't wearing any panties either. He removed my jeans, leaving me completely naked, no more than two feet inside his apartment "I swear to God, woman, you are going to be the death of me." Carson stood back and admired the view, his hand automatically running through his hair.

We didn't make it to his bedroom. We fucked right there on the floor just inside his doorway, and then again on his kitchen table.

15

It was just after one when I got back to our apartment. I had stopped for a coffee and bagel after I left Carson's.

I knew Dani had said she didn't want to know about my affair, but I wasn't sure how I was going to handle spending ten hours with her and not say anything. My guilty conscience needed someone else to know about my indiscretions. I couldn't be the only one keeping this secret. But I didn't want to ruin our entire day, so I had to try.

I took a shower and let my hair air dry into loose waves. I pulled on clean jeans and my Oregon hoodie, and then sat down at the kitchen table to do some work until Dani got there. I didn't want to fall behind after taking the afternoon off yesterday. I had seventy-five emails. You would've thought I had been gone three days, not three hours.

I had answered, deleted, or archived all the emails and had started on my personal letter to the hiring committee by the time Dani texted me to let me know she was downstairs.

I pulled black boots on over my skinny jeans, grabbed an extra jacket and my purse, and headed downstairs.

"It's a damn good thing you have on an Oregon hoodie, otherwise I was going to have to kill you," Dani said as I got in the car.

"I told Quinn I was going to wear red, you know, to support Utah," I said.

"That's not even funny."

"It's just a football game, it's not that big of a deal."

"Are you trying to get yourself kicked out of my car before we even get on the interstate?" she said, and I laughed.

"Is that an option?" I asked, and she glared at me. "Calm down, I'm only teasing."

Dani and I talked about work for a while. It'd been so crazy lately, I hadn't even gotten a chance to tell her about my temporary-but-hopefully-permanent promotion.

"Oh my God! How have you not told me this yet?"

"It's been nonstop craziness since it happened. I'm sorry … I meant to call you." *That's not the only news I've sat on,* I thought. "I promise if I get the job for real, you'll know immediately," I said.

"Of course you'll get it. Why would they give you a trial if they weren't planning on giving you the job eventually?" she asked.

"I could still fuck it up." I shrugged.

"You won't fuck it up. You were made for this job. You're going to kick ass. I'm so fucking proud of you."

Dani told me about a couple she'd done an ultrasound for the other day. The dad had cried when she'd told them they were having twin girls.

"Like sad tears, not joyfully happy tears," Dani said, exasperated. "His poor wife was so excited. I wanted to punch him in the face and tell him at the very least he should pretend to be excited for his wife."

"Yeah, he's probably sleeping on the couch for the rest of his life," I said.

"I love watching Dad's reactions the best. The mom's always try to act excited even when I can tell they are disappointed they didn't get the gender they wanted. But dads never fake it; you always get the raw reaction."

"I still don't know how you can even tell anything on an ultrasound. It all just looks like a blurry, black and white blob."

"I can't even draw a straight line, so we're even."

We fell into a comfortable silence, and I dozed off. When I opened my eyes, we were pulling into a parking lot a few blocks from the stadium.

"Well, hello again, sleeping beauty," Dani said sarcastically.

"I thought you said we were going to get dinner?" I was still in my post sleep haze and confused why we were at the stadium when the game didn't start for another two hours.

"We are, but there is a great burger place just a couple blocks from here, I figured we could get a parking spot before shit gets crazy."

"Aah, sounds like a good idea."

"All my ideas are good, duh," Dani laughed as she parked the car.

"Mmm, remember when you got a pixie haircut sophomore year after you broke up with Jason? That's two bad ideas … Jason and a pixie cut."

"You must be thinking about someone else. I would never do that." Dani turned and looked at me, and we both burst out laughing.

We laughed and reminisced about old times all through dinner. By the time we got back to the stadium, my stomach hurt from laughing so much.

Our tickets were on the 50-yard line, six rows up from the field. Even I was impressed.

"How did you get these tickets? Did they cost you a fortune?" I asked.

"Actually they were free. One of the doctors I work with is a season ticket holder, but he's out on vacation this week, so I begged him mercilessly for weeks, and he finally gave them to me."

"I might come to games more if we had seats like this. Look, you can see the sweat on that guy's face from here!"

"Oh my God, are you actually getting excited about football?"

"No, being excited about football and being excited about being within ogling distance of dozens of super fit 20-somethings is very different."

Dani just shook her head and laughed. There was still 45-minutes until kickoff when Quinn texted me.

Quinn: Meet me on the concourse in five, I've got a few minutes.

Me: Awesome, see you in a minute!

"Quinn has a few minutes, so I'm going to go meet him. Do you want me to get you anything?"

"A beer," Dani said. I held out my hand. She looked at me like I was a psycho, and then slapped it away. "I'm not giving you money."

"That was the deal … you buy all the beer and don't make me come to another game for two years," I reminded her.

She mumbled under her breath as she dug in her pocket and handed me a twenty.

"Thanks, I'll be back in a few."

I could see Quinn waiting at the top of the steps.

"Hey," I said. He greeted me with a deep, passionate kiss. Someone to my left yelled at us to get a room.

"Hi babe," Quinn said when he finally pulled his mouth off mine.

"Hi," I said again, a little out of breath from the kiss.

"It's a good thing you're not wearing red."

I pulled the edge of my jeans to show him the red panties I was wearing.

"I'd show you the matching bra, but that might be inappropriate," I laughed. Quinn just shook his head.

"Let's make a bet," he said, a wicked grin spreading across his face. "Since you are hell-bent on supporting Utah, one way or another, let's make a bet."

"I'm listening..." I folded my arms across my chest.

"If Oregon wins, you have to put on the Oregon lingerie I bought you and wait up for me tonight," he said, then added, "And you have to wear an Oregon shirt the next time we visit your parents."

"And if Utah wins?" I raised my eyebrow.

"Anything you want, babe."

"Anything?" I asked.

"Yup."

"Deal," I said, sticking out my hand. I didn't know what I wanted out of the bet, but I knew having something like that to hang over Quinn's head would be so much fun.

"What do you want if Utah wins?"

"I haven't decided yet."

"You have to tell me so I know what I'm getting into!" Quinn protested.

"That wasn't part of the deal." I leaned in close and whispered in his ear, "You just better hope your precious Ducks can pull off the win."

"You're evil, you know that, right?"

"Come on ... I told Dani I'd get us some beers." I took his hand as we stood in line for beer.

"I love you, babe." He gave me another kiss, this one much tamer, and left to head back to the booth, as the game was about to start.

"I love you too."

I took the steps back down much slower, careful not to spill our beers.

"What the fuck ... did you guys go have a quickie in the car or something?" Dani said when I returned to our seats. "I thought I was going to have to come up there and get my own beer."

"No, we were making a bet."

"What kind of bet?" she asked. I filled her in on the details.

"So what are you going to ask for if Utah wins? Which they won't by the way," Dani said after she finished glaring at me for wearing red underwear.

"I honestly don't know yet. But it'll be fun to make him squirm while I figure it out."

"Maybe you should ask for a 'hall pass,' or I guess at this point a 'get out of jail free card' would be more appropriate," she said, her voice icy. She took a sip of her beer and didn't look at me.

"That's fucked up." I couldn't believe she was bringing this up now.

"You're the one who did it." She sounded angry. Even after all these years I sometimes couldn't figure her out.

"You're a bitch sometimes," I said. "Why did you even bring this up? Are you trying to ruin the good time we are having?"

"I watched you make out with Quinn at the top of the steps," she said. I waited for her to make her point, but she didn't keep going.

"So what?" I snapped. "He's my husband … I'm allowed to kiss him."

"I just don't know how you can carry on with Quinn and pretend like nothing happened," she said. "I guess I'm still just disappointed in you."

I started to respond, but at that moment, the Oregon fight song began playing loudly over the speakers, and Autzen stadium shook as fans cheered and stomped and welcomed the Ducks, wearing their God-awful neon yellow uniforms, to the field. Thank God. I didn't know what else Dani was going to say, but the way our conversation was going, it wasn't going to be pretty. Fighting with her about my affair in a crowded stadium was not my idea of fun. I had been on the verge of telling her everything in the car ride down, so now I was glad I hadn't. She didn't need even more ammo against me.

It took every ounce of restraint I had to not cheer loudly in Dani's face when the Utah players ran onto the field. I didn't care who won the game, bet or not, but she'd pissed me off, and now I was going to cheer for Utah just to make her mad.

Who the fuck did she think she was? Like she'd never made any bad choices. *Yeah, but she's never slept with her husband's best friend … repeatedly.* I wanted the little voice in my head to fuck off, but she was right. If we were ranking bad choices, I was definitely winning.

My phone vibrated in my pocket.

Quinn: LET'S GO DUCKS!!

I'd just heard the Utah cheerleaders do a stupid cheer, so I responded to Quinn's message with it.

Me: U-T-A-H Fight, Fight, Fight!!

Quinn responded with a puking emoji, and I laughed. I caught Dani watching me out of the corner of my eye.

"I'm sorry," she mouthed, her words drown out by music and cheering.

"It's okay, I probably deserved it," I said in her ear as I pulled her in for a hug.

The rest of the game was surprisingly pleasant. It turned out football was more fun when I had a reason to care. Although, I got a few weird looks from the fans around me when I groaned every time Oregon scored.

With forty-five seconds left in the game, Oregon was up by one and Utah had the ball. Dani was jumping up and down screaming things like, "wrap him up" and "hold the line" and lost her shit when Oregon got called for a penalty that put Utah in field goal range with five seconds left.

"Damn it! Utah's kicker never misses. They call him fucking Automatic Andy," Dani groaned.

"That's good for me!" I said. He had made two field goals already this game.

"I can't watch. Goddamn it, I'm going to be sick." Dani covered her eyes as Utah setup for the field goal, but then peeped through her fingers as the kick went up. It sailed to the right of the goal post, and the stadium erupted.

"He missed! Automatic Andy missed! Oh my God! Yes!" Dani jumped up and down and yelled with the other 50,000 Oregon fans in Autzen Stadium.

Poor Andy sank to his knees on the field and held his helmet in his hands while Oregon players swarmed and celebrated. I wanted to go out there and give him a hug.

Dani shook me back to reality, and I tore my eyes off the Utah kicker.

"That was awesome!"

"No! Now I have to wear that stupid lingerie Quinn got me."

"You get to have super-hot sex tonight. I don't think you can really complain about losing this bet," she said.

I shrugged; she was right. It felt strange to be giddy and excited about a night with Quinn when earlier in the day I had had the same feeling on my way to see Carson.

I checked my phone as we made our way to the car. There was a text from Quinn.

> *Quinn: Can't wait to see you in Oregon's colors when I get home. Get ready for a night you'll never forget.*

I was a terrible road-tripper. Dani had to nudge me awake when she dropped me off at our apartment.

Although it was almost two AM, my nap in the car had refreshed me, and I was awake and excited. I lit some candles in the bedroom, then dug around in my dresser until I found the hideous bright yellow lace teddy and matching thong. The fabric had big green "O's" all over it. I laughed.

"Well, that's appropriate," I said to no one. I slipped out of my jeans and hoodie and took off the red bra and panties I had been wearing. It was a shame, since they looked way better than what I was about to put on.

I glanced at myself in the mirror and laughed again—it looked ridiculous. I crawled on the bed and laid right in the middle, propped myself up with all the pillows, and read a book on my phone. I didn't have to wait long; I hadn't even made it five pages when I heard Quinn's key scrape in the lock.

Quinn didn't even bother putting his stuff away; he just dropped it on the floor and walked toward the bedroom.

He stood at the foot of the bed, a huge grin on his face as his eyes raked over my body.

"I didn't think you'd actually do it," he said.

"I thought about it, but a bet's a bet. Fucking Automatic Andy screwed me over." Quinn raised an eyebrow at me and pulled his polo shirt over his head.

"Oh, you know their player's names now?"

"Only that one … and only because of Dani," I admitted sheepishly.

"I was sweating when they got in field goal range. He never misses a kick that close." Quinn undid his pants and let them drop to the floor.

"That's what everyone keeps saying, but of course when I had skin in the game he missed." I shook my head.

"I'm damn glad he did. Seeing you here, all sprawled out and looking hot as fuck is better than Christmas."

"This lingerie looks ridiculous," I said.

"I know someone who would disagree." He winked and took off his boxers, his already hard cock sticking straight out.

Quinn crawled toward me on the bed, a look of pure lust in his eyes, and my heartbeat quickened. He straddled me, his hands on either side of my head, his knees between my spread legs, his cock hard and stiff against my stomach.

Quinn lowered his head and kissed me, soft and tender, like he was savoring every taste of me.

"I could spend the rest of my life kissing you and be completely happy," he said when he finally pulled away.

A ball of guilt formed in my stomach at his words. It threatened to bubble up and spill out of me. I silenced it by grabbing Quinn's face and pulling him back down for another kiss. This time more feverish. Quinn dragged his mouth off mine and ran his tongue over my nipple. The warmth of his tongue and the rough lace fabric created a delicious friction, and I let out a moan.

"Oh my God, Quinn," I whispered. Quinn sat back on his heels and looked at me like I was a piece of meat he was about to devour.

"You are so fucking beautiful," he said. I squirmed under the intensity of his gaze. His hands roamed up my stomach and over my breasts and rested on the neckline of the ridiculous yellow teddy. I let out a small scream when he ripped the lace in half, pulling it off my body and discarding it. Then his mouth was on me again, licking, kissing, and tasting every inch of skin from my neck to the top of my lace thong. When he got there, he ripped it off, too, and then resumed his tour south. I moaned when his tongue flicked over my clit and swore loudly when it dipped inside me.

"Holy shit, baby," I mumbled and arched my back off the bed. His hands gripped my hips and held them in place while his tongue did things I didn't know were possible. I was on the brink of an orgasm when he lifted his mouth off me and smiled. He did it three more times, bringing me to the edge of pleasure before pulling me back.

"Quinn, please," I begged. "You're killing me."

"Just wait … it'll be worth it," he said, the words a tickle against my most sensitive area. This time he didn't stop. His tongue knew just what to do, and my body was primed and ready. My world went black as my orgasm crashed into me and washed over me like a wave breaking against the rocky Oregon coast. My nails dug into Quinn's shoulders, and I yelled incoherently as the waves of never-ending pleasure continued. Quinn finally pulled his mouth off me, leaving a trail of kisses up my stomach as he crawled his way back over top of me.

"That ... was ... holy fuck..." I struggled to make a coherent sentence in my post-orgasm daze.

"I'm just getting started, baby." Quinn smiled and leaned down to kiss me again. I moaned against his mouth moments later when he entered me slowly, burying himself inside me before pulling back out again. In and out, in and out, so slow and delicious. He sat back up again, grabbed one of my legs, and put it over his shoulder before lowering himself back down.

"Chloe, fuck, you're amazing," Quinn said through gritted teeth. "I've been thinking about this all day."

"Fuck, Quinn, it feels so good," I moaned. I ran my hands down his back and grabbed his ass, pulling him in even deeper.

I bit my lip and moaned as Quinn swirled his hips. He did it again and a shiver ran down my spine. Quinn closed his eyes and groaned, his body tense, his movements slow and deliberate. I reached a hand between our bodies and circled my clit with two fingers. My body tightened around Quinn's, and I could tell he was close too. We came together moments later, both of us moaning as we got lost in the pleasure.

Quinn rolled off me and collapsed on the bed. We lay there in the glow of the candlelight for a long time, both of us breathing hard. After a few minutes, I thought Quinn must've fallen asleep. I pulled the covers over me and blew out the candles on my side of the bed.

"Sorry about your lingerie," Quinn said finally. I rolled over on my side and looked at him.

"Please … you did me a favor!" I laughed. "Now I'll have to put back on my Utah-red panties and bra." I moved like I was going to get out of bed but Quinn pushed me back down into the plush mattress.

"Don't even think about it."

"Why not? I think they're good luck, Oregon won."

"You're not going to need clothes for a while." He winked at me and disappeared under the covers.

Thank God Andy missed.

It was just after noon when I finally woke up. Quinn was still sound asleep beside me. I stretched, but didn't get out of bed. I wasn't ready to leave the warm covers and soft bed. I was reading emails on my phone and catching up on Instagram when my phone vibrated.

Carson: When can I see you again?

I lifted my head and looked at Quinn; he was on his stomach, but his breathing was slow and even, and he was definitely still asleep.

Me: Seriously? I'm in bed with Quinn.

Carson: Lucky bastard.

Carson: Soo... seeing you again, that's happening, right?

Me: God you are impatient. I saw you yesterday.

Carson: And it was fucking amazing.

Carson: Doesn't Oregon have the Thursday night game this week?

Me: How the fuck am I supposed to know that?

Carson: They do. I looked.

Me: So what's your point?

Carson: I'll come over Thursday, bring you dinner, maybe I'll let you beat me at Mario Kart again.

I giggled at the memory of Carson pouting when I beat him before.

Me: Oh please, I beat you fair and square, except when you cheated.

"Who are you texting?" Quinn said. I visibly jumped and stuck my phone under my body. Quinn laughed. He was still laying on his stomach, his head turned toward me now. I was pretty sure from that angle he wouldn't have been able to see my screen.

"Jesus, you scared me."

"Sorry, but that was funny. You hid your phone so fast, you would've thought I caught you watching porn or something." *Or something,* I thought to myself. *Something worse than porn.*

"Nah, you just scared me," I lied. Quinn rolled out of bed and walked to the bathroom butt naked. I couldn't help but stare as he walked away. What was wrong with me? Here I was making plans with Carson, when I already had Quinn, and he worshiped me. Quinn was amazing, and we had a great sex life. I never knew there was anything missing until Carson. Quinn knew me intimately, knew everything I loved, but it didn't feel like enough anymore. With Carson, it was always rip-your-clothes-off passion and intensity; there was a sense of urgency that somewhere along the way had gotten lost with Quinn.

I picked my phone back up and had three more messages from Carson.

Carson: I don't recall any cheating.

Carson: Playing a little dirty is just my style.

Carson: Hello? Am I making plans with myself now or what?

I shook my head. He was acting like a needy child.

Me: My God, seriously. I'm at home with Quinn. You have to stop acting like an impatient teenage girl. Unless you want to get caught.

Carson: What happens if we get caught? Would you choose him or me?

I glared at my phone. What the hell? Was he seriously asking me that?

Me: Fuck you, Carson.

Carson: Whoa, calm down, just playing.

Me: It's not a joke, okay?

Carson: Got it. So Thursday?

Me: I'll let you know. Work has been crazy lately.

Carson: So that means yes. I'll be there at 8.

Me: I didn't say yes.

Carson: I'm not taking no for an answer, so say whatever you want, I'll still be there at 8.

Me: Fine, whatever.

I heard the toilet flush and deleted the string of text messages before I pulled the covers off and got out of bed. I was standing by the bed, naked, and stretching, when Quinn came back in the room. He had put on a pair of basketball shorts.

"Are you trying to get me back in bed for round two?" he said.

"Round two? I think we passed round two and three last night."

"I didn't hear any complaints."

"Oh, no complaints here, only rave reviews."

"Is that right?" Quinn walked over and stood in front of me.

"I'd never leave a false review," I whispered. Quinn leaned in to kiss me, but I ducked sideways and walked over to my closet. "But no, I'm not trying to start something. I need to go for a run."

"You didn't get enough cardio last night?" Quinn pouted. I pulled on a pair of leggings, a sports bra, and jacket.

"I've only got a few more weeks of nice weather, then I won't be able to run outside, and I'll participate in all the indoor cardio you want." I sat on the edge of the bed and laced up my tennis shoes.

"All right, fine."

"I'll be back in a little while." I kissed him on the cheek, grabbed my headphones off the table, and left.

For forty-five minutes, I tried to make sense of what I was doing. Tried to understand why, when I was happy with Quinn, when our relationship was everything I'd ever dreamed of and more, I was willing to risk everything for a fling with Carson. But nothing made sense. There was no sane explanation for my actions.

The passion between Carson and me was all-consuming—an overwhelming wave of lust and desire. You didn't ignore that kind of connection. I knew it sounded crazy. I knew no one would ever understand. I didn't need anyone to understand … I didn't need to explain it … I just needed to not get caught.

16

Carson

I was a grade-A douche bag. No, I was worse than a douche bag. If being an asshole were an Olympic sport, I'd have more gold medals for being an asshole than Michael Phelps did for swimming.

What kind of man had an affair with his best friend's wife? What kind of man tracked her down and pushed her to fuck him, even when she tried to stop him? *Let's be real, she didn't try very hard,* a nasty little voice in my head said.

That was true, it had been easy, too easy. But that wasn't the point, it didn't matter if she practically threw herself at me, I should have walked away.

It had started out as just sex—the best sex of my life—but now I found myself wanting to spend more time with her. Even though we'd been friends for years I realized there was a lot I didn't know about Chloe. Now I wanted to know everything about her.

This wasn't how it was supposed to be. It was just supposed to be sex, nothing else. But I was falling for her. Hard. If I wasn't careful, I was going to end up in love my best friend's wife. What the fuck would I do then?

My dick stirred at the thought of Chloe. Fuck. I knew it was wrong, but I didn't care. I was addicted to her—her soft skin, her touch, her taste, her smell, the way it felt to be buried inside her, and the way she screamed my name when she came.

I set my razor down, put both hands on the sink in front of me, and looked at myself in the mirror. I didn't look like the kind of guy who ruined marriages. With blond hair and blue eyes, I looked innocent as fuck. I ran a hand through my hair and blew out a breath, then laughed when I remembered how she'd noticed my tic. Damn it, everything I did made me think of her.

We'd made plans for Thursday, but now that seemed too far away. I picked up my phone and texted her.

Me: What are you doing?

Chloe: Working.

Me: At 7:30 in the morning?

Chloe: Yes. I've basically got two jobs at the moment.

Me: What are you wearing?

Chloe: I'm at work.

Me: I'm not. I'm standing in my bathroom, naked and hard, thinking about you.

Chloe: What do you want me to do about it?

Me: Go in the bathroom, send me a picture.

Chloe: Not a chance in hell.

I imagined her sitting at her desk, giggling, as she refused to play along. That turned me on even more.

Me: Don't worry, I don't need a picture. The image of you naked on my kitchen table, legs spread wide, wet and ready for me is burned into my memory.

I ran a hand down my shaft as I imagined it. Chloe lying there on my table, hair tousled, biting her lip and rubbing her nipples. Fuck, I let out a groan as I moved my hand up and down.

Chloe: Are you trying to torture me?

Me: Is it working?

Chloe: I'm so wet right now. How am I supposed to work like this?

Me: Now you know how I feel. I can't concentrate on anything because I'm constantly thinking about your perfect pussy and the things I want to do to it.

I stroked myself, while I waited for her reply, and watched my eyes grow dark in the mirror as I got closer and closer to the edge.

Chloe: Purple lace panties, that are now soaking wet thanks to you, a black bra, a navy blue sleeveless dress.

It took me a minute to realize she was finally answering my question about what she was wearing.

Chloe: It's short enough that if I spread my legs under my desk I can touch myself.

I let out another moan, my strokes coming faster and harder now. I tried to text her back but my brain and my fingers weren't currently working together.

Chloe: No one else is here yet. I could dip a finger inside. Touch myself just the way you like.

I had to grip the sink for balance as my legs started to tremble.

I imagined Chloe, legs spread as she fingered herself under her desk, murmuring my name as she made herself come. The image was enough to send me over the edge. I stroked harder and faster and groaned her name as I came.

17

Sexting Carson made me so horny I couldn't focus all day, and, as a result, I got almost nothing accomplished at work.

I did, however, finally manage to get my application submitted. It was perfect, the best portfolio I'd ever put together. That, combined with me being named interim team lead, gave me a damn good shot at the position.

I didn't even bother trying to stay late to catch up on work I'd ignored all day while I'd daydreamed about Carson. At 4:59, I shut down my computer and left. I texted Quinn on my way to car.

Me: Are you home?

I resisted the impulse to hike up my dress right there in my car and finally satisfy the urge that had been building all day.

Quinn: I'm picking up some dinner and then I'll be home.

Me: Good. I'm going to rip your clothes off as soon as I see you.

Quinn: Is that a promise or a threat? ;)

Me: Both. Can't wait to see you.

I made it home before Quinn did. The apartment was dark and quiet when I opened the door. I started undressing in the kitchen, leaving a trail of clothing down the hall to the bedroom. I didn't turn on any lights, but lit a few candles in the bedroom and laid down on the bed, naked. It didn't take long before Quinn opened the door.

"Chloe?" he called from the living room.

"In here," I said. I heard him chuckle as he made his way to the bedroom.

"What are you doing?" I could hear the smile in his voice.

"I started without you." I ran a hand down my stomach and between my legs.

"Oh really?" Quinn appeared in the doorway, a huge grin plastered on his face. His eyes narrowed when he saw me. "Dinner is going to get cold."

"Fuck dinner," I said, my eyes never leaving his face, my fingers tracing lazy circles around my clit.

"I'd much rather fuck you," he said and pulled his shirt off over his head and unbuckled his belt. I groaned when he removed his boxers and his hard cock sprang free.

Quinn spent the next hour satisfying what I'd been fighting all day—his body erasing the memory of Carson's and my conversation earlier in the day.

I used to wonder how people who had affairs found the time to sneak around and still have a normal life. How they came up with lies and excuses for where they had been and what they had been doing. How they kept it from their spouses without being suspicious. In the last few weeks, I'd decided those people were either exceptional liars, or maybe they had significant others with jobs like Quinn's.

I never had to lie to Quinn's face, never had to make excuses for where I had been, because every time I was with Carson, Quinn was at work. He was gone every Saturday and worked past midnight on random Thursdays and Fridays. It was more than enough time for Carson and me. It was easy. Maybe too easy. There was no sneaking around, no lying. I spent time with Carson and never felt like it was taking away from my time with Quinn.

So far, keeping up with both Quinn and Carson hadn't been a problem. The more sex I had, with either of them, the more I wanted to have. Each of them fueled the desire I had for the other.

Carson came over on Thursday night, like he'd said he would, even though I'd never agreed. He'd brought dinner, but we'd never gotten around to eating it.

We'd played strip Mario Kart, but had only made it three games before Carson was naked and then he couldn't keep his hands to himself. He hadn't even bothered trying to cheat—just tackled me, pulled my clothes off and rolled us both onto the floor. When he'd left three hours later, I'd made him take the uneaten dinner with him so Quinn wouldn't ask questions.

With work and everything, September flew by, and before I knew it, it was the middle of October.

I knew the ease of maintaining a happy marriage with Quinn and having a super-hot affair with Carson had an expiration date. I knew any day it could all come crashing down around me, but the risk wasn't enough to make me stop. For now, the risk was worth the reward.

18

I was still lying in bed Saturday morning when my phone rang. Quinn was in the shower; he had a rare Saturday off. Oregon had a bye this week and Rick had let him off for the Oregon State game. I pulled my phone off the nightstand and looked at it. My brother's face filled the screen.

"Hi Derek," I answered.

"Hey sis."

"What's up?"

"Don't you have something to tell me?" he asked. For a quick second, my stomach twisted in knots … how could he know? No one knew, except Dani, but even she thought it was a one-time thing that had ended weeks ago.

"Ummm ... I don't know, do I?"

"Hello! You get a sweet new job and you can't even call your only brother?" he asked. I let out a sigh of relief. "I have to hear it from Mom weeks later."

"Oh, yeah! Sorry, it's been crazy since it happened and it might not be permanent. Technically, I'm just the interim team lead."

"Still! That's pretty cool."

"How's Adrienne?" I asked.

"She's good. We get to find out if we're having a boy or girl pretty soon, we'll probably tell everyone at Thanksgiving."

Derek tried to convince me to come to Mom's for Thanksgiving.

"That's unlikely, since Quinn will have to work. I'm pretty sure he told me Oregon is playing on Friday and I don't want to leave him alone over Thanksgiving." I heard a crash in the background and then yelling.

"I've got to go," Derek said. "Max and Dylan are destroying things again. But congratulations. And don't make me find these things out through Mom anymore, or I'll have to come to Portland and kick your ass."

"Promise?" I laughed. There was more yelling in the background.

"All right, I have to go. Love you!" Derek said and hung up.

I had a text message from Carson when I hung up.

Carson: I don't know if I'm going to make it two weeks without seeing you. I'm having withdrawals.

Me: Don't be such a baby.

Carson: That's easy for you to say. You still get laid.

Me: So go have sex with someone else. You're hot … it wouldn't be that hard.

An unexpected twinge of jealousy surged through me at the thought of Carson having sex with someone else.

Carson: I don't want someone else.

Me: Quinn's off today. I can't help you.

Carson: Meet me somewhere. We can be quick.

Me: No.

Carson: Please.

Me: No. I'm not lying to Quinn.

Carson: Oh, because you've been 100% honest with him up to this point?

Me: Fuck off. I don't see you telling him about it either.

Carson: Fair point. But come on. Just meet me. Tell him you're going to yoga or something.

Me: I'll think about it.

Carson: Don't think … just do it.

Quinn appeared in the bedroom doorway, a towel hanging off his hips, his hair wet and tousled. I looked up from my phone and smiled.

"Good morning, babe," Quinn said.

"Good morning."

"I have an idea." He stood in front of the dresser and pulled off his towel.

"Does it involve you bringing that ass over here so I can squeeze it?" I asked. He pulled a pair of shorts out of a drawer and put them on.

"No, but you'll probably like this idea even better." I raised an eyebrow and waited.

"Well, it's been a while since we..." Quinn paused, like he was trying to figure out how to say what he wanted without actually saying it. "Since we … had a threesome."

"Yeah, so?" I sat up in bed and crossed my arms. I had hoped Quinn was over it. I had wondered why he hadn't said anything since the last time, but I wasn't about to bring it up.

"So, I was thinking we should do it again."

"Why?" There was no way that was happening again. Not with Carson at least.

"It was fun. We both enjoyed it," Quinn said, then added, "I love seeing how excited it makes you. I've wanted to ask you for a while, but work has been so busy I haven't had anytime to think about it."

"With someone new?" I already knew the answer, but it was worth a shot.

"No, with Carson."

"What did he say?"

"I haven't asked him yet. I wanted to see if you'd even consider it before I got his hopes up."

"I don't know." I got out of bed and walked over to him. "I barely have time to see you, so when we get a chance, I want it to be just you and me," I lied. Quinn kissed me lightly on the lips, then turned and walked over to his side of the bed and grabbed his phone.

"Just think about it."

"When do you want to do it?"

"Tonight."

"What? And how long do I have to think about it?" My voice rose a little.

"Calm down, babe. I don't have another Saturday off work until who knows when. Seriously, you have no idea how much it turns me on to see you so completely lost in the pleasure. It's unbelievably hot."

Fuck, fuck, fuck, what was I supposed to say to that? I didn't even know how to begin to argue when he made points like that. All I knew was it couldn't happen with Carson again, so I took the low road.

"Are you going to pout all day and be moody for a week if I say no?"

"Maybe." Quinn smirked. I balled my hands in fists and forced out a breath.

"Ugh, you are infuriating sometimes. You spring this on me and expect me to make a decision in five minutes." I was starting a fight on purpose, anything to get Quinn to drop it. I pulled running clothes out of my closet and threw them on the bed.

"You started this," he said.

"Oh, shut up about that, will you? It was months ago." I pulled on running leggings, yanked the T-shirt I had been wearing over my head, then put on a sports bra and jacket.

"You act like you hated it."

"I didn't hate it, but that's not the point." I sat on the edge of the bed and laced up my tennis shoes.

"What is the point then?" Quinn asked.

"The point is…" he looked at me like he couldn't possibly understand why I was so upset. I couldn't explain to him why I was mad because it was all an act. I couldn't tell him the truth, and we couldn't have another threesome with Carson.

"Never mind, I'm going running." I grabbed my phone and walked out the bedroom door.

"Chloe, wait…" Quinn followed me down the hall to the front door.

"I'm going running. I'll be back in an hour or so. I'll think about it." I didn't wait for an answer before I pulled open the door and left. Even though I had pretended to be mad, Quinn's words had turned me on. When I was in the elevator, I pulled out my phone and called Carson.

"Meet me at your office in half an hour," I said when he answered.

"Why?"

"Don't ask questions … just meet me there."

"Okay, I'm leaving now," he said. I hung up, put my phone back in my pocket, pulled out my headphones, and turned up my music. I ran hard. It was a little over four miles from our apartment to Carson's office. I didn't know where else to meet him. It had to be within running distance because my car couldn't go missing.

Carson was standing outside, leaning on the hood of his Jeep, when I rounded the corner into the parking lot. I was out of breath and sweaty. I pulled my headphones out of my ears as I approached him.

"What are we doing here?" he said. I swear to God, all the men in my life were being stupid today.

"Take me somewhere and fuck me." The look of confusion on his face was replaced with one of surprise, and his eyes darkened. Carson stood there for a second like he wasn't sure if I was serious.

"Now, please," I said. "Don't make me ask you twice."

"Okay, you got it." He led me into the deserted building. Suddenly, I was a little nervous.

"Is anyone going to be here?" I asked.

"Not where we're going," he said. I followed Carson down into the basement. He used a key card in his wallet to enter a room at the end of the hallway. It was a mailroom-slash-supply closet. He flipped on a light and looked at me. "Are you going to tell me what's going on?"

"We don't have time. You wanted to meet me, and here I am. Now shut up and kiss me." Carson stepped closer to me, pushing me back until my ass rested against a small table. He looked like he was going to say something else, but I pulled on his shirt until his mouth crashed against mine.

Carson didn't need any more prodding. He lifted me and set me on the table, unzipped my jacket, and pushed up the fabric of my bra, exposing my breasts. I let out a moan when he pulled one of my nipples into his mouth. Then his mouth was back on mine, his tongue greedily exploring.

I undid his belt buckle and jeans and pushed them off his hips, then wrapped my hand around his cock. He groaned against my mouth as I moved my hand up and down.

His fingers pulled at the waistband of my leggings, tugging at them until they slid down my thighs and hung around my ankles. He pushed my hand away and spread my legs with his knee and entered me all in one fluid motion.

"Oh God…" I dug my fingers into his back. The small table creaked and slammed into the wall with every thrust. "Holy fuck, Carson," I moaned. I clenched around him, and he swore under his breath.

"Do that again," Carson demanded. I did. "Holy shit, that feels good," he murmured. Carson reached a hand between our bodies and pressed his thumb against my clit and fucked me even faster.

"Jesus Christ, yes ... don't stop ... oh my God," I moaned as my orgasm hit me out of nowhere. My whole body pulsed around Carson as I came.

"Holy fuck, Chloe!" he yelled a few moments later when he buried himself inside me and came, drawing out the pleasure for both of us.

He didn't move from between my legs, instead, resting his hands on either side of my head and leaning against the wall as we both caught our breath. Finally, he pulled back, his cock dropping out of me as he bent over and pulled up his pants.

"Quinn wants to have another threesome," I said as Carson zipped his jeans.

"What?" He turned to face me. I was still sitting on the table, my pants around my ankles, my bra twisted up by shoulders, my jacket hanging open.

"He asked me this morning."

"Oh, so that's what this was all about." It wasn't a question but a statement. "So what did you tell him?"

"I said I'd think about it while I was running." I slid off the table and pulled up my pants.

"So did you think about it?" Carson smiled.

"I had other things on my mind." I smirked and fixed the rest of my clothes. "I'm surprised he didn't call you already."

Carson pulled his phone out of his pocket.

"He did. I've got a missed call and two texts from him." I looked at the time … my hour was almost up.

"Let's go. You're going to have to drive me partly home, or I'll never make it back before Quinn starts to wonder where the hell I am."

"I think we have to say yes," Carson said as we made our way back up the stairs.

"Why?"

"How are we going to explain it if we both refuse?"

"Fine, I'll say yes … you refuse."

"How about the other way around?" Carson said as we climbed in his Jeep.

"No, you don't have to live with him. Quinn can be impossible and pouty when he doesn't get his way. At least if you say no, he won't be mad at me."

"I don't think he'll buy it. How am I supposed to explain why I won't do it, when we've already done it twice?"

"Just tell him you're busy," I said, fastening my seat belt.

"He knows I'm not. He asked me yesterday if I had plans, and I told him no."

"Fuck!" I yelled and pounded the dashboard with my fist. "What are we supposed to do now?"

"Calm the fuck down," Carson said, his voice rising with mine as he pulled out of the parking lot and into the Portland traffic. We sat in silence, both of us trying to come up with a solution. When Carson spoke again, it was quieter, the anger and frustration gone from his voice.

"Why can't we do it? What's the big deal?"

"Are we going to be able to pretend like we haven't fucked a dozen times since last time?" I asked, my voice quieting to match his. "It just seems like a recipe for disaster."

Carson pulled his Jeep to a stop a few blocks from our apartment.

"You overthink things," Carson said. "I'll call him, but I'm not making any promises. If I can't convince him, we're just going to have to see how good your acting skills are."

"My acting skills? What about yours?"

"My acting skills are great." Carson smirked. "I've wanted to fuck you for the last eight years and you never had a clue, so I'd say I'm a pretty good actor."

"Fuck, you are no help to me." I unbuckled my seatbelt and opened the door.

"Umm, what about the last half hour? I think that was pretty helpful."

"Nah, that was for you." I winked, put my headphones in, and shut the door. I sprinted the half-mile back home. I was sweaty and out of breath enough when I got there to make Quinn believe I really had been running for the last hour.

"Carson said yes." I was barely inside the door, one headphone still in my ear, when Quinn spat the words at me, jumping off the couch and coming over to me.

"What?" I had heard him perfectly, but was hoping he'd made some sort of mistake.

"Carson, I talked to him, he said he was in for tonight." I wanted to scream. Not only did Carson not handle it like he'd said, he'd done the exact opposite of what he was supposed to do.

"Oh … he did?" I forced my voice to remain calm.

"Yeah, I talked to him just a few minutes ago."

"I don't know, babe. Aren't we good enough on our own?" I knew it was a bitchy thing to say, especially considering I was in the middle of an affair, but it was my last line of defense.

"Come on, you know it's not like that."

"Why is it so important to you?" I hadn't intended to turn this into another full-blown argument, but that's the way this conversation was going.

Quinn's voice was cold when he answered me. "Why are you so against it? Aren't you the one who 'wanted it more than anything'?"

"Are you going to throw that night in my face for the rest of our lives?" I spat back. "We did it, it was awesome, now I'm over it, let's move on."

"That's fucking ridiculous," Quinn laughed, but there was no warmth to the sound. "I think you're lying. I can't figure out why, but something's off here." Knots instantly formed in my stomach. I let out a sigh, forcing the anger out of my voice before I spoke again.

"I'm sorry. I've just been stressed with work and the application process, and I just wanted to spend time with you. I feel like we haven't seen each other in weeks," I thought I sounded apologetic enough as I lied to my husband's face. Quinn's face softened as he walked over and stood in front of me.

"I'm sorry, too. I shouldn't have pushed you. I'll call Carson and tell him I changed my mind."

"Wait." I put my hand on his chest. I was going to break his heart someday, the least I could do was indulge him for now. "Let me take a shower … I'll think about it some more."

"It's really okay if you don't want to, I was being selfish, I'm sorry."

Guilt raced through me. He was being selfish? I don't think he even knew what selfish meant.

"No, it's okay, don't apologize, just give me a half hour." I swallowed the lump that had formed in my throat and turned away. Tears stung the corners of my eyes and threatened to spill over and down my cheeks. I shut the bathroom door, stripped off my sweaty clothes, and turned on the shower.

"What the fuck is wrong with you, Chloe?" I said out loud to myself, but I didn't have an answer. Guilt flowed through me. "Quinn doesn't deserve this," I whispered, as tears spilled down my cheeks and got lost in the water from the shower.

For a brief moment, I considered getting out of the shower and confessing to Quinn right then, coming clean about everything, but even that was selfish. I shouldn't tell him just so I could stop feeling guilty. If I was going to confess, it should be because I was ready to face the consequences of my actions. But I wasn't ready for that. I wasn't ready to stop. I wasn't done with Carson yet.

19

Quinn

Something was off. I couldn't figure out what it was, but Chloe was acting strange.

It wasn't like her to run away like she did this morning, and it definitely wasn't like her to start a fight over something so stupid. She was constantly on her phone, she seemed more irritable than usual, and she never wanted to hang out with Carson anymore. I didn't understand why she was so pissed about having another threesome.

Chloe had told me to wait until she got out of the shower, but I picked up the phone and called Carson again anyway.

"Hey, what's up?" Carson answered on the second ring.

"Chloe is acting weird."

"Oh, how so?"

"She just started a serious fight about this threesome shit. I don't understand, since it was her idea in the first place, but now she is totally against it."

"I don't know, man, it's probably just PMS or something," Carson said. "Maybe it's just work stuff, and she's taking it out on you. She has been working a lot, hasn't she?"

"I don't know, she loves her job. Even with all the extra hours lately, she never complains; she just rambles on excitedly about design shit I don't understand."

"I'm sure it's nothing."

"It's fucking weird, dude. She's always been into the kinky stuff. I swear, now she'd be fine if we only did it missionary style for the rest of our lives."

"Don't be stupid, you know that's not true," Carson snorted. "I think you're over-thinking things. Give it some time, I'm sure everything will go back to normal when all the work stuff gets figured out."

"Yeah, you're probably right," I said.

"So, are we still on for tonight or not?"

"I don't know. She said she was going to take a shower and then let me know. I'll let you know as soon as she tells me one way or the other."

"Why don't you guys go out tonight, just the two of you? Between football season and everything else, I'm sure it's been forever since you took her out."

"Are you sure?" I asked.

"Yeah, don't worry about me. I'll be fine, trust me. Spend your Saturday night off with your wife."

"All right, thank you, man. I'll talk to you later."

Carson is a good friend, I thought to myself. He was right. Chloe and I needed a night out. I pulled open my laptop and started to make plans. By the time I heard the shower turn off ten minutes later, I had made dinner reservations and bought movie tickets.

Chloe emerged from the bathroom with a towel wrapped around her body. I smiled at the sight of her. She was beautiful, even in just a towel and with no makeup on.

"I'm sorry," she said. "I didn't mean to start a fight earlier. We can do it if you still want."

"No, it's okay, I made other plans."

"What kind of other plans?" She eyed me suspiciously.

"A night out, just you and me. We'll get dinner, go to a movie, and whatever else we feel like doing."

"That's a great idea." She walked over to me, and I stood up, wrapping my arms around her and pulling her close.

"It was actually Carson's idea, but it was a damn good one. We haven't been out in a long time."

"Damn football season." She laughed and looked up at me. I loved the way her green eyes lit up when she laughed.

"I know it's been rough, but I appreciate you not complaining too much. Thank you," I said. She waved a hand dismissively.

"Don't worry about it." I planted a soft kiss on her lips.

"Thanks, babe, you're the best."

20

Well, I'll be damned. Carson actually did come through. The knot that had been in my stomach since that morning finally released when Quinn said we were going out tonight, just the two of us, and I breathed a sigh of relief.

I texted Carson while I blow dried my hair.

Me: Thank you.

Carson: I didn't do anything. Just made a simple suggestion. Quinn ran with it.

Me: But still, thank you.

Carson: Well, in that case you owe me ;)

I didn't respond. I deleted the messages from Carson and finished with my hair. It was straight and shiny by the time I was done.

Quinn and I ran a few errands and grabbed some lunch from the bakery down the street before we came home and spent the afternoon doing our own thing. Quinn played some video games, while I read and caught up on some work emails. That was one of the best things about our relationship. There was no need to fill the time and silence with stuff—we could just be together. It was comfortable and content and happy.

I looked up from my computer and studied Quinn. I wondered how everything would change if he knew what was happening. I would be naive to think things could continue on like they were. I knew that would never happen. But could we still be together? Would he want a divorce? Fear coiled in my belly at the thought of divorce.

I was going to break the heart of the beautiful man sitting in front of me. I didn't want to, but I knew I would; I could feel it in my heart. I needed to end things with Carson, now, before it got to that point. The fear in my stomach grew, but this time for a different reason. I couldn't image my life without Quinn, but a piece of me wilted a little at thought of never seeing Carson again. He brought something inside me alive. It was an invigorating feeling—an adrenaline rush; I was addicted to that feeling, to the rush. I craved more when we were apart. But I couldn't have what I wanted. I wanted them both—forever.

They were so different. Quinn was tall, dark, and handsome, literally. He was smart, and loving, and tender, the kind of man parents dreamed their little girls grew up and married. Carson looked innocent with his blond hair and blue eyes, but he was anything but. He was rough and demanding, and took what he wanted and didn't apologize for who he was. It was hot as fuck. My heart swelled a little at the thought of Carson, and fear raced through me again, because I couldn't have real feelings for him. My heart belonged to Quinn.

"Why are you staring at me?" Quinn asked. I snapped out of my trance. I hadn't realized I was still looking at him.

"Can't a girl just admire her hot husband?" I winked. Quinn laughed and shook his head.

"Sure, I guess."

"What? It's true." I got up from my seat at the table, walked over to couch, and sat down next to Quinn. I snuggled into his chest. "I love you." It wasn't a lie, but I was afraid maybe Quinn wasn't the only one in my heart anymore. I shoved the idea deep down inside me and forgot about it. I loved Quinn, nothing could change that.

"I love you, too," he said.

It was Tuesday night, and I'd actually gotten off work at five for a change. I was sitting on the couch, drinking a glass of wine, waiting for Quinn to get home with dinner when Dani called.

"Hello."

"What up, bitch?" Dani said when I answered.

"That's not a very nice way to address your best friend," I said sarcastically.

"Please, I haven't talked to you since Automatic Andy helped you get laid, which was like a million years ago. I don't know if I can even consider you my friend anymore."

"I'm sorry! I know, I've been a terrible friend."

"What have you been doing anyway?"

"Work is nuts, dude. Being interim team lead is a bitch. I love it, but that and my regular job is a lot to handle."

"Come on, you aren't working 100 hours a week! What about all those Saturdays Quinn is working?" Dani said. "You haven't even bothered me about yoga, and you're always trying to get me to go to yoga with you."

"You really should come with me, you'd love it."

"It's too fucking early in the morning. Take me to a class at, like, noon, and I'd do it, but you didn't answer the question. What the fuck have you been doing?"

"Nothing, I swear. Just work and everyday life stuff."

"And Carson," she said, like it was the most obvious thing in the world. I nearly spit out my wine.

"What? No!" I didn't sound convincing, even to myself. There was no way Dani would believe me. "Why would you even say that?"

"Because you won't tell me if I don't pry it out of you."

"I thought you didn't want to know!" I yelled and checked the time. Quinn would be home any moment.

"So, you are having an affair then?"

"Jesus Christ, Dani, is this why you called?"

"I can't believe you honestly thought you could hide this from me," she said, sounding mad.

"You are impossible!" I yelled. "You told me not to tell you, so I didn't, even though I wanted to call you a million times. I left you out of it just like you wanted, and you're still mad? How is that fair?"

"How is what you're doing to Quinn fair?"

"Leave Quinn out of this. How did you even know? Why do you even care?"

"We've been friends for ten fucking years, Chloe, and you think I can't tell when something is up? You haven't so much as texted me in weeks, that's not like you. Obviously something shady is going on," she said. "And don't pretend like you don't know why I care. You know exactly why I care."

"You don't understand."

"Fuck that. I don't need to understand. You disgust me."

"Are you going to tell Quinn?" I asked, suddenly afraid.

"That's between you and him, and Carson, I guess."

I didn't know what to say, but I could feel tears forming through my anger. How dare she ask me to keep my infidelity a secret from her, and then blow up when she figured it out on her own?

"What happened to 'you'll always be there for me'?" I was grasping.

"Don't you turn this around on me. You're at fault here, not me." A tear rolled down my cheek at her words. This couldn't be happening. I couldn't be losing my best friend over this.

"I haven't done anything to you!"

"That's not the point. Quinn is my friend, too."

"Not like us." My voice caught in my throat.

"Are you crying?"

"What else am I supposed to do? My best friend is breaking up with me. I don't think there are enough tears in the world for that."

"Don't be all dramatic, I'm not breaking up with you," Dani said. "But I don't think what you're doing is right. Quinn doesn't deserve that."

"So you just called to tell me you think I'm being a shitty person?" I asked. This was the strangest conversation I'd ever had with Dani.

"That's what best friends are for. Who else is going to call you out on your bullshit but still love you when it's all said and done?"

I let out a deep sigh. I had wasted weeks hiding from Dani, thinking she'd hate me if she found out. Tears rolled down my cheeks as I thought about all the times in the past few months I could have used her advice.

"Are you going to tell me what's going on?" Dani's voice broke through my thoughts.

I heard Quinn's key turn in the lock.

"Not now, Quinn's home, I have to go." I heard her snort on the other end of the line before I disconnected the call. I wiped my eyes and took a big gulp of wine and prayed Quinn wouldn't notice anything was wrong.

Quinn, as it turned out, was unobservant. He didn't notice anything was wrong when he got home that night, he didn't notice the sudden increase in my texting habits, and he didn't notice how every time he brought up Carson, I found a way to change the conversation before it even got started. At least that was what I thought.

It was a little disheartening. I had always thought we were more in-sync, that he would notice minor shifts in my personality and habits.

Quinn's less than stellar observation skills made me brave. I started doing things I said I would never do, things that were reckless and dangerous.

21

I couldn't get enough of Carson. I'd seen him Saturday for a marathon sex session where no body part was left untouched, no desire left unsatisfied, and now I wanted more; it was all I could think about. But it was only Tuesday, and I wouldn't be able to see him again until at least Saturday, maybe longer, depending on Quinn's schedule.

Now that it was November, and Oregon State was out of contention for winning the Pac-12, Rick was focusing a lot more on just Oregon, meaning Quinn had to work fewer late nights and super long Saturdays. It was cutting into the time when Carson and I could get together safely.

I texted Carson on my lunch break.

Me: What are you doing after work?

Carson: You ;)

Me: That's what I was hoping you'd say.

Carson: Feeling a little frisky are you?

Me: Do you want me to come over or not?

Carson: Yes, please. I'd leave work right now if you asked me too.

Me: That's not necessary. I'll be there at 6:00.

Carson: I'll be waiting.

Carson's apartment was twenty minutes farther from Nike than ours. I might have to leave a little early to get there by six, given rush-hour traffic.

I picked up my phone and called Quinn.

"Hey, babe, what's up?"

"Hey, I just wanted to let you know I have to work late tonight," I said, filing my voice with remorse as I did the one thing I had sworn I'd never do.

"Oh, how late?"

"I don't know … probably 'til at least seven, maybe later. We have a big project we are presenting at the staff meeting tomorrow, and it's not anywhere near ready."

"Oh man, I was going to cook that tortellini soup you love so much."

"I'm sorry, that sounds amazing, but I'll probably order pizza or something for the team."

"Look at you, sounding all official ordering dinner for the team." Quinn laughed.

"I just hope they make it official soon. They've had the applications for over a month now, and I haven't heard a peep."

"Don't worry, babe. Of course you'll get it … you've been killing it lately."

"Thanks, I've got a meeting in a few minutes, so I've got to go," I lied. "Sorry about tonight, I'll call you when I'm on my way home."

"I love you, Chloe."

"I love you, too."

The conversation with Quinn almost made me change my mind. I was a terrible person. I was worse than terrible—despicable—and I knew it. I put my head in my hands and hunched over my desk. I had already jumped down the rabbit hole, there was no going back now, but my conscious kept popping up and making me feel guilty. I was now *that* person. The one who lied about having to work so they could fuck their lover, and I didn't like the feeling it gave me.

I'd had the same thoughts a hundred times. Maybe I should end it now, maybe I could get out before any real damage was done, maybe if I stopped now, no one would get hurt. But then a memory of Carson would float through my mind, my thighs would clench, and I'd forget all about stopping. This time was no different—a shiver went down my spine at the memories from Saturday. But Quinn...

"Chloe..." I visibly jumped at the sound of Chelsy's voice. I lifted my head and saw Sean's intern standing next to my desk, giving me a strange look.

"Are you all right?" she asked.

"Yes, I'm fine, I just have a little headache," I replied.

"Sean wants to see you." I opened my calendar to schedule a meeting with him.

"When?"

"Right now."

"Oh okay." I was sure I looked as surprised as I felt.

"Are you busy?"

"Nothing that can't wait a few minutes." I locked my computer screen and stood up, straightened my dress, and tucked a stray hair behind my ear.

"Okay great!" She sounded excited about it, like she had expected me to say no.

I was anxiously awaiting any word about the application process, so I wasn't going to turn down a meeting with Sean, even if it meant putting my ever-growing to-do list on hold for a few minutes.

I followed Chelsy to Sean's office. He was on the phone, and I waited outside until he waved me in, finishing up the call as he motioned for me to take a seat.

"Hello, Chloe. Thanks for meeting me on such short notice," he said, straightening a pile of papers on his desk.

"Of course," I replied. I felt like I should say more, but I was nervous and wasn't sure what was going to come out of my mouth, so I just waited in awkward silence until Sean continued.

"How is the team doing?"

"Great, sir," He glared at me, and I remembered his earlier request to call him Sean. "I mean, Sean. They are doing great. We'll be ready to present sketches of some of the spring line at staff meeting tomorrow."

"That's good to hear, and you, how are you doing?"

"Good." I kept it brief, didn't want to complain about my workload. "Things are going well; I think I've finally got my feet under me and the team seems to be adjusting well."

"Great. That's what I needed to hear. The hiring process is taking a bit longer than we had hoped, and I just got word that it'll probably be another couple months before we make a final decision. Interviews likely won't start until December sometime."

"Oh…" I tried to hide the disappointment in my voice. "May I ask what the delay is?"

"I wish I could tell you," He shook his head like he was a frustrated. "I've been pushing to get things moving. I wanted someone in place by now, but I keep getting push back from people above me. I don't know what the issue seems to be, but I wanted to keep you in the loop, since it directly impacts you."

"Thank you, I appreciate that."

"Keep up the good work. I think everyone has been impressed with your leadership so far."

"Thank you," I said again.

"That's everything," Sean said, and I stood up to leave. "Chloe?"

"Yes?" I turned back around, my hand still on the doorknob.

"Take the day off on Friday. I know you've been working lots of late nights; you deserve it."

"I'll do that. Thank you."

I breathed a sigh of relief as I walked back to my desk. I had expected the worst. The waiting was killing me, but at least now I knew I wasn't out of the running.

When I sat back down at my desk, I had a sad emoji text from Quinn, and the soul searching I had been doing before Chelsy interrupted me came back in full force. I had to end this now. I couldn't meet Carson tonight.

Me: I don't think I can come tonight.

Carson: Of course you can come. I'm really good at that ;)

I giggled at his idiotic joke. Then remembered I was supposed to be ending things and got more serious.

Me: You know that's not what I meant. I can't come over. We have to stop.

Carson: Don't make me call you at work.

Me: I'm serious Carson, we can't do this anymore.

Even as I typed and sent the words, I didn't feel the conviction behind them. I was weak, and Carson knew if he pushed me I'd fold, like I always did. My phone vibrated in my hand, and I looked down to see Carson calling me.

"Damn it, Carson," I whispered under my breath. I stood up and looked around, and then jogged into the nearest empty conference room. I shut the door behind me before I answered. "What?" I said, trying to sound annoyed.

"Don't get all sassy with me," he said.

"Carson, I'm at work, what do you want?"

"You, sitting on my face, moaning my name as I fuck you with my mouth." A wave of desire rolled through me at his words. Goddamn it, why did he always know just what to say? "You sprawled out on my bed, biting your lip, my hands on your beautiful body, my—"

"Stop," I cut him off. "I get it."

"So you're still coming over then?"

"No."

"Are you wet right now?"

"What? No!" I blushed, even though he couldn't see me.

"That's a yes."

"What does that have to do with anything?"

"It has to do with everything, babe. I'll see you at six." Carson hung up before I could respond.

Carson was right, and at 5:50, I pulled my car into the parking lot of his apartment building. The door opened almost before I knocked. Carson stood there, still in his polo and dress pants from work, the biggest grin I'd ever seen on his face.

"I thought you weren't coming?" He laughed.

"Shut up and let me in," I snapped.

"Whoa," Carson backed up from me a few steps. "Someone is feisty." I glared at him. I was on edge about this. It was different knowing that Quinn was at home, thinking I was at work, waiting for me to come home, and it made me nervous. Carson walked over to me and ran a finger down my cheek. "It's okay, I like feisty," he whispered.

Carson leaned down and kissed me, gently at first, then he grabbed my face with both hands and kissed me harder. He ran his hands down my arms, pushing my cardigan to floor before he reached down and pulled my dress over my head in one motion, leaving me in my high-heeled, knee-high boots, bra, and panties. Carson took a step back, looked me up and down, and ran a hand through his hair. I bit my lip coyly and bent down to take off my boots.

"Oh, fuck no, leave those on, they are hot as hell," Carson said. I yelped when he picked me and carried me down the hall to his bedroom. He threw me on the bed and stood there looking at me like he'd never get enough. The look in his eyes sent a tingle down my spine and straight to my core.

"Are you going to just stand there or are you going to take off your clothes and join me?" Carson jumped on the bed on top of me. "You didn't take off your clothes!" I squealed from underneath him.

"That okay, my clothes don't matter right now," His breath was hot against my neck, as he trailed kisses down my collarbone before he pulled my bra down and sucked a nipple into his mouth. My back arched off the bed, and I moaned at the contact. He kissed down my stomach, tasting every inch of skin until he reached the top of my panties.

He kissed over the silky fabric before he pulled it to the side and slid a finger inside me. I moaned again.

"Have you been this wet all day?" Carson asked. "God, I love how your body responds to just my words. I love how wet you get for me."

His words sent my mind reeling. I had heard Quinn say the exact same thing before. The thought of Quinn was an unwelcome visitor.

"Stop talking," I said.

"So demanding," Carson teased, his finger moving in and out of me lazily.

"There are way better uses for your mouth."

"Like this?" he asked and flicked his tongue over my clit.

"Yes," I breathed. "Like that." He did it again. "Just like that." My hands fisted around his sheets as he slipped another finger inside me. His tongue and fingers moved in unison, bringing me closer to the edge.

"Oh my God, Carson," I moaned, as my eyes closed and my head rolled back.

I felt the pleasure between my legs grow until every muscle in my body contracted and my orgasm washed over me.

Carson hooked his thumbs in my panties and pulled them off as he stood up off the bed and made quick work of his clothes, dropping them in a pile at the foot of the bed before he crawled back over me.

My breathing was erratic, and my heart threatened to beat out of my chest. Carson made me feel like a drug addict. I couldn't get enough of him, I always needed more, just one more hit, just one more taste. I bit my lip and stared up into his deep blue eyes.

"God, you make me crazy," he whispered before he bent down and kissed me. I wrapped my arms around his neck, pulling him closer. He grabbed my waist and rolled us over, so I was on top of him, our faces just inches apart. I could feel his heart beating against mine, pounding fast and steady, and it lit a fire in me.

I shifted and slid down on his cock, eliciting a growl from Carson. I pushed off his chest so I was sitting, my knees on either side of his body. I sat there, adjusting to the fullness of him buried deep inside me.

"Are you trying to torture me?" Carson asked.

"Maybe." I smiled.

"It's working," he said. I laughed, and then moved my body up and down, slowly sliding on and off his cock. Carson's eyes rolled back in his head, and he groaned. I swirled my hips in a circle, first in one direction and then the other.

"Holy fuck, Chloe." Carson breathed. "You feel so good."

I picked up speed and Carson arched his hips off the bed, his thrusts meeting mine.

"Oh God," I moaned. Carson gripped my hips and held me in place, thrusting. I leaned back and enjoyed the ride. He ran his hands up my back and pulled me down, so we were face to face again. When he thrust again, pleasure rippled through me, the change in angle hitting my g-spot.

"Jesus Christ, that feels amazing," I whispered. Carson held me in place, his hands strong on my back as he fucked me. With every thrust, the pleasure built, higher and higher. A string of incoherent words tumbled out of my mouth as I came, my body clenching around Carson's.

"Oh fuck, Chloe," Carson yelled, when he came seconds later. I rolled off Carson and laid on the bed. When I realized I was still in my bra and boots, I laughed out loud.

"What?" Carson turned and looked at me.

"I look fucking ridiculous."

"False. You look hot as fuck." I noticed the clock on the nightstand behind his head; it was after seven.

"Shit, I've got to go," I said. Carson grabbed my arm when I tried to roll off the bed.

"I wish you could stay."

"Well, I can't." I couldn't let my mind go down that road, couldn't think about if I wanted to stay or not. I had to go home to my husband. I pulled my panties back on and walked back out into the living room, pulled my dress over my head, and picked up my phone off the table. I already had a missed call from Quinn. Carson came into the living room, wearing a pair of basketball shorts and nothing else.

"When can I see you again?"

"I don't know. Maybe this weekend. I have Friday off, but I don't know what Quinn's schedule is like. It's been all over the place lately." I swung my purse over my shoulder and pulled open the door.

"I want just one night," he said. "One chance to spend the whole night with you." Damn him. He made me want to close the door, turn around, spend the night with him, and deal with the consequences tomorrow. But I couldn't, and he knew it.

"Sorry, you know that's not how this works."

"A guy can dream."

"I've got to go. See you later." I didn't wait for a response before I walked out, shutting the door behind me.

Quinn was watching one of those custom car shows when I got home half an hour later.

"Hey babe," he said when I walked in, but didn't look up from the TV.

"Hi, sorry I'm so late."

"That's okay." He shrugged. "Did you get everything done for the meeting tomorrow?"

"Yeah, everything is ready to go." It wasn't a total lie, seeing as everything was ready for the meeting … it had just been ready since four o'clock.

"Do you want some Chinese? I didn't eat it all," Quinn said, lifting a container from the coffee table. My stomach growled at the sight.

"Yeah, I'm starving." I sat down on the couch by him and ate the rest of his beef and broccoli and an egg roll.

When I was done, I leaned back onto the couch and closed my eyes for a moment. Quinn ran a hand up my thigh, under my dress, and my eyes snapped open. I stood up suddenly. Quinn looked at me like I'd lost my mind.

"I'm going to change my clothes," I said. "I've had these boots on for way too long today."

Once in our bedroom, I took off my boots, pulled my dress off, and unhooked my bra, letting it fall to the floor. I was standing in nothing but my panties when I heard Quinn come in the room. He walked up and wrapped his arms around me. He kissed the back of my neck and ran his hands over my bare breasts.

My body reacted involuntarily, but my mind protested loudly. I couldn't do this, not with my panties still wet and Carson's cum still inside me. I pulled a T-shirt over my head and pulled it down, pushing

Quinn's hands with it. I turned around and gave him a soft kiss on the lips.

"I have a headache," I lied. I played the oldest card in the book and reached a new low in this twisted game I was playing. "I'm sorry." Quinn looked disappointed but shrugged and gave me another kiss.

"It's okay. You're mine for life, I'll get plenty of other chances." He grinned, and my heart broke in two. I was a monster.

22

I needed to get away. I couldn't think, couldn't make decisions with both Quinn and Carson so close. I needed distance and perspective and someone to slap some sense into me. I needed Derek.

I picked up the phone and called my mom.

"Hi, Chloe," she answered.

"Hey, Mom. Am I still invited for Thanksgiving?" I cut right to the chase.

"Of course! It's a little last minute, flights will be expensive, but you are always invited. Quinn too," she added.

"Quinn probably won't come, he's got work, but I think I might."

"We'd love to have you. Your brother would be thrilled." I pulled my laptop off the coffee table and switched it on. My mom launched into a story about the twins, but her words were lost to my sudden obsession with finding a flight to L.A. *Maybe I should talk to Quinn first.*

"Hey Mom," I cut her off mid-sentence. "I've got to go. I need to call Quinn and find flights if I'm really going to come next week."

"I can't wait to see you."

"It's not set in stone yet, but I'll let you know if I book a flight."

"Okay, love you, Chloe."

"Love you too, Mom."

I tossed my phone on the couch and resumed my flight search. When I found one I wanted for less than $500, I got up to get my credit card and called Quinn, hoping he wasn't busy. I wanted to book the flight before it was gone.

"Hey babe," he answered after three rings.

"Hi, are you busy?"

"Not right now, just getting the equipment all packed up for the game tomorrow. What's up?"

"I have a question."

"Oh?" I could imagine him raising his eyebrow.

"I want to go home for Thanksgiving. I know that means you'll be alone and working and sad, but I haven't seen Derek and the boys in over a year, and I'm not sure when I'll get another chance, and I found a decently priced flight, but I don't want to leave you all alone on Thanksgiving..." I rambled on, nervous about what he would say. "So is that okay?"

"Of course," he said.

"Really?"

"Yeah, I think you should go. I'm going to be swamped Friday and Saturday anyway, and you'll have a much better time chasing Max and Dylan around than you will sitting here doing nothing." *Pretty sure I would be doing Carson,* I thought, and then shook my head. Getting away from Carson was the whole reason I was going.

"Are you sure?" He was taking this better than I expected.

"I promise, I'll be fine."

"You seem awfully eager to get rid of me," I teased.

"I never want to get rid of you," Quinn said, his voice barely above a whisper, his sultry tone making me temporarily forget what we were talking about. "I'll miss you, but if you really want to go, I think you should. Your mom has been begging you to come visit."

"That's true. Maybe she'll finally leave me alone if I do."

"Go, I promise I'll be fine for a few days. I don't think Carson is going home, so we can order Chinese and watch football all day ...

it'll be great." My stomach turned at the mention of Carson; I definitely needed to get away.

"Okay, I'm going to book a flight then. Thank you."

"No problem, see you in a few hours, I love you."

"I love you, too." I felt guilty saying the words. Even though I meant them, it didn't feel right to say I love you when I my actions said anything but.

I booked a flight and swore my mom to secrecy. I wanted it to be a surprise.

Everyone was gathered in the backyard of my parents' L.A. home Wednesday evening when my Uber dropped me off from the airport. I stepped out into the warm night air. It was in the low 70s and perfect. This was what I missed about Southern California. The warmth. The sunshine. I loved Portland, but sometimes the dreary weather got to me.

I left my bag at the front door and walked to the back of the house. The doors were open, and the sounds of laughter and squeals from small children filled the air. My heart instantly relaxed as the peace only home could bring washed over me.

Derek saw me coming before I could get to the doorway.

"Chloe?" he said, confused, and everyone turned to look at the doorway in unison.

"You guys couldn't possibly be having this much fun without me," I said sarcastically.

Derek handed his drink to Adrienne and rushed over to me as I came down the small set of stairs onto the back deck. He crushed me in a hug, the way he did every time I saw him. I had to blink back unexpected tears that had formed in the corners of my eyes.

"What are you doing here?"

"I had to defend my title in the Thanksgiving Day Mario Kart Tournament. I couldn't let you win by default."

"I'm going to win anyway, but you can try." He put an arm around my shoulders and led me over to the rest of the group. Max and Dylan were running circles around the yard, oblivious to my arrival. I hugged my Dad next.

"Chloe! I'm so happy you're here," He beamed. "No Quinn?" Guilt pierced through me at the mention of his name.

"No, he has to work Friday and Saturday—big days for college football."

"Ah yes." My dad nodded. I hugged my mom, too, the only one not surprised by my sudden entrance. Uncle Jason and Aunt Denise were here from San Diego, and Jackson and Christina from down the street were here as well. I gave them all quick hugs before reaching Adrienne.

Derek hadn't been lying—even with over three months left in pregnancy she already looked like she was carrying a basketball under her shirt. But, true to form, she was still in skinny jeans, high heels and looked flawless.

"Adrienne! You look beautiful. How's that baby girl?" Her eyes got wide, and she glared at Derek.

"I didn't tell her, I swear!" He held up his hands.

"Oh! Are you really having a girl?!" I squealed. "Derek really didn't tell me … that is just what I was hoping it would be." I hugged her tight. "I'm sorry for spilling the beans."

"It's okay," she said. "We were going to tell everyone tomorrow anyway."

I wrangled hugs and kisses out of Max and Dylan, who were now chasing the next door neighbor's cat around the yard, while everyone said their congratulations to Derek and Adrienne.

"Way to ruin the surprise." Derek nudged me when I rejoined the adults.

"I knew it was a girl," I laughed. "But I am sorry … I was just playing around."

"Do you want a drink?"

"Please." Derek grabbed a beer out of the cooler and popped the top off for me. A few minutes later, Derek kissed the boys goodnight, and Adrienne disappeared to put the little monsters to bed. Everyone was deep in conversation about politics or something I had no interest in being part of. I sat down on a bench and sipped my beer.

"So, why did you really make an impromptu trip down here?" Derek asked as he sat down beside me.

"I just wanted to see you all. Quinn is going to be busy anyway. It was the perfect time to get away, get some California sun, and see those crazy boys."

"Uh-huh."

"What? Do I need some top-secret reason to come see my family for Thanksgiving?"

"No, but you're not normally this spontaneous. I was just curious."

"You're just nosy."

"I'm your older brother, it's my job to be nosy."

We both laughed. Derek was the whole reason I was here. No one—except maybe Dani—gave me better advice than him.

I needed to tell him about Carson, needed to get his opinion, needed a perspective that wasn't clouded with lust and love and sexual tension. But now was not the time for that. Mom looked over at us every few minutes, and she had hearing like a fox. If she picked up anything that sounded interesting she would swoop in and demand to know all the details.

The fire had all but died down, and everyone but me had gotten a jacket before Jason and Denise, and Jackson and Christina said their goodbyes and left. I stood up and stretched.

"I think I'll go to bed," I said. "See you all in the morning." I kissed my parents on their cheeks and made my way up to the room I'd had as a teenager. The walls were still yellow, but the bed had been upgraded to a queen, and all my old photos and knick-knacks were packed away in the basement.

I changed into a T-shirt and brushed my teeth. I collapsed on top of the covers and sent a text to Quinn.

Me: "Goodnight, I love you."

I was asleep before he responded.

Thanksgiving at my parents' was a big deal. Mom put out a spread of bagels, muffins, fruit, yogurt, and coffee in the dining room for breakfast, and then threatened anyone who came anywhere near the kitchen for the rest of the day. Dinner was served at seven, and you were expected to be dressed up. I had tried to wear jeans to Thanksgiving dinner once when I was a teenager and almost got thrown out of the house.

We spent the day playing tag or wrestling or hide-and-go-seek in the backyard with Max and Dylan. They were like the Energizer Bunny times two, just whirlwinds of energy and noise. When they finally passed out for an afternoon nap, I went upstairs to call Quinn. I already had a text message from him.

Quinn: Happy Thanksgiving babe. I miss you. Hope you're having a good time with the family.

He answered after two rings.

"Hey babe,"

"Hi," I said. "Happy Thanksgiving!"

"Thanks, you too. How's the family?"

"They are great. What are your plans for the day?"

"Just watching football and drinking beer. Carson's coming over later with some dinner and we're just going to hang out." I was glad I was hundreds of miles away. I couldn't spend another afternoon with Quinn and Carson.

"That sounds fun. If you were here, you'd have to put on a tie for dinner."

"Your mom still makes everyone get dressed up?"

"Oh yes, she threatened me this morning. Told me if I wasn't wearing at least dress pants I was never getting invited to Thanksgiving again." Quinn laughed, the deep happy sound that made me smile. I heard my mom calling me from downstairs. "I'm being summoned to the kitchen. I better go."

"Okay, have a happy Thanksgiving."

"You too."

"I love you, Chloe."

"I love you, too."

My mom wanted help rolling out pie shells. It was apparently the only task she thought I could handle without messing up. After the pie shells were rolled, cooked, and filled with everything from pumpkin to coconut cream, I was excused to go "make myself presentable for dinner."

I showered and blow-dried my hair. Then I took my time putting on make-up. I thought about Quinn and Carson the entire time. I wanted them both, but knew that wasn't an option. How had I let this happen? How had I let Carson push his way in, so deep that I couldn't get him out?

I thought about leaving Quinn, a thought that had crossed my mind 1,000 times. My stomach dropped and tears immediately begin to form in my eyes, threatening to run down my cheeks and ruin my perfectly applied make-up. It was the same reaction I had every time

I considered it. I loved Quinn, needed him, wanted him. I couldn't let him go.

I didn't even know if a relationship with Carson could work, seeing as we barely knew each other. He knew every inch of my body, but he didn't really know me.

By the time I pulled on my sweater dress and high-heeled booties, my mind was more conflicted than ever. I put in a pair of earrings and headed downstairs for dinner.

Derek was coming out of the bedroom down the hall, adjusting his tie.

"Why does Mom do this to us?" he complained. "This is like the only time all year I wear a tie. Why can't we eat in our sweats and pass out on the living room floor like the rest of America?"

"Oh God, I can just see the look of horror on Mom's face if we all showed up to dinner in sweatpants and T-shirts. She would die."

"It's not like there are neighbors coming over. If it's just family, who gives a shit if we look nice?"

Adrienne emerged from the bedroom wearing a black maxi dress and a red cardigan that showcased her baby bump perfectly. Derek walked over and kissed her on the cheek.

"You look beautiful," he said to her.

"Let's go eat. I'm starving. I've been trying to sneak something out of the fridge for an hour now, but your mom has it locked down."

Just then, tiny voices floated up the stairway.

"Mom! Mom!" Max and Dylan bounded up the stairs, looking adorable in their matching khaki pants and button-down shirts. "We hungry!" Dylan said.

"Let's go eat then. Grandma said dinner was ready," I said and ushered the two toddlers back down the stairs and into the dining room.

The table was full of everything you could ever want on Thanksgiving. A huge turkey, mashed potatoes, sweet potatoes, green bean casserole, roasted veggies, salad, corn bread, rolls, cranberry dressing, and turkey gravy. There was a whole other table full of pies. My stomach growled, and my mouth watered at the feast before me.

Dinner was amazing. Everything my mom cooked was pure gold. Two hours later, I was full of food and wine and pie. The dishes had been cleaned up and put away and the boys were in bed. My aunt and uncle had joined us for dinner, and we all sat around in the living room talking about nothing in particular.

"Oh!" Adrienne placed her hand on her belly. "She's kicking!"

"Can I feel?" I had never seen Adrienne when she was pregnant with the twins, so I didn't get to feel their tiny kicks.

"Of course." I got up, and she placed my hand gently on her stomach. It only took a moment before I felt a tiny little kick against my hand and then another.

"Oh, I feel her! That's amazing!"

"You know, Chloe," my mom spoke up from behind me. I rolled my eyes, knowing where this was going. Adrienne tried to stifle a laugh at the look on my face.

"What, Mother?" I said in the driest voice possible.

"That could be you soon." I didn't know if it was all the wine or the turbulence in the rest of my life, but I wasn't up for this shit tonight.

"Actually, Mom, it couldn't, as I'm still actively trying not to get pregnant. I'm happy with my life, without a baby." My mom looked taken aback but remained calm.

"Chloe, I'm just saying. You're—"

"You're not going to be young forever. I know, Mom, but some of us have bigger goals for ourselves than staying home raising babies." It was a low blow, but I'd had enough. My aunt gasped at my statement.

"Chloe," my dad warned.

"No." I stood up, nearly spilling my wine. "I'm done with this shit. I don't need to be berated every time she talks to me about when I'm going to have a baby. News flash, Mom, I'm probably never having a baby. Fucking deal with it."

"Chloe Louise. Watch your language or you can be excused," my mom snapped.

"I don't need to be excused. I'm done." I stomped out of the room and made my way back upstairs. My face was hot and flushed, a combo of the wine and my angry outburst. I opened the window in my bedroom and climbed out onto the roof, like I had done so many times as a teenager.

It didn't take long before I heard the door to my room open and close, and then Derek knock on the window sill.

"Can I join you?"

"Are you going to pester me about having a baby, too?"

"No, of course not. I don't give a shit if you ever have a baby."

"Fine, then you can come out," I said.

Derek laid down on the roof beside me. We had to look ridiculous, two grown adults in our Sunday best, laying on the roof of our parents' house. We laid in silence for a few minutes, nothing but crickets and the sound of the freeway in the distance.

"What was that all about?" Derek broke the silence.

"I'm having an affair." The words tumbled out of my mouth unexpectedly. I thought I was going to say something about Mom getting on my nerves, but that was what came out instead.

"What?" Derek sat up on his elbow and looked at me.

"I'm having an affair," I repeated, even though I knew he heard me the first time. "With Carson, since September." I saved him the trouble of asking for the details.

"Shit, that was not what I was expecting," he said after a few moments of quiet.

"Save yourself the trouble if you are going to yell at me for being a terrible person … I already got that from Dani. And I know." Derek didn't say anything; he just laid back down and looked up at the sky, no stars visible under the orange glow that was L.A.

"Why?" he asked after a while.

"I can't explain it. There is a connection I have with Carson that's unlike anything I've ever experienced. I love Quinn, but Carson sets me on fire." I fully expected him to laugh at me, but he didn't say anything. "Are you going to tell me how ridiculous I sound?"

"Do you want to have this conversation by yourself, or are you going to let me tell you what I actually think?"

"Sorry," I mumbled.

"How did this even happen?"

Derek didn't need to know the details of my sex life, so I told him the next best thing.

"Years of pent up sexual tension finally broke us down," I said. "I know it was wrong—it is wrong—but it felt so right. I love Quinn, I really do, but I can't explain the way Carson makes me feel."

There was more quiet.

"I understand," he said finally.

"Understand what?"

"What you're feeling. I felt that same way when I met Adrienne," he said. "You probably don't remember, but I had been dating Lisa for, like, two years. I was about to propose to her. We were perfectly happy, but then I ran into Adrienne at the gym. We had an instant connection, which I couldn't explain, but I wanted her like I'd never wanted anyone before."

"Oh my God! You were going to marry Lisa? No, she was awful!"

"I thought you liked her?"

"I lied. I never thought you wanted to marry her, though, or I would've been honest with you."

"Can I finish my story?"

"Yeesss," I drew the word out dramatically.

"I tried to forget her. Tried to just be happy with Lisa, and I was, but I couldn't stop thinking about her. I looked for her every time I went to the gym, and the next time I saw her I asked her out."

"You were still dating Lisa?"

"Yes, we were living together."

"Oh good, so I can tell Dani it's not my fault, but that I come from a family of cheaters. It's genetic."

"I didn't cheat."

"Oh really?" I said.

"Well, not really. We went on one date, and when I took her home, I kissed her, and that was it. I broke up with Lisa that night." Derek said. "I knew Adrienne was the one; I didn't even try to make it work with Lisa."

"So are you saying I married the wrong person?" I asked defensively and sat up and looked at him.

"I'm not saying anything … just telling you my experience," he said calmly.

"I've known Carson almost as long as I've known Quinn, and I've never felt anything until now."

"Never? Come on, there had to have been some signs before."

"I have maybe had a crush on him for a while."

"A crush? What, are we in middle school again?"

"Shut up. That's the best way to describe it. I've always liked Carson; we've always gotten along, but somewhere along the way I started to imagine more. When I started to notice him flirting with me, I let my imagination run wild. Then I had a chance to make it all a reality, and I took it." I sighed. "And it backfired on me like a bitch."

"Did it really though?"

"What the hell is that supposed to mean? Yes, it did. I'm in the middle of a three-month affair with my husband's best friend, with no idea how or when to end it."

"Or if you even want to," He said matter-of-factly. I glared at him, hating him for knowing what I was thinking.

"All right, Dr. Phil. So what the hell am I supposed to do?"

"I don't have a fucking clue."

"What would you do? Say you and Lisa did get married, and you were happy and in love and everything was going great, and then you met Adrienne."

"I think my story would've turned out the same. I was meant to be with Adrienne."

"Don't take the easy way out. Would you have even asked her out if you had been married instead of just dating? Would you really have divorced Lisa? Or cheated on her?" I wanted him to make me feel better about myself, to tell me he would have cheated too.

"I don't know, Chloe. I can't go back in time and change what happened. Who knows how it would've played out if I hadn't met Adrienne until a few years later."

"Do you still love Quinn?" he asked.

"Of course I do," I said defensively.

"Do you love Carson?"

"No," I said immediately, then reconsidered. "I don't think so. It's just sex." Was it just sex? I didn't know anymore. I couldn't deny that my feelings for Carson had grown, but I wasn't ready to call it love.

"Is sex with Quinn bad?"

"No, it's good. It's always been good. I thought it was amazing until Carson."

Derek sat in silence for a minute.

"Do you want to leave Quinn?" he asked then.

"No." My stomach knotted instantly at the thought. "I can't. Just thinking about it makes me sick. I love him."

"Then you have to break it off with Carson." The thought of that made me nervous too.

"What if I can't do that either?"

"You already know the answer to that. You can't have both, Chloe. It doesn't work that way."

"What about Carson?"

"What about him?" Derek asked.

"He's Quinn's best friend! I'm not going to be able to avoid him for the rest of my life. If I see him..." I didn't finish my sentence; Derek knew what I meant.

"You have to have a little bit of self-control," he snorted.

"Yeah, you see how that's worked out so far."

"He'll get over it. You're not his to have. If he's any sort of man, and you end it, he'll back off and keep his distance—maybe not from Quinn, but from you at least," he said, then reconsidered. "But then again, I don't know very many men who would fuck their best friend's wife in the first place."

My heart skipped a beat when I heard the door to my bedroom open, but I relaxed when I saw it was Adrienne. She came to the window, but didn't even try to climb out and join us.

"Are you two all right up here?" she asked.

"We're good," Derek said.

"Well, thanks for leaving me all alone with your family."

"Sorry, baby. I didn't even think about it," he replied.

"Don't worry, I was my usual charming self, and they love me, but you owe me. I just came to tell you I'm going to bed."

"Okay, I'll be in soon. I love you."

"Love you too. Goodnight."

I sat on the roof, pulled my knees to my chest, and rested my head on them.

"What are you thinking?" Derek asked when Adrienne was gone.

"This is going to be hard."

"Are you going to tell Quinn?"

"I think I have to. He deserves that much."

"He deserves it? I think the guy would probably be better off never knowing his wife and his best friend fucked for three months." I groaned at his statement. "And there's nothing to guarantee that Quinn won't walk away if you come clean. There is a very real chance he won't want to stay with you. I know I wouldn't."

I looked Derek in the eyes and knew he wasn't lying.

"Even if it was Adrienne?" I asked, lifting my head.

"I love her, but having an affair with my best friend? Pretty sure that is a deal-breaker."

"That's reassuring," I said sarcastically.

Derek scooted closer and put his arm around me.

"I don't know how you got yourself into this fucked up mess, but I'll be here when the whole thing implodes and you need someone to have more roof-time talks with."

I rested my head on his shoulder and sighed. "Thanks, Derek."

"For what?"

"Perspective. Everything looks different from the 10,000-foot view. I was in too deep to see things clearly."

"That's what older, smarter brothers are for." He smirked.

"And for helping smooth things over with Mom tomorrow?" I asked. He jerked away from me and laughed.

"Not a chance, you're on your own for that one." He stood and started to climb back in the window.

"Come on! You have to help me. She's probably already writing me out of the will for saying *fuck* to her."

"Sorry, I have to draw the line somewhere. I don't want to get written out of the will too."

"Thanks a lot!"

"Goodnight, Chloe." Derek laughed and left my bedroom.

"Goodnight."

I stayed out on the roof for another hour, imagining the days that were ahead, and hoping I was strong enough to get through them.

23

Three weeks later, nothing had changed. I came back from California and went right back to doing everything I'd sworn I was going to stop—sneaking around, seeing Carson whenever I could, and keeping Quinn in the dark.

Derek's words about not wanting to end it with Carson haunted me. If I had done anything in the past three weeks, it was prove his theory right.

Quinn was in Las Vegas covering Oregon State's bowl game.

I was standing in the kitchen, trying to decide what I wanted for dinner, when there was a knock on the door. I opened it to see Carson standing there, a box of pizza in one hand and a six-pack of beer in the other.

"What are you doing here?" I said.

"How about, 'Hi Carson, come in, thanks for bringing dinner'?" he said sarcastically.

"Maybe I already ate," I said, but then my stomach growled loudly.

"Either you or your stomach are lying." He laughed.

I rolled my eyes. "Come in, thanks for bringing dinner." I moved aside and let Carson in. He followed me into the kitchen, and I reached for the pizza, but he held it above his head, out of reach.

"Maybe I should make you earn your dinner." He smirked. I stood on my toes and tried unsuccessfully to grab the box out of his hands. My stomach growled again.

"Come on, I'm hungry," I pleaded.

"Kiss me first," he demanded.

"Carson! I'm going to starve."

"No kiss, no pizza," he said, still holding the pizza over his head.

"Fine," I fake-whined. I stood back on my tippy toes and pressed my lips to his. A spark shot from our lips down through my body, and suddenly the pizza didn't matter anymore.

Carson pulled away long enough to put the pizza down, and then he kissed me again, cupping my face between both hands and devouring my mouth.

My stomach growled loudly in protest, and Carson pulled away, laughing.

"I guess we better eat."

"Or we can just ignore my stomach."

"Nah, let's eat. You're going to need energy for later." He winked, and my knees went weak.

We sat on the couch and ate, the episode of *Keeping up with the Kardashians* I had been watching earlier playing the background. I inhaled two pieces of pizza and a beer, and then leaned back onto the couch, feeling much better.

"How do you watch this shit?" Carson said, taking a long swig of his beer.

"Eh, it's my guilty pleasure, don't judge me." I shrugged.

"Oh, I'm definitely judging you," he said. "But it's all right … I still like you." He leaned over and kissed me.

His hands roamed over my body, pulling and tugging at my clothes as he kissed me like he might never get another chance. He crawled on top of me and pushed me back onto the couch, his kisses moving from my mouth to my neck to the top of my camisole. I clawed at his shirt and pulled the fabric up over his head, forcing him to break the kiss for a moment, then his mouth was on mine again.

He ran a hand under my shirt and brushed his fingers softly over the lace fabric of my bra. My nipples hardened under his touch, and I moaned against his mouth. My fingers struggled with his belt. He shifted his weight to give me a better angle and kicked a beer bottle off the coffee table. It shattered on the floor in a spray of foam.

"Goddamn it," Carson swore, as he jumped up off the couch, careful to avoid the glass. His breathing was ragged, his hair was a mess, and I could see his erection straining against his pants as he stood there staring at the glass.

I giggled.

"What's so funny?" He looked at me, still sprawled out on the couch, and ran a hand through his hair.

"You look so perplexed," I said.

"Well, fuck, things were just getting good," he said. I stood up on the couch and walked to the other side, not wanting to get glass in my bare feet. I wrapped my arms around his neck and pulled him close.

"Forget the glass and take me to bed," I whispered in his ear. He wrapped his arms around my waist and kissed me.

"I'll take you to bed, but I can't promise there will be much sleeping."

"I didn't say anything about sleeping." I laughed as he picked me up from the couch, but he didn't take me to the bedroom. Instead, he sat me down just inside the bathroom.

"I thought we were going to bed?" I raised my eyebrow at him.

"We probably need to wash the beer off ourselves," he said matter-of-factly.

"I don't have any beer on me," I protested. Carson reached down and pulled my shirt off over my head.

"Oh, you definitely do … there is beer everywhere." He laughed and pulled my pants down.

"Are you sure this isn't just an excuse to get me naked and wet?"

"I was going to get you naked and wet no matter what," he said and turned on the shower. "But the shower will make it better." He pulled off his own pants and stepped under the warm water before he grabbed my hand and pulled me in after him.

I awoke the next morning, weak December sunlight streaming through the windows, Carson's body tangled up in mine. My heart sank a little. I hadn't meant to let him stay, to let him sleep in our bed, where Quinn should be. My two worlds weren't supposed to mix like this.

Carson moved beside me. His eyes opened, then closed again. He pinched his arm, opened one eye, and looked at me suspiciously.

"What are you doing?" I asked.

"Making sure this isn't a dream. I never thought I'd get to wake up with you beside me."

"Well, don't get used to it; it was a one-time thing, which shouldn't have happened," I said, anger lacing my words.

"Don't be so uptight." He wrapped an arm around my shoulder and pulled me into his chest. "Quinn won't be back until tomorrow, we're fine."

I hated his nonchalance, how nothing seemed to matter to him. Sleeping with someone else in Quinn's and my bed was a big deal. It was the ultimate betrayal. As if everything I had done up to this point wasn't enough, I had to bring my lover into our bed too.

"Stop thinking," Carson whispered. "I can feel you stressing about it." He pulled the covers over his head suddenly.

"What are you doing?" I asked, lifting the covers so I could see his face. He had slid down and was grinning up at me from between my legs.

"I'm going to make you relax." He winked. Then his mouth was on me, and I forgot all about Quinn and our bed and everything but Carson's mouth and tongue and the incredible things they were doing to me.

An hour later, we were still lying in bed, my head nestled into Carson's chest, neither of us wanting to move and ruin the rare peaceful moment we had together.

"Be with me," Carson said suddenly.

"What? I am with you."

"No, I mean, really be with me. Leave Quinn," he said. I pulled back from him, pushing his arm off my shoulders and untangling my legs from his.

"Are you fucking kidding me?" I searched his eyes for some sign that he was joking.

"You can't tell me the thought hasn't crossed your mind?"

"No!" I yelled and jumped out of bed, taking the sheet with me. That was a lie, but I couldn't believe he had the balls to actually ask me. "It actually hasn't. I'm perfectly happy with Quinn."

"Oh really?" Carson didn't move out of the bed. "If you are perfectly happy, then what are we doing here?"

"Get out." I pulled on a T-shirt and yoga pants.

"What?"

"You heard me. Get out." I wasn't going to let him question me or my marriage.

"Chloe, come on. Forget it … forget I said anything."

I picked up his clothes off the floor and threw them at him.

"No. Get the fuck out of my bed and leave." A tear trickled down my cheek. I couldn't deny that Carson had a point. What were we doing here if I was perfectly happy?

I shook my head; no, he was wrong for asking me to leave Quinn, the husband I still loved. Carson pulled on his jeans and came around the bed to me, but I stormed out to the living room. Carson followed me, grabbed my arm, and spun me around.

"Chloe. Stop. Stop freaking out." He pulled his shirt over his head. "It was just a suggestion."

"Well, it was a fucking stupid one. How dare you ask me to leave Quinn for you? Who do you think you are?"

"We've been together for three months now; you know I'm not crazy for assuming this could be something more. We've made love dozens of times..."

"No, we've been fucking. That's it. This has nothing to do with love."

"Do you even still love Quinn? Why would you keep coming back to me if you did?"

I slapped him across the face. He looked taken aback as he rubbed his cheek, a red mark forming where my hand had been.

"Don't you dare question my love for Quinn. You don't even know me."

"Chloe..."

"Get the fuck out. Now."

"Chloe..." he said again. "I'm sorry." He held up his hands in surrender, but it was too late. I was furious. This wasn't how it was supposed to end. We were supposed to come to some sort of mutual closing that let everyone move on happily. There wasn't supposed to be yelling and raw emotions.

"Leave. We're done. This is over."

Carson's eyes widened in shock, and then filled with hurt and disbelief.

"I'm not ending my marriage for you, Carson, and you can go to hell for even asking. This was sex, and that's it."

"Wow," he said, grabbing his jacket and keys. "You can't possibly believe that, can you? Is that what you have to tell yourself so you can sleep at night?"

"Fuck you," I spat at him. I walked over to the door and yanked it open.

"I don't know how you can stand there and tell me that none of this meant anything when you know damn well it did."

"Don't play the victim here, Carson. It's not a good look on you."

"So that's it?" My mind raced back to the morning after the first threesome when he'd asked me the same question.

"It never should have been anything in the first place," I said. "It was all a mistake."

Carson walked over and pushed the door closed.

"No, fuck that!" he yelled. "It wasn't a mistake, and you know it. You don't just cheat on your husband for three months for no reason. You felt something too, didn't you? Didn't you?" he yelled again.

"You can yell at me all you want, but it doesn't change my answer. I'm not ending my marriage for you."

"Your marriage is a sham!" I slapped him again.

"You don't know anything about my marriage!" I yelled back. "Don't stand there and act like I'm the only one who did something shitty. Quinn is supposed to be your best friend, but apparently, that doesn't mean shit to you. I'm not the only one who did something wrong, Carson. But two wrongs don't make a right."

"I can't believe this."

"What did you expect? That I'd leave Quinn and we'd ride off into the sunset and live happily ever after? This isn't a fairytale, Carson, pull your head out of your ass and look around. We sneak around, and hide, and lie. I've lied point blank for you. Quinn is the victim here, not you." I felt like I was going to be physically ill.

"What about us?" he asked.

"There was never an us. I was never yours to have, not then and not now."

"Chloe..." I didn't know what he was going to say, but I didn't care anymore. I pulled the door open again.

"Just leave, it's over."

He shook his head and gave me one last long glance filled with pain and heartbreak before he walked out the door. I let it slam behind him and heard him kick the wall just outside the door and swear loudly before he stomped off down the hall.

I crumpled to the floor and cried.

24

Three days later, I was sitting at my desk, the office mostly dark around me, no one else was still working at seven.

I hadn't spoken to Carson since he'd left Saturday morning, and I had been avoiding Quinn as much as I possibly could, given that we shared a one-bedroom apartment. I didn't know how to start the conversation we had to have. How do you tell your husband you've been cheating on him? With his best friend, nonetheless?

My phone vibrated on my desk, and Dani's face filled the screen.

"Hey," I answered, but she apparently wasn't calling to chit-chat.

"Quinn just called me, asking all sorts of questions about you working late and being all distracted lately," she said without a hello. "I swear to God, if you are with Carson right now, I'm going to come over and kill you both."

"I'm not, I really am at work, I swear."

"Why? It's after seven, three days before Christmas. What could you possibly be doing? Never mind, I don't really give a shit, but I'm not going to cover your fucking tracks for you."

"Dani..." I didn't really know what I was going to say, but it didn't matter, because she cut me off and kept going.

"Either you tell Quinn, or fucking end it, because I'm not lying for you again."

"I already ended it, three days ago."

"You ended it? Or you're just waiting for Quinn to go out of town again?"

"I don't owe you an explanation," I said. "Don't sit over there and act like you're better than everyone else, like you've never fucked up before." I was tired of her bullshit; I didn't do anything to her. Every conversation we'd had had since she'd found out about the affair went the same way. She'd make some snide comment about how she didn't agree with what I was doing, I'd get mad, she'd get mad, and then I'd apologize to keep the peace.

"Fuck you, Chloe. I just lied to your husband for you. Told him I had no idea what was going on, that you must just be really stressed at work when really I wanted to tell him you are a lying, cheating asshole. And now you're going to yell at me?"

"It's over, okay? It's done. I'm sorry Quinn called you … I'm sorry you got dragged into this." The words were supposed to sound sincere, but instead they sounded bitter and resentful.

"Either figure out a way to tell Quinn, or stop being shady, because I won't lie for you again, and it won't be pretty if he finds out from me." She hung up before I could respond. I resisted the urge to throw my phone across the office and scream.

Instead, I packed up my things, pulled on my coat, and walked to my car.

I tried to rehearse what I was going to say on the drive home, but every time I tried to say the words, I choked up and started to cry. There was no way I was ever going to get through this conversation. What was the point anyway?

I still loved Quinn. I knew no one would believe me if I told them. Like Carson had said: who had an affair if they were perfectly happy? But it didn't matter what anyone else said, I did love Quinn. I didn't want to break his heart. It was over with Carson. I decided I wasn't going to tell Quinn.

I checked my make-up in the stainless-steel wall of the elevator and walked to my apartment, ready to pretend like nothing was wrong.

Quinn, unfortunately, had other plans.

"Where have you been?" he said before I even got in the doorway. He stood from the couch, turned off the TV, and walked over to me.

"I'm sorry, I was at work," I said.

"Until eight? Christmas is in three days … you can't possibly have any big projects due this week," he said. I was suddenly annoyed at him and his questions.

"Yes, work is busy," I said, my tone condescending. "I'm still doing the job of two people and sometimes that means I have to work late and you'll just have to deal."

"You told me you'd be home two hours ago, I was worried. Is that okay? Or am I not allowed to be worried?"

"I just don't want to come home and get interrogated." The more I tried to make it seem like he was the one in the wrong here, the more Quinn pushed back on me.

"What is your problem lately? You're all moody and distracted, you literally run away any time there is even the slightest bit of conflict, you work late all the time, and that's not like you. What is going on?"

I stood there, silent, trying to find the right words. Quinn waved a hand out in front of him as if to say, *Well, I'm waiting.* A million lies bubbled to the surface, but the words that came out were the truth.

"I was having an affair," I whispered, but the words echoed through the quiet apartment like I had shouted them.

"What?"

"Please don't make me say it again," I pleaded softly.

"With who?"

"It doesn't matter. It's over now. It's done."

"Chloe," Quinn said, anger building in his voice. "Who?"

A tear rolled out of the corner of my eye and down my cheek.

"Please, it doesn't matter, it was nothing," I begged. Everything would be worse if he knew.

"Fucking tell me," he said through gritted teeth.

"Carson," I whispered again.

Quinn stumbled backward, like I had punched him in the stomach, and grabbed on to the couch for support. His head dropped, and he took a few deep breaths. When he looked up at me again, his eyes were full of confusion and pain.

"Please tell me you're lying," he said. I shook my head, unable to speak.

"You are. You are lying … Carson would never do that to me."

"Quinn, it's the truth," I choked out. He shook his head like he couldn't believe the words that were coming out of my mouth.

"How long?" he asked, not looking at me.

"Quinn, please, none of that matters. It's over now. I ended it."

"It all matters, Chloe. Don't make me drag the information out of you," Quinn said in a voice I'd never heard before. Low and controlled but full of fury. "How long have you been fucking Carson?" He said the words like they were poison.

"Three and a half months."

"Jesus Christ." He ran his hands over his face. "I never thought in a million years this was what was wrong with you. I called Dani because I was worried about you, worried that you were overworking yourself, or something was wrong and you wouldn't tell me. But this? I never would've guessed this."

He turned his back on me and leaned on the couch. I wanted to say something, but I didn't know what. Nothing I could say would make this moment any better, so I just stood there in silence.

"Why?" Quinn's voice cracked on the single word.

"I don't know!" I choked back a sob.

"Was our marriage bad? Did I miss something? Are you not happy?" Every word that came out of his mouth sounded pained.

"No, Quinn, nothing was wrong." Tears rolled down my cheeks as I spoke. "Everything was amazing, you are amazing. I was a fool … I made a mistake."

"A mistake?" Quinn shook his head and walked to the bedroom. I called after him as I followed him down the hallway.

"Quinn, it's over. It's done," I repeated.

"You think that matters? A three-month affair isn't a mistake, Chloe. It's a fucking betrayal … it's unforgivable."

I watched as he grabbed a backpack and started stuffing things inside it.

"Quinn, please, don't go. I love you." He spun around, his half-packed backpack in his hand, and looked at me.

"Don't talk to me about love," he said. "I've always loved you, Chloe, but apparently, that wasn't good enough for you. What did you think was going to happen? Did you think you would tell me, and I'd just forgive you and everything would still be perfect? Or were you just going to hide it for the rest of our lives? Don't even answer, I don't even care." He grabbed a few more things from the bedroom, shoving them into the backpack, and then stomped out into the living room, where he grabbed his keys and wallet and laptop and shoved them inside, too. "I can't fucking believe this. I would've done anything for you, Chloe. I loved you with everything I had, and this is how you repay me? I hope you fucking burn in hell."

Then he yanked open the door and was gone. My husband was gone—the man I had loved for the last eight years, the man I had thought I was going to grow old with was gone. And I didn't know if he was ever coming back.

25

Carson

I was in love with my best friend's wife. There was no other explanation. No other reason why I would ask her to leave Quinn for me. I was tired of sneaking around and only seeing her once or twice a week. I should have just been happy with what we had, but I wasn't. I wanted all of her, not just the sex. I wanted to get to know her and lay in bed on Saturday mornings talking about nothing. I wanted everything. Asking her to be with me was the only option I had. I couldn't share her with Quinn anymore.

She apparently didn't feel the same way. I had been so sure she would say yes. Not only had she said no, but now she wouldn't talk to me. It had been the longest three days of my life. I needed her. Was this what it felt like when you were with your soul mate? I didn't even know if I believed in soul mates, but I knew I didn't want to imagine my life without Chloe.

I had just finished cleaning up dinner, and was standing in my kitchen trying figure out how I could get her to talk to me again, when my phone rang. It was Quinn.

"Hey, what's up man?" I answered.

"What the fuck is wrong with you?" The sound of his car moving down the road crackled through the phone.

"Whoa, what's wrong?" I swallowed the lump in my throat, not sure I wanted to know the answer.

"How can you even call yourself a man? I thought we were friends, I thought we were brothers!" He continued yelling.

"What are you talking about?" I asked, even though I already knew the answer.

"Don't fuck with me Carson, I know! I fucking know about you and Chloe."

"Quinn..." I started, but then realized I didn't have a fucking clue what to say.

"Please, tell me she's lying … please say, that for some twisted, unexplainable reason, she is lying about this?" His voice was calmer now, but cold as ice.

"She's not lying," I coughed. "Whatever she told you is true."

"What the fuck is wrong with you?" he yelled again. "How could you look me in the eye and act like my friend for the past three months, when the whole time you were fucking my wife?"

"I can explain."

"There is no explanation, no excuse." And then the line went dead. I sunk into a kitchen chair and held my head in my hands.

I felt like someone had punched me in the gut. My heart raced, and I couldn't breathe. I picked up the phone to call Chloe. If I felt like this, I couldn't imagine how she felt, couldn't imagine the conversation she'd had with Quinn.

She, of course, didn't answer. I left her a message, and then sent her a text message. She didn't respond to that either. I thought about getting in my car and going to find to her. To hold her and tell her I loved her. But my ego was still too fragile from being rejected before. I couldn't handle it if she told me no again.

I grabbed a beer out of the fridge and sat on the couch. I had known all along that if Quinn found out, our friendship would be over. I thought I had been prepared to lose him as a friend, thought

I was ready to give him up for Chloe, but I was wrong. I wasn't prepared—hadn't expected it to feel like this.

I knew Quinn would never talk to me again, I couldn't blame him, but that didn't mean I liked it. I rubbed a hand across my face. I had no idea it would hurt this bad to lose my best friend. I prayed to God that Chloe would give me a chance to show her how much I loved her. I couldn't lose both of them.

26

It was two AM before the tears finally stopped, before I dragged myself to bed, alone. I didn't sleep much, dreams of Quinn slamming the door as he left haunted me. When my alarm went off at 6:30, I felt like I had been hit by a bus.

I did my best to cover my swollen eyes with makeup and went to work, hoping for a distraction from the pain that radiated from my chest into my entire body. At some point in the day, I tried to call Dani, but when she didn't answer, I started sobbing again and left her a tear-filled voicemail I wasn't sure she'd even be able to understand.

I was on my way home from work when she called me back.

"Hi," I answered.

"Do you need somewhere to stay?"

"God yes," I sighed. "Quinn won't answer any of my calls, so I have no idea where he is or what he's doing, but I can't stay at our place right now."

"Come stay with me," she said.

"Aren't you going home for Christmas?"

"This is more important."

"Thank you, Dani, seriously…" I paused, the realization of everything that had happened yesterday hitting me out of nowhere. "My God, what did I do?" A sob tore through my words.

"Get some stuff and come over, we'll talk it out."

"I'll be there soon," I said and hung up. Quinn wasn't at the apartment, and it didn't look like he'd been there since last night. I grabbed a few things and left as fast as I could, the memories of our conversation less than twenty-four hours ago haunting the space. I sent Quinn a text to let him know I'd be staying at Dani's, just in case he wanted to come back to the apartment. Like every other message I had sent him that day, he didn't reply.

Dani answered the door wearing a sweatshirt and yoga pants. She took one look at me and pulled me into a hug. My shoulders shook as I stood on Dani's doorstep and sobbed. She didn't say anything, didn't try to get me to come inside, even though it was cold outside; she just stood there in the doorway and let me cry. A breeze picked up, sending a shiver down my spine, and I finally peeled myself out of Dani's embrace so we could go inside.

"What happened?" Dani asked ten minutes later when we were both sitting on her couch with glasses of wine. I curled my feet up under me and stared out her back window into the dark night.

"My time ran out," I sighed. "I knew it would. I just didn't expect it to all blow up so violently."

"Why did you end it with Carson?" Dani asked. I closed my eyes and took a deep breath. Dani was going to ask me all the uncomfortable questions, make me find the answers I'd been ignoring for too long.

"He asked me to leave Quinn for him."

"Are fucking kidding me?" Dani shook her head. "What an asshole."

"He questioned my love for Quinn, and our marriage, so I slapped him across the face, told him it was over, and kicked him out."

"He's not entirely wrong, you know."

"What is that supposed to mean?"

"You can't honestly sit there and pretend like none of it meant anything, can you? You slept with the guy for four months and lied to your husband the whole time … I would've questioned your marriage, too. If your love for Quinn is everything you say it is, what was the point?"

Anger swelled in me. I still loved Quinn, damn it, why didn't anyone believe me?

"We got to that question faster than I thought we would," I snorted and took a long sip of my wine.

"We can come back to it," Dani shrugged. "I've got nothing but time. What happened with Quinn?"

"I got home from work after you called me, and he started badgering me with questions. He wasn't buying any of my bullshit anymore, so I just told him the truth." Tears welled in my eyes as I remembered the look on his face when I'd told him, the way his knees buckled when I'd said it was Carson. "It broke him, Dani. I saw it. I watched the light in his eyes change, watched the way he looked at me change, everything went dark and cold."

"Oh Chloe," Dani sighed.

"I did that. I broke the man I loved," I said. "Why? Quinn loved me more than anything else in the world, why would I do that to him?"

"Only you can answer that question."

"I don't know," I whispered.

"Yes, you do; you might've buried it too deep to dig up right now, but you know the answer. You don't cheat on your husband for no reason."

I rested my head on the back of the couch and let the tears roll down my cheeks.

Thank God I had a few days off work for the holidays. It was a struggle to drag myself off Dani's couch for anything more than the necessities. Every day, I tried to call Quinn. I left him voicemails until his mailbox was full, then apologized a million times via text, but heard nothing from him.

Meanwhile, Carson seemed to be employing the same tactic with me. His calls and texts were incessant, but I ignored him. It was at least fifty percent his fault that I was in this mess.

The week after Christmas flew by in a blur of tears and work. It was slow at work, and I still hadn't heard about the team lead position, even though I'd interviewed weeks ago. I tried to keep myself busy with planning for spring projects and organizing. Once I had organized my desk, I did the copy room and the supply closet.

Finally, it was Friday, and I could resume my Netflix binge and couch surfing at Dani's. She was working an overnight shift at the ER, and as I watched old episodes of *Sex and the City*, loneliness crept in. Even though I had been with Dani, Christmas without Quinn had been miserable. I missed him. I missed his voice and his smile and the way he liked to snuggle in the morning before we got out of bed. Was it all gone forever? I wondered if Quinn could ever forgive me, if we could ever have the same amazing relationship again. Would he want a divorce? I took a shot of tequila to keep from thinking about it.

Somewhere around shot number three, I decided I'd go to the apartment tomorrow and get fresh clothes and some other things I needed. I couldn't stay at Dani's forever. I'd have to go home eventually … now was as good a time as any. After two more shots, I started crying again. I'd ruined my marriage and broke my husband's heart; my life as I knew it was gone, and I didn't know if I'd ever get it back.

27

I hadn't expected Quinn to be at our apartment on Saturday afternoon—I don't know where I thought he would be especially since football season was over—but when I unlocked the door to our apartment, I was surprised to see him standing in the kitchen.

"What are you doing here?" His voice was cold. "I'd thought you'd be off somewhere fucking Carson."

"Quinn, don't, it's not like that."

"Not like what? Have you not been sneaking around, fucking the guy I thought was my best friend, for months? Months, Chloe!" he yelled, and I flinched. Quinn never yelled; it was a side of him I'd never seen before.

"I know, I fucked up, big time."

"No, fucked up doesn't even begin to describe what you did. You took everything we had, everything we've built, and crushed it. And then you did it again and again until there was nothing left. You threw away eight good years. And the whole time you just pretended like everything was still perfect. Did you fuck him in our bed?"

I couldn't answer, but tears streamed down my cheeks as I nodded.

"Jesus Christ, Chloe. And then you let me make love to you in the exact same bed? I don't even know who you are."

"I'm still me, I still love you," I whispered.

"Is this how you treat people you love? How many times have you told Carson you love him?" He ran his hands over his face and blew out a frustrated, angry breath.

"Never. I never did, I've always loved you, I never…" I was going to say I never loved Carson, but the words wouldn't come out. I did love Carson. The realization hit me like a tidal wave, and I had to grab on to the kitchen table to keep from falling. I loved Carson. I loved Quinn. I loved them both.

"You never what?" Quinn asked, then waved me off. "Never mind, it doesn't even matter anymore."

"Quinn please," I took a step toward him and placed a hand on his arm. I still wanted him. I might be in love with Carson, but Quinn was part of who I was now. I didn't know what life would look like without him. I didn't want to know. He jerked away like my touch burned him.

"You were it for me, Chloe. You were everything I ever wanted." He was no longer yelling, his voice now hollow. "We were going to grow old together."

"We still can," I choked out between sobs. "Please, let me fix this."

"How? I can't even look at you, can't trust a fucking word that comes out of your mouth. How am I ever supposed to go to work again and not wonder every second I'm gone if you're off fucking someone else?"

"There isn't anyone else. It was just Carson; it was just sex, and we're done." I didn't believe the words even as I said them. None of them were true. How was I just supposed to walk away from Carson now?

"Until the next time you decide our sex life isn't good enough."

"Quinn, please, you know that's not true."

"Do I? If it was really just sex, why wasn't I good enough? Why weren't we enough? Weren't those your exact words when I wanted to have a threesome again? 'Aren't we good enough on our own?'" he mocked. "I'm such a fucking idiot. Everything is perfectly clear now … you were fucking him then, weren't you? That's why you didn't want to do it."

"It wasn't like that," I whispered.

"What was it like? Please, tell me. Did you just stumble on his dick over and over again? Don't fucking treat me like I'm an idiot, Chloe, when you've already been lying to me for months."

"Quinn," I begged. "Please, I still love you. I want to be with you." My heart was breaking. One way or another, I was going to have to give up one of the men I loved.

"Maybe you should've thought of that when you were fucking Carson in our bed."

I flinched at his words and stood in the middle of the kitchen and sobbed. I had nothing left to say. Everything he said was true. I didn't deserve a second chance, but here I was begging for one anyway. I had to try and make it work with Quinn. I'd loved him first. At one point, I had loved him with everything I had, everything I was. My heart fractured again at the thought of giving up Carson. But this was the right choice, wasn't it?

"You know," he said, his voice barely above a whisper, "I could've maybe understood it happening once. I still would've beaten the shit out of Carson, but I could have forgiven you. People make mistakes, I get that, but you kept doing it. You kept going back over and over again … you kept lying and hiding and cheating."

"I know," I whispered. "I'm sorry. I'm so sorry."

"Sorry isn't good enough, Chloe. How am I ever supposed to trust you again?"

"I don't know. Please, I'm sorry," I begged. Sorry was the only thing I could say.

Quinn just shook his head and started toward the door.

"Quinn, please don't go, please stay," I cried.

"I can't stay here. You've tainted everything in my life. You broke my heart, Chloe. Don't think I'm going to hand it back over so you can do it again."

He opened the door and walked out, the door slamming shut behind him.

"Quinn, please, please don't go, come back, I love you," I yelled after him.

"I always loved you," I whispered. I sunk to my knees in the middle of the kitchen and sobbed, praying that Quinn would come back, but knowing he wouldn't. An hour later, I dragged myself off the floor and collapsed on the couch, unable to lay in our bed, and cried until I fell asleep.

28

Quinn

I stood outside the door and listened to her yell at me to come back, and then sob, my own tears running down my cheeks. I listened to her cry long enough that the hallway grew dark as the sun set, the dim hall lights replacing the bright glow of the sun.

I wanted to go back inside, wrap my arms around her, and tell her I'd stay. I loved her. Despite everything she'd done, I still wanted her. But I couldn't stay. If I did, nothing would ever be the same. I wanted the old Chloe and Quinn back, but they were gone, a ghost of who we used to be left in their place.

What I'd said had been true—I couldn't trust her, I would wonder every time I wasn't with her what or who she was doing. I couldn't live like that, no matter how much I still wanted her.

Everything was so clear now. All the times she'd fought me about having a threesome again, never wanting to hang out with Carson and me, the late nights at work—everything made sense. How had I been so blind? How had I never noticed the way they looked at each other? All the times Chloe must've lied to my face played over in my mind. But she really wasn't a very good liar. I should've picked up on something sooner. It shouldn't have taken four fucking months. I loved her so much, I never thought anything like this was possible. Whoever said *love is blind* had it right.

God, I was such an idiot. All these years I'd thought my best friend and my wife being so close was a good thing. Fuck, was I wrong, and now I'd been betrayed by the two people I loved the most. I had never questioned why she had chosen Carson to have a threesome with, but even that made sense now. My stomach churned, and I felt like I was going to be sick.

I finally turned and walked away, unsure when I'd be back. I would have to get my stuff at some point. I'd need to find a new apartment and file for divorce. *Divorce?* My heart broke a little more at the thought. I had really thought she was it, the one I would spend my whole life with, maybe have babies with, get old and gray with, but now it was all gone. None of that would ever happen.

"Jesus Christ, how did we get here?" I murmured to myself, and ran my hands over my face. The elevator dinged, announcing my arrival on the ground floor. The doors slid open, and I lifted my head and looked into the face of the man I had once considered a brother.

"What the fuck are you doing here?" I sneered.

"Quinn ... I ... I..." Carson stumbled over his words.

"You what? Didn't think I'd be here? Didn't think I'd catch you coming to fuck my wife?" I lunged out of the elevator at him. Our bodies collided and flew backward. "How could you?" I yelled.

We crashed to the ground, and I felt the air heave out Carson's chest. I got two punches in before Carson caught his breath and blocked me. But I didn't stop—just kept swinging, punching every surface I could connect with—yelling the whole time.

"How could you do this to me?"

"You were like my brother!"

"You could have any woman you want, and you had to have her? Why? Why did you have to have her?"

It took me more than a minute before I realized Carson was barely fighting back. He was blocking me enough to keep me from breaking his nose, or doing any major damage, but for the most part he was just lying there, letting me use him as a punching bag. It made me even angrier that he wasn't fighting back.

I rolled off him and rested with my head between my knees, my breath coming in short bursts.

"Quinn," Carson said. I couldn't look at him. I might go ballistic again. I wanted to inflict as much pain on him as he had on me. I wanted to rip his world to shreds, until nothing was recognizable, like he had done to mine. I pushed myself to my feet. I wasn't going to stay here. Carson and Chloe deserved each other, fucking liars and cheaters.

"Quinn," Carson said again as he stood and blocked my exit.

"What can you possibly have to say to me?"

"I'm sorry."

"God, did you two practice your apology speeches together? I don't give a fuck if you're sorry. There is literally nothing you can say that will justify what you did. My wife, Carson! You were my fucking best man at our wedding! How could you do this?"

"I'm not going to stand here and give you some half-assed apology speech about how I wished it never happened, and tell you that if I could go back in time I'd change things, because that's bullshit. I'd do it all again tomorrow if I had a chance," he said. I inhaled sharply, and our eyes locked. He wasn't lying, which, at the very least, was appreciated. I was tired of being lied to. "I tried to stop more times than I can count, but Chloe…"

"Don't," I said. "Don't stand here and tell me about my own fucking wife, like I don't already know. You are disgusting, both of you."

"I know, and you're right. I came here today with every intention of being with Chloe. I thought you'd be at work."

"Why are you telling me this?" I couldn't understand why he was still talking.

"Because you're my brother."

"*Were*," I corrected. He winced, like the words physically hurt.

"I deserve that, but before you leave and never speak to me again, you have to listen to me."

"Why should I listen to you? How am I supposed to know every word you say isn't a lie?"

"Quinn, she still loves you. She doesn't want me." He shook his head like he couldn't believe the words that were coming out of his own mouth. "I'm the one who started this. I pushed her when I shouldn't have, kept coming back when she tried to keep her distance. It's my fault."

"Come on!" I yelled. "Don't make her out to be innocent here. She participated willingly, for months."

"I'm not saying she's innocent, but when she says she still loves you, it's true." Carson exhaled deeply. "I can't believe I'm about to tell you this, but I asked her to leave you. Asked her to be with me. You know what her response was? She slapped me, and then threw me out. That was two weeks ago, and I haven't talked to her since. She won't answer my calls or respond to my texts. She doesn't want me."

"Am I supposed to feel bad for you?" I balled my fists at my side. The fact that he had asked her to leave me made me want to tackle him again. How had I ever thought he was my friend?

"No, man, but you should think twice before you do something drastic."

"Something drastic? You mean like having an affair with my best friend?" I asked. "That's what she did. It doesn't matter what you say, I'm not giving her a second chance. She doesn't deserve that. Neither of you do." I pushed my way past Carson and out into the parking lot.

"Have a nice life, Carson," I said. "Actually, have a shitty life … I don't really care anymore."

29

A knock on the door woke me from my fitful sleep. A small glimmer of hope swelled inside me. I jumped off the couch and opened the door, but it wasn't Quinn. Carson's blue eyes stared back at me, and my heart skipped a little. I didn't know it was possible to still feel love when I felt so broken inside.

Carson had a red welt under his right eye and a cut in the corner of his lip.

"Are you okay?" I asked instinctively.

"Yeah, I'm fine."

"What happened?"

"I ran into Quinn on my way in."

"Oh my God! I can't believe he hit you."

"I can," Carson said. "He caught me coming to fuck his wife, I would've hit me too."

"Is that why you're here?" I glared at him.

"I came to check on you. You haven't said a word to me in weeks, and after what happened with Quinn, I was worried about you."

"Well, isn't that nice of you," I said nastily. I turned away from the door and walked farther into the apartment. Carson followed me in and shut the door.

"What is that supposed to mean?"

"I don't need you to swoop in and rescue me. In case you forgot, you're the reason we're in this mess in the first place."

"Oh, so it's all my fault?" He raised his voice a little.

"Yes! You couldn't just leave me alone like I asked. You couldn't just walk away from the threesome and leave it at that. You had to keep pushing me and testing me until I broke."

"That is total bullshit, Chloe, and you know it. You wanted it just as bad as I did. I just had the balls to do something about it."

"That's not a good thing!" I yelled.

"And don't try to pretend like you didn't start this whole thing! You and your fucking threesome. Who does that?"

"Oh, please, don't judge me. You jumped in willingly."

"So did you, babe, so did you," he said. "All it took was one kiss and you were begging me to fuck you."

"You are an arrogant bastard."

"You didn't seem to mind a few weeks ago."

"My God, do you hear yourself? Do you realize what we've done? Quinn hates us both. He's never going to forgive us. He's fucking gone. Gone, Carson. You'll never play Mario Kart or watch football or see who can eat more hot wings in five minutes again. It's over. Your friendship, my marriage, we fucking ruined it."

"You think I don't know that?" Carson yelled.

"And for what? A couple of months of hot sex?" I turned away. I couldn't look at him. He turned me on and made me furious all at the same time. I wanted to tell him I loved him, but I couldn't, not when I still felt so raw from arguing with Quinn.

"It was worth it," Carson said, his voice calm and even. I spun back around.

"What?"

"You heard me. It was worth it," he said, his words dripping with sexuality. He took a step closer, his body just inches from mine. I tried to keep my breathing even, tried to quiet my heart that was pounding in my chest. "I'd do it again in a heartbeat."

"Carson, please." I pushed against his chest. I needed him out of my space, where I couldn't smell his body wash and feel the heat radiating off him. He took a step backward and ran a hand through his hair.

"I didn't mean for this to happen," he said. "It was just supposed to be some kinky fantasy that I got to play a part in. But then I got a taste of you, and I was addicted." The look in his eyes made my knees go weak.

"I couldn't stop. I can't stop," he said and took a step toward me again, running a hand up my arm and tucking a piece of hair behind my ear.

"Carson," I whispered. It wasn't right, not so soon after Quinn left. I pushed against his chest again, but he grabbed my wrists and held them tight.

"Let me fix it," he said, his breath soft against my lips.

Then his lips crashed against mine. Passion and fire burned through my veins, consuming all the hurt and anger and pain from the past week until there was nothing left but lust, desire, and Carson. There was nothing but my body and his and too many clothes between them.

Our hands tore at each other's clothes. Carson pushed me back against the kitchen table. He pulled my leggings and panties down in one motion, then lifted me up and set me down on the table and kissed me again. His fingers dug into my hips as he thrust into me, but didn't move beyond that. He rested his forehead against mine, fully inside me, where he fit perfectly.

"I missed you," he whispered. Then he lost control and fucked me. He held me in place on the table as he drove in and out of me in long, hard strokes. "This. Is. Worth. It." He grunted out. "Worth.

Every. Fucking. Moment. You are so fucking beautiful, Chloe," he breathed against my mouth, never slowing his rhythm.

"You talk too much," I said, and grabbed his face with both hands, pulling him down for a kiss.

Carson pulled away, dropped to his knees in front of me, and sucked my clit into his mouth. I leaned back and ran a hand through his hair.

"Holy shit, Carson," I moaned. His tongue traced circles over my clit, the pleasure building with each pass. "Oh my God, yes." I gripped the edge of the table with both hands as my orgasm exploded through me. Before it had subsided, he thrust into me again, dragging out the waves of pleasure. He pulled me to the edge of the table, burying himself as deep as he could go.

"Oh fuck," I moaned. Carson tightly held on to me as he fucked me hard and fast. He buried his face in my neck and mumbled incoherently when he came. Neither of us moved as we caught our breath.

Carson turned away and started to get dressed. I slid off the table and pulled my leggings and shirt back on. Carson was trying to button his shirt when I stood back up.

"You are missing some buttons." I smirked.

"That would be your fault." He smiled back.

"Hey, let's not lay blame here," I laughed, and put my hands up to show I was innocent. Carson looked at me, but there was no laughter on his face.

"So now what?" he said. "Where do we go from here?"

"I don't know," I said quietly, as the hurt and pain seeped back through me. Carson ran his hand over his face. That wasn't the answer he was looking for, but I wasn't ready to jump into a relationship with him. Not when the wounds from Quinn were still fresh and raw, not when a tiny part of me still believed there was a chance we could make it work again.

"You're seriously still going to push me away?" His voice rose. A tear spilled down my cheek, and his face softened. "I'm not done with you, Chloe, and I don't think you're done with me either," he said. Grabbing his jacket, he walked over to me. He looked down at me and ran a finger across my cheek. "I'm not going to let you push me out." He kissed me gently before turning and leaving.

"It's not up to you," I murmured as the door shut behind him.

30

Is it possible to love two men at once? It had been a week since I'd let myself admit that I loved Carson. The two sides of my heart felt like they were in a wrestling match. I still loved Quinn, but it wasn't with my whole heart anymore. Without even realizing it, I had let Carson in. I had let him steal a piece of my heart.

I sat in the lobby of Dani's and my favorite restaurant, waiting for her. I had needed to get out of the apartment, but other than work, I hadn't left since the day I fought with Quinn, and it was making me crazy. I constantly replayed the events of the last few months, trying to figure out where it had all gone so wrong. How I had let everything spiral out of control? Was Derek right? Had I married the wrong person? Had I always loved Carson? A small part of me thought I had always loved him, from the very beginning. I smiled as I thought about the first time we met.

It had been my third or fourth date with Quinn. I had reluctantly agreed to go tailgating at an Oregon football game with him. Quinn had gone to the bathroom, and I was standing awkwardly off to the side of the group that had gathered. I didn't know anyone else and knew nothing about football. I really liked Quinn and didn't want to embarrass him by saying the wrong thing.

"You must be Quinn's new girl?" I spun around and saw Carson for the first time. His blue eyes sparkled with mischief as he ran a hand through his hair

and looked me up and down. I didn't say anything … was I Quinn's new girl? "I'm Carson." He stuck out his hand, and I shook it.

"Chloe."

"Chloe," Carson said and draped an arm around my shoulders. I saw Quinn coming toward us, but Carson didn't remove his arm, instead leaning in closer.

"If you ever get sick of Quinney-Boy and decide you want a real man, come find me," he said loud enough for Quinn to hear.

"Get off, man," Quinn said as he slapped Carson's arm off my shoulders. "Chloe, I see you met Carson. My idiot best friend."

"Hey, just giving the lady options," Carson laughed.

"Chloe," Dani's voice snapped me out of my daze. I looked up and saw her standing right in front of me. "Sorry I'm late. Traffic was a nightmare."

"It's okay … I haven't been here long."

When we were seated at a booth in the corner, and our orders had been taken, I said, "I know the answer to your question."

"Oh?" Dani took a drink of her beer. "This should be interesting. So, what's the answer … why did you do it?"

"I love Carson," I sighed.

"Are you sure?" Dani looked shocked.

"Yes. Carson, damn him, weaseled his way in, and somewhere along the way, I fell for him. I didn't want to admit it, because then I had to admit that it wasn't just sex, that I had betrayed Quinn on every level possible."

"You still love Quinn?"

"I'll always love Quinn, but it doesn't matter … he's moving out tomorrow." I wiped a tear from the corner of my eye; I wasn't going to cry about it here. I'd shed more tears than I had imagined possible since Quinn called and told me he wanted a divorce. I had begged him to reconsider, told him I'd do anything to make it right, but nothing I said made any difference.

"Oh, Chloe." Dani put her hand on top of mine. I shook my head.

"It's okay, this is what I deserve," I said. "I couldn't just be happy with what I had. I had to have more. I had to live out my fantasies, no matter the cost."

"How could you have known having a threesome would lead to this?" God bless her. Dani was trying so hard to be supportive and make me feel better, when all I wanted was to wallow in my own grief. I didn't feel like pointing out that I did know. After the first time, I knew nothing would ever be the same; I knew what would happen if we went down that road again, but I did it anyway. "What are you going to do now?"

"What do you mean?" I looked up from my drink. Dani was looking at me with sad eyes, an expression I'd never before seen on her face. I frowned; my sadness was rubbing off on her, and I didn't like it.

"Do you want to be with Carson?"

"I honestly don't know," I said. "I've been with Quinn for a long time. I don't know how to have a relationship with someone else."

Our food came, and neither of us said anything for a few minutes.

"Thank you for listening to me and not judging me. I know your feelings about cheating, and I appreciate you keeping them to yourself while I figure this all out."

"Look, I hate what you did to Quinn—nothing you say about loving Carson or anything else will ever change that—but we were friends first, and nothing will ever change that."

"I hit the best friend jackpot with you." I smiled.

"Well, duh," Dani laughed. "I've been telling you that for years."

31

I stood in our apartment, surrounded by boxes, a never-ending river of tears flowing down my cheeks. Quinn was moving out. We'd spent the last few hours dividing our possessions, the occasional conversation about who should keep what breaking up the deafening silence.

I had been dreading this day, and now it was almost over. Quinn had already taken most of the stuff down to his car. He was leaving all the furniture. He told me he didn't want any furniture Carson and I had fucked on, which he figured meant all of it.

I walked through the apartment, my heart heavy with guilt as I looked at the fragments of our life together, pictures and random things Quinn didn't want. I sat down on the edge of the bed and crossed my legs.

The bedroom was mostly empty. Quinn's side of the closet was cleaned out, and all the artwork on the walls was gone. It had all been Quinn's before we met. Even his Oregon throw blanket that had been on our bed since before we got married was gone. I hugged a pillow to my chest. I would have to move too. I couldn't stay here; there were too many memories, good and bad, too much pain and hurt inside these walls.

"Well, I guess that's it," Quinn said from the doorway. I looked up into his eyes, and my lip quivered, a new round of tears spilled down my face. He walked over to me and wiped a tear from under my eye.

"You have to stop crying. You know this is the right thing to do," he whispered. I was the one who had lied and cheated, but he was still consoling me. Why hadn't I realized how amazing he was? Why did it take losing him to see everything I had taken for granted before?

"That doesn't make it hurt any less," I said. I knelt on the bed so we were face-to-face. "Please stay."

"Chloe, please, I can't have this conversation again," he said, irritation lacing his voice.

"I'm so sorry." I hung my head and sobs racked my shoulders. "I never meant to hurt you."

"I know." He lifted my chin, and our eyes met. There was so much sorrow in those deep brown eyes. "I'll always love you, Chloe Louise."

"Quinn," I whispered, unable to get any other words out. He cupped my face gently with both hands and wiped the tears from under my eyes before he planted a soft kiss on my lips. I wasn't ready for him to leave. I leaned forward and kissed him again, his hands never leaving my face as he kissed me back.

He laid me back on the bed and kissed me slowly before he peeled off my clothes, and then his own. I moaned when he thrust into me. I knew this would be the last time. For one last time, we were one—husband and wife, lovers. But it wasn't the same. It was slow and beautiful and heart breaking, but there was no spark, no fire. The flame that used to burn between us had been snuffed out. With every thrust, my heart shattered into thousands of tiny pieces. I didn't think it would ever be whole again. He took a piece of my heart every time he pulled out.

And then he left without another word. I watched him go from the bed, our eyes meeting one last time as he paused at the door. Then he was gone. I let him go without a fight this time—let him walk out the door with the pieces of my broken heart, knowing I had no one to blame but myself.

32

There was a reason they were called fantasies; they don't belong in the real world. They should stay tucked safely away in the corners of your imagination where they were bright and shiny illusions of what could be. In the harsh light of reality, they were dark and dirty, spreading like the plague until nothing looked the same.

I laid in bed, staring up at the dark ceiling, smoking a joint, the sheets tangled around me. I hadn't made the bed or washed the sheets since Quinn had moved out several days ago. They still smelled like him. I pulled the covers over my head and inhaled deeply. For a moment, the scent was enough to make me believe I could uncover my head and see Quinn's goofy grin smiling back at me; that I would wake up and this nightmare I had created would be over.

My phone rang, the screen bright in the dark room, the sound echoing through the quiet apartment. It was Derek. I pushed IGNORE and rolled over. He called three more times before I finally answered.

"I wasn't sure you were still alive. Are you at work?" he asked.

"No."

"Why not?"

"I didn't feel like it." I had used four days of my vacation time in the last two weeks, on days when dragging myself out of bed and interacting with other human beings seemed like too much to deal with.

"So, what are you doing?"

"What do you want, Derek?" The words came out angrier than I intended.

"Don't get snippy with me. I called to check on you; you haven't responded to any of my texts or calls in two weeks," he snapped. "Let me guess, you probably haven't gotten out of bed today, other than to go the bathroom, and you're probably either drunk or high most of the time, lying there feeling sorry for yourself? Does that sound about right?"

"Fuck you."

"So that's a yes. Get over it, Chloe. Get your ass out of bed and do something! You did this to yourself; you made your bed, now you have to lay in it."

"How original," I said sarcastically. "Besides, laying in my bed is exactly what I'm doing."

"You have to move on."

"How am I supposed to move on from the man I've been with for eight years? The man I thought I'd grow old with?"

"I don't feel sorry for you. You should have thought about that months ago."

"I thought you understood?" I asked.

"Just because I understand doesn't mean I have to have sympathy. I know it's hard, I know you feel like your world is over, but it's not. And you can't stay in bed for the rest of your life," he said. "What about Carson?"

"What about him?" I snapped. Dani was still the only one who knew I loved him, but right now it wasn't enough. Pain pushed out any feelings of love.

"Does he still want to be with you? Move on with him if you have to."

I couldn't pretend I hadn't thought about it. I'd wanted to call him a million times in over past few weeks, or answer one of his incessant texts, especially after our rendezvous. I wanted to tell him I loved him. But my heart was too broken and mangled and only wanted Quinn. I had held onto a glimmer of hope that he might forgive me and we could make it work, but it had died the day he'd moved.

I had tried to make myself hate Carson, tried to blame him, but I couldn't do that either. I had been the selfish one. I was one who couldn't just be happy with what I'd had. I had let him in; he was just an asshole and took advantage of it.

"I can't," I choked out.

"Maybe he's it for you, like Adrienne was for me."

"He's not. Quinn was it, and I fucked it up. I threw it all away."

"Chloe," Derek said matter-of-factly. "If Quinn was really it for you, you would've never slept with Carson; it doesn't matter how strong he came on to you, or how intense the lust was, Quinn would've been enough and nothing else would have mattered."

"That's bullshit."

"Shut-up and let me finish. It's not bullshit and you know it. That's why it took you almost four months to break off the affair, and, to be honest, I think if Carson hadn't asked you to leave Quinn, you never would have."

"But I was happy—" I interjected. Derek cut me off.

"You were happy with Quinn, I know, but that doesn't mean he was your soulmate. Plenty of people have perfectly happy marriages, live their whole lives together without the kind of spark you had with Carson."

"So what, that makes everything better?"

"No, it is still going to be shitty for a while. And you still did an awful thing to Quinn, there is no denying or justifying that, but it doesn't have to be the end of the world."

"God, are you a psychologist or a cop?" I rolled my eyes and took one final hit of my joint.

"I was always the smart one," Derek said, and I snorted.

"Yeah right."

"Hey, I'm not the one lying in bed, getting high on a Wednesday."

"Do I have to get out of bed today?"

"No, but tomorrow you do. You have to go to work and continue being kick-ass Chloe. Shouldn't they be deciding about the team-lead soon? Calling out this many times can't look good for you," he said, and I groaned, because I knew he was right.

"I didn't even think about that. Goddamn it, now I'm not going to get the job either."

"Don't be all dramatic," Derek said. "But you should probably go to work every day for the foreseeable future."

"Fine."

"I'm calling you at 7:30 tomorrow morning to make sure you are up and on your way."

"Great, can't wait."

"I love you, Chloe."

"I love you, too." I laid back down in bed and pulled the covers over my head.

I thought about what Derek had said, about Carson, and I wondered if we could really have a relationship; at least then, this whole shit-show wouldn't have been for nothing.

I dozed off and dreamed about Quinn and Carson, like I had every day for the past few weeks, but none of it made any sense.

A few hours later, my phone rang and woke me out of my deep, pot-induced sleep. I bolted upright in bed and looked at my phone … it was Sean.

"Fuck," I mumbled under my breath and tried to wake myself up.

"Hello," I said, hoping I didn't sound like the zombie I felt like.

"Chloe, I'm sorry to bother you on your day off," Sean said. "I hope you're feeling all right. I've been worried about you being gone so much recently."

Dread crept through me. *Yup, I'd fucked this up too.*

"No, I'm fine, just family stuff. Thank you for being concerned," I lied.

"I need to meet with you, in person," he said, sounding rushed.

"When?"

"Today, if possible. I have to go to New York tonight and would really like to speak with you before I leave. The hiring committee has made a decision."

That woke me up.

"I can be there," I said hastily and looked at the clock. It was almost one. "Can you give me a few hours?"

"Can you be here by 2:30?" I jumped out of bed and stumbled toward the shower.

"Yes, I will be there," I said.

"Great, see you soon."

I hung up and turned the shower on cold and stepped under the spray. The cold water woke me up and swept the cobwebs from the corners of my mind. Then, I turned the water to hot and washed the smell of weed off myself.

I pulled my hair into a low bun, put on a little makeup to hide the red rims around my eyes, brushed my teeth, and put on a pair of dress pants and a sweater.

At 2:15, I pulled into my office building. Whatever was about to happen would be a big deal, and I had butterflies in anticipation. Either I was being promoted, or I was being demoted from my temporary position.

I stopped in the bathroom and checked my reflection one last time before I walked to Sean's office. I knocked on the door and heard

Chelsy protest from her desk behind me, but Sean waved me into his office.

Another man I didn't recognize was sitting in the corner. Even though he was sitting, you could tell he was tall, and he was handsome. His broad shoulders pulled at his suit jacket. His black hair and turquoise eyes made it hard not to stare, but I forced my attention to my boss as I shut the door behind me.

"Chloe, I'm glad you made it," Sean said. "Please, take a seat." He didn't make any mention of the stranger in his office and didn't introduce us. I sat down, perplexed. Was this guy taking my job?

"Chloe, I'll get right to the point. We've chosen someone else for the women's team lead here in Oregon."

It was like someone punched me in the gut; all the air left my lungs, and I struggled to breathe. This couldn't possibly be happening. Everything in my life couldn't fall apart at the same time. I couldn't look at Sean, I was afraid I might cry.

"But we have another opportunity for you," he added. I looked up slowly and saw him smiling.

"I don't understand," I said.

"Chloe, this is Adam. He heads the design team in our New York office." Sean finally motioned toward the man in the corner. The man—Adam—nodded, but didn't say anything. "He has an opening on a team for a special project, and he wants you."

Adam jumped into the conversation.

"We are completely overhauling our NFL line, designing new looks for all the teams that will debut in Thursday night games next season. We also have a new contract with the Syracuse Athletics Department, and need a whole new line of gear designed for each of their varsity teams. We anticipate both projects together will take about a year. I've got most of the team in place, but I need someone to lead the projects."

"I have never worked in uniforms before. Are you sure this isn't a mistake?" I said.

Sean raised his eyebrow at me. I didn't understand what was happening.

"I was on the final hiring committee for the women's position and saw your work. That is part of the reason this decision has taken so long. Sean was ready to give you the job here, when I called and said I wanted you. We had to start over again," Adam said. "I think you are a perfect fit for what we need. You have vision and focus, and will be able to lead a team in creating cohesive, original designs."

"It is an amazing opportunity, Chloe," Sean said.

"You are offering me a job in New York City?" I asked, to make sure I was following the conversation.

"It would only be for a year, maybe eighteen months," Adam interjected.

"What happens after that?" I asked.

"Your job on the women's team would still be here when you get back, assuming Adam doesn't come up with some other project he needs you for," Sean said with a smile. "We're in negotiations for the 2020 and 2022 Olympic game contracts, and will need a team lead for those projects as well. You could be considered for positions like that after this."

"But we need you in New York in the next month," Adam said. "We are already behind our timeline for the NFL uniforms."

"I know you'll need to talk it over with Quinn," Sean said. I waved my hand and dismissed him. Tears formed in my eyes, because I didn't need to talk to Quinn. I was the only one making decisions now.

"Of course I'll do it," I said. "I can't turn down an opportunity like this. I'm honored to even be considered."

"Great!" Adam stood, and looked like he was ready to shake my hand. Sean held up his hand and looked at me intently.

"Chloe, are you sure you don't need more time? I can give you a few days to think it over. This is a big decision."

"No," I said confidently. "I'm positive this is the right decision for me."

It was the right choice—the chance to start over, far away from Quinn and Carson and the memories of them both on every corner. Adam and Sean exchanged glances, and then Sean nodded.

"Welcome to the team, Chloe." Adam stood in front of me, and I rose to shake his hand. "It was a pleasure to meet you, but I've got to run, I have a plane to catch. One of our agents, who has moved dozens of employees across the country, will be in touch tomorrow and will help you get the details all figured out." He pulled an envelope out of his briefcase and handed it to me.

"This is the contract. Please look it over tonight and let me know immediately if you see any issues."

"I will, thank you," I said. With that, he strode over to the door.

"See you in New York, Chloe."

Twenty minutes later, I sat in my car, my head spinning. I had instinctively called Quinn, but hung up before it went through. I would have to tell him eventually, but right now I needed someone to share my excitement with.

I picked Dani. When she didn't answer, I sent her a text.

Me: I have amazing news! Call me ASAP.

I pulled out of the parking lot, and my phone rang before I got to the street—Dani.

"Oh my God, Dani, you're never going to believe it! Nike offered me a job in New York City!" I said as soon as I answered.

"You are moving to New York?! Are you shitting me?"

"It's real," I said. "I have the contract with me right now. I'm planning on reading it tonight, and signing it in the morning."

"When are you going?"

"I don't know yet … soon. Within the month."

"That is fucking amazing! I'm coming over right now, and we are going to celebrate! New York City! Oh my God, I can't even believe it."

"It's still pretty surreal, but I'm excited," I said. "I'm sure that will change when I call my mom, since she already gives me so much grief for being in Portland. I can't imagine what she is going to say if I'm 3,000 miles away."

"Don't worry about that now, just be excited! You can deal with her tomorrow."

"Aaahhh!" I yelled. "I'm so excited."

"Me too," she said. "I'll see you soon."

I'd only been home 10 minutes when Dani arrived with two bottles of wine and food from our favorite Indian place.

We ate and drank and caught up on the things I hadn't had a chance to talk to her about yet. I told her every detail from the day I'd left her house, to the heart-breaking sex I'd had with Quinn when he'd moved out, to the rude phone call from Derek this morning.

"I knew I liked Derek," she said. "But seriously, it's a damn good thing he called you. I was about to come over here and drag your ass out of bed. I've never seen you like this before."

I had ignored pretty much everyone since Quinn had moved out, Dani included.

"I've never had to come to terms with the fact that I cheated on my husband and tore apart our marriage."

"God, I would've loved to have been a fly on the wall for the fight between Quinn and Carson," Dani said through a mouth full of food.

"Carson didn't tell me much, but I imagine it wasn't pretty."

"Have you talked to him?"

"No, I can't bring myself to call him. I want to, but to say what?" She looked at me like I was delusional.

"Ummm, I don't know ... maybe I love you?"

"What's the point now? I'm moving." She shrugged and let it go.

"Are you going to tell Quinn?"

"I have to. We're not officially divorced yet. Besides, I think he'd want to know."

"Divorced. Fuck, it sounds so..." Dani struggled to find the right word.

"Ugly," I supplied.

"Yeah, that'll work."

"I've got others. Sad, lonely..."

"A second chance," Dani interrupted. "Think about it. If none of this had ever happened, would you be moving to New York? Taking the job of your dreams?"

"Maybe..."

"I will never, ever condone what you did, but if you were still with Quinn you wouldn't be able to accept the job on the spot like you did. He just got his new show..."

"He did?" I interrupted.

"Oh, yeah, I heard him on the radio the other day. It was damn good. But that's not the point. He got a new show, so I doubt he'd just drop it to move across the country."

It was true. I hadn't even stopped to consider what would've happened if Quinn and I were still together. For the first time in weeks, I felt a little bit of hope.

"I'm going to miss you," I said. Dani looked me straight in the eyes, and, for a moment, I thought I saw a tear forming in the corner of her icicle blue eyes. She shook her head and swore at me.

"Damn it! I didn't come here to cry. We are supposed to be celebrating, not mourning. Besides, it's just a year, and you better believe I'm coming to visit you."

Dani got up and opened the second bottle of wine, and even though we both had to work in the morning, we stayed up laughing and talking and celebrating my new start until two in the morning. I hugged Dani tight when she left and felt a little piece of my broken heart heal itself.

I had my best friend and a kick-ass new job in the fashion capital of the world. I went to bed feeling lighter and happier than I had in weeks.

33

I waited outside the radio station, leaning against Quinn's car. I shivered in the early February breeze and clutched my coffee cup tighter, hoping the warmth would spread from my hands to the rest of my body. Quinn, not surprisingly, wouldn't return my calls, no matter how many voicemails I left him.

I was leaving for New York next week, and he still didn't know I was moving. I couldn't give him the news via voicemail or text, so this ambush was my last resort.

The door swung open, and Quinn stepped out into the winter air, his head down against the wind, and my stomach tightened at the sight of him. Quinn's eyes narrowed as he looked up and saw me. He stopped walking and started to turn around, like he was going to go back inside.

"Quinn, wait," I called after him and jogged over to where he was still standing.

"What are you doing here, Chloe?"

"You wouldn't answer my calls."

"Maybe that's because I don't want to talk to you. I want to move on, but you keep fucking with my head."

"I never wanted you to move on; I wanted to fix it. If it was up to me, we'd still be married, not going through divorce proceedings." I shook my head; this wasn't why I came here. I didn't come to argue with him, to try to win him back … again. "I'm sorry, that's not why I'm here," I said with a sigh.

"Why are you here then?" he said, frustration in his voice.

"I'm moving to New York," I said, and took a sip of my coffee. "I thought you should know."

"When? Why?"

"Next week. I got a job working on a couple of special projects for Nike, but I'll only be there for a year or so."

"Chloe! That's amazing!" For a fraction of a second, I saw the old Quinn in his eyes, the one who was always so proud of me. Then the flash was gone, and the new, more stoic Quinn was back in place. "That is really great."

"I heard about your new show … congratulations. I told you they would be stupid to not give you a chance. I even listened to it a couple times. You are amazing, as always."

"Thank you. It's been great."

We stood there awkwardly, unsure what to say to one another. The breeze picked up, and I shivered again. I reached in my pocket and handed him a business card with my New York address written on the back of it.

"That is my new address; you can send any divorce papers there, and I'll do my best to get them back to you as soon as I can. I don't want to hold up the process for you."

My voice cracked on the last word, and I had to fight the urge to beg him for another chance. I couldn't do it again. He'd made it clear he was done and moving on. I had to accept it. In the weeks since I'd taken the job in New York, I'd made peace with my decisions and was ready to start this new chapter of my life, but seeing Quinn standing here brought back all the feelings of regret and despair.

"Chloe," He took a step closer to me. I turned away, afraid I might cry.

"I'm okay," I said, turning back around to face him. "I'm sorry for everything. I want you to be happy. I know we had that, and I threw it away, but I hope you can find it again, with someone who deserves you and everything you have to offer, because God knows I don't."

"I'm happy for you," he said. "You're going to kick ass in New York."

"Thank you." I took a step closer and kissed him on the cheek before I turned and walked to my car.

"Chloe." I turned back around at the sound of Quinn's voice. "Good luck in New York."

"I can't wait to hear you on ESPN Radio one day," I said. "Goodbye, Quinn." I gave him one last long glance, before turning my back. A single tear ran down my cheek as I got in my car and closed the door on my past.

Before I knew it, it was the night before the move. My apartment was mostly empty—my clothes, books, kitchen wares, and the few pieces of furniture I was taking were already gone. Everything else was packed up and waiting for the moving guys who would come tomorrow and take it all to storage.

Dani was on her way, I'd already ordered Chinese, and had a six-pack of beer in the fridge. I sat down on the couch while I waited, going over my checklist for the thousandth time to make sure I wasn't missing anything, even though I knew everything was done.

There was a knock on the door, and I checked the time on my phone.

"That was fast," I mumbled to myself as I went to answer the door. I hadn't expected Dani or the food to be here for another twenty minutes.

My heart nearly stopped when I opened the door to see Carson standing there. I hadn't answered a single one of his calls or texts in the weeks since I'd told him I wasn't ready to give him my heart. And there had been plenty of them. I couldn't talk to him, couldn't have his blond hair and blue eyes clouding my already questionable decision-making skills, couldn't be distracted by the spark between us and the way he made my stomach flip.

"Carson," I stammered.

"Surprised to see me?" he said, a cold edge to his voice. "I know Quinn moved out and filed for divorce weeks ago, and you still haven't answered any of my calls or texts."

I opened my mouth to ask how he knew that, but decided it wasn't important. He had to leave before Dani got here, or she would lose her shit.

"Are you going to let me in?" He peered around me. His eyes narrowed when he noticed the boxes and missing furniture. "Are you moving?"

I moved aside and let him in. He turned and looked at me; a fire I'd never seen burned behind his eyes. He was mad.

"Chloe, are you moving?" he said calmly, but I could tell it was taking a lot of restraint for him to keep his composure.

"Yes," I said, and then added in a whisper, "to New York."

"Wait? What? Did I just hear you right? You're moving to New York? Like, New York City?"

"Yes. I got a job offer from Nike to lead up some special projects there."

"When are you leaving?"

"Tomorrow." I turned my head. I didn't want to see the look on his face. The growl-like sound that came out of his mouth told me everything I needed to know.

"And you weren't going to tell me?" He was hurt. I looked at him again. The anger in his eyes had faded, confusion and hurt in its place.

"Carson, I can explain. It's all happened so fast, and then everything with Quinn. I didn't know where we stood." Anger flashed back across his face.

"That's a fucking lie!" he yelled, then balled his hands. "When did they offer you the job?" he said, lowering his voice.

"Three weeks ago." He ran a hand through his hair and paced back and forth in the kitchen, taking deep breaths as he walked.

"I can't fucking believe this," he mumbled. "You were seriously going to move across the fucking country without telling me?"

"Carson, what did you want? It wasn't going to change anything; I would've taken the job no matter what. I'm going no matter what."

"I wanted to know! Maybe spend some time with you, other than just fucking. Maybe figure out what the hell we do now."

"It doesn't even matter. I'm moving 3,000 miles away. I'll be gone for over a year … what good would three weeks of half-assed dating done?" I asked.

"Don't you get it?" Carson asked. "I love you, Chloe."

The words slapped me in the face. That was not what I was expecting to hear. I had spent the last month terrified of telling him my feelings, afraid he wouldn't feel the same way.

"Don't say that."

"Why not? It's true."

"No, it's not. You might love having sex with me, but you barely even know me." I brushed off his words, unwilling to accept what he was saying. His love would only make everything more complicated. "You don't—" I started to say, but he cut me off.

"Don't tell me how I feel." Carson started pacing again. I checked the time; Dani would be here any minute.

"Carson," I said quietly. He spun around and looked at me. "You have to leave. Dani will be here any minute, and she will kill us both if you're here."

"I don't give a fuck about Dani."

"Carson, please," I begged. "I don't want to fight with her my last night here."

"What about me?" he yelled. I closed my eyes. Things might have been different if I weren't leaving for New York. I might've ran into his arms and kissed him and told him I loved him too. But I couldn't leave half my heart in Portland.

"I'm not ready for what you're offering," I said calmly. "New York doesn't change that. I've barely had time to process the fact that I'll be divorced soon. I've been with Quinn for eight years, and I need time to let go. I need time for me, to figure out what I want. It would only make everything worse to rush into something neither of us are really ready for. It wouldn't be fair to pretend I can give you what you need right now, when I can't, especially not from a distance." Even though I knew I loved him, the words were true. I couldn't jump into a relationship with him. I needed to focus on my job in New York. I couldn't expect him to wait for me to be ready.

"I don't want to let you go," he said. "I was just getting started."

"It's already done. I have to go. It's what I need, what I want."

His face softened a little, like maybe he could understand where I was coming from. Our eyes met, and I swear we had a million conversations in those few seconds. Carson nodded and walked over to the door.

"Goodbye, Chloe." He opened the door and was gone before I could say anything else.

Less than five minutes later, Dani knocked on the door, carrying the food.

"I ran into the delivery guy on the way in," she explained as she dropped her purse on the floor and put the containers on the kitchen counter.

"I thought I saw Carson pulling out of the parking lot when I pulled in," she said as she grabbed the two paper plates I had left on the counter and opened us both beers.

"You did," I said, taking a drink of my beer. She spun around and glared at me. "Don't freak out, it's not like that. I've been ignoring him for weeks. He came looking for me, I told him I was moving to New York, he told me he loved me, I told him I wasn't ready for that, and he left."

I summed up our entire conversation in one sentence.

"He told you he loved you?" Dani raised an eyebrow at me. "And you didn't tell him you loved him too?"

"I couldn't. It's not fair to tell him I love him, and then move across the country."

"That's basically what he did to you. Threw it in your face when he already knew you were moving."

"I don't think he was saying it just to get me to stay," I said. Dani gave me a look that could have frozen over hell. "But I really think he meant it."

"Well, he's a little too late," she said matter-of-factly.

"I wasn't considering staying for him," I said.

"Good, I would've beaten the shit out of you if you were."

"Are you trying to get rid of me?" I teased.

"No! But not taking your dream job in New York City because of a guy you fucked a few dozen times would be a bad decision."

We drank beer and ate in silence for a few minutes, and I thought about all the random nights we'd had dinner together or laughed for hours about nonsense.

"I'm going to miss you," I said, a tear rolling down my cheek.

"Don't start this already!" Dani yelled through a mouthful of lo mein. She turned away, and when she looked back at me, her eyes were swimming with tears. "I can't believe you're leaving tomorrow."

"I know, but I'll be back."

"Yeah right. They'll get you there and will see what a creative genius you are and keep inventing new projects for you, just so you have to stay."

"Then you'll just have to come with me. I'm sure they need ultrasound techs in New York too."

"Nah, I'm not cut out for that weather," Dani said. "It's like fifteen degrees there right now and one hundred in the summer. No thanks, I'll keep my cool Portland weather and come visit you in the spring or fall when the weather is perfect."

"Well, jeez, I'm glad the perfect climate is more important to you than your best friend."

"The truth's a bitch," Dani laughed. "But seriously, you better not move there permanently and abandon me. How will I ever find a guy without my wing girl?"

"Oh, please! How many dates have I ever helped you get? I am pretty sure zero."

"It's not your fault I always sabotage it on purpose." She shrugged.

"I knew it! I knew I couldn't have been that bad of a wingman!" We both burst out laughing again.

We laughed and reminisced all night. It was the perfect way to say goodbye. We fell asleep side-by-side in my bed, both of us talking until neither of us could keep our eyes open anymore.

Dani had agreed to stay the night and drive me to the airport in the morning since I had sold my car a few days before. I got up before her, got ready, and finished packing my suitcase. Dani was up by the time the movers came and stood in the doorway of the bedroom listening while I gave them instructions about the storage unit and my stuff. She'd agreed to check on it all later this afternoon to make sure it all got there.

We drove to the airport in silence. When we pulled up to the drop off, she got out of the car without saying anything. She stood on the curb with my bag, her eyes full of tears once again.

"I'm going to miss you so much," she said, pulling me in for a hug.

"I'm going to miss you too. I wish you could come with me." I swung my purse over my shoulder.

"Don't worry, as soon as it's not fifteen degrees and snowing, I'll come visit."

"Do you have to keep reminding me that it's freezing there?"

"Just trying to prepare you." She laughed and hugged me again. "Call me when you land."

"I will. Thank you."

"For what?"

"Everything."

"I'm leaving before you make me cry again," she said, and walked back around her car. "I can't wait to visit you in the big city. Knock 'em dead, Chloe."

She smiled and got in her car. Even though it was overcast, she put on her sunglasses to hide her tears and waved as she drove away. I stayed on the sidewalk until I couldn't see her car anymore.

"Goodbye Portland," I murmured as I turned and walked into the airport.

34

I stepped out of the subway and shivered against the piercing East Coast wind. I thought Portland was cold, but it was nothing compared to New York in February. I pulled my coat tighter around me, and picked up my pace, my boots clicking against the frozen sidewalk.

I'd only been here three days, and already, the hustle and bustle of the streets was starting to heal my broken heart. I had finally found peace in the city that never sleeps. This was what I needed. A new city, a fresh start, a world of possibilities before me.

Everything was new. There were no memories here, no ghosts of the past lurking around every corner. I felt more alive and happier than I had weeks.

Warm air welcomed me as I ducked into the restaurant where I was meeting Adam. The hostess showed me to our table, but Adam hadn't arrived yet. I pulled my phone out of my purse and texted Carson.

Me: I'm sorry for the way I handled things. It was selfish and immature.

Carson: That makes two of us. I never should've pushed you.

Me: Don't go down that road. What's done is done. I'm here, you're there. There is no need to make ourselves crazy thinking about what could've been.

The truth was, I'd already done that a million times. What if I had stayed in Portland? Could Carson and I have had a real relationship? Did he really love me? What if we'd never had an affair? Would I still be here in New York with this new exciting job? There were too many possibilities to consider.

Me: But I should've told you sooner, and for that I really am sorry.

Carson: I'll miss you, Chloe. But kick ass. Those New Yorkers aren't going to know what hit them.

Adam arrived at our table just then, and I tucked my phone back in my purse.

"Chloe!" He beamed. "It is so good to see you. I'm glad you made it and haven't frozen yet." He hung his coat on the back of his chair.

"It's been close a few times; I wasn't prepared for how cold it is. I've already had to go shopping." I stood up to shake his hand, but he pulled me in for a hug and kissed both my cheeks.

He had grown a beard since I saw him last. It fit with the look he had going on—a knit sweater, jeans, and boots. His turquoise eyes glimmered with laughter.

"Shopping in New York? You poor thing."

"I didn't say it was a bad thing!"

We sat down, and the waiter brought menus. We talked easily about the move, about the weather, and he told me about the things I needed to do and see in New York

The conversation, laughter, and wine flowed freely. We briefly discussed work. I was starting on Monday, although I'd visited Nike yesterday, and got settle into my new office with the help of the IT guys.

It was the first time in as long as I could remember that for two whole hours I didn't think about Carson or Quinn—the first time my heart didn't hurt, and I didn't long for things to be like the used to be.

We finished dinner and walked outside.

"Let me walk you home," Adam said.

"No!" I protested. "It is kind of a long way, and it's freezing. I'll just take the subway."

"There is no way I'm letting a New York virgin ride the train home this time of night," he said. "Walk with me to my apartment only a few blocks away. We can have a nightcap, and then I'll call you a cab."

I studied his face the best I could on the semi-dark street. His eyes showed no hint of mischievousness; no dishonorable intentions or desires lurked behind the pools of turquoise.

"That sounds great," I said finally. We turned and walked away from the restaurant, but only made it a few feet before I stepped on a patch of ice and nearly fell. Adam grabbed my arm to keep me from landing on the street below.

"Easy there," he laughed. "You haven't got your New York winter legs yet."

"It hardly ever snows in Portland!" He laughed, a booming friendly sound that echoed through the streets.

"Hey, don't feel bad. I probably fell at least once a week the first winter I lived here. It's rough." He wrapped my arm in his to keep me from slipping again, and we started walking toward his apartment.

It was the perfect night—comfortable, easy, and filled with promise. Promise for a fresh start, promise for my new job, promise that with every day my heart would heal, and the light would shine a little brighter; Promise of a new chapter, and maybe one day, a new love.

Epilogue

The Portland air felt good on my skin. It wasn't the hot, sticky New York air that had arrived in May and never left.

I'd spent the last two days unpacking, getting stuff out of storage, and getting my new apartment set up. I needed a break.

The Saturday morning St. John's Farmer's Market had been just the thing I needed to get out of the house. It wasn't too far from my new University Park apartment. I had picked up a coffee and pastry for breakfast and was quickly filling my grocery bag with fresh produce.

After my job in New York ended, I'd taken a trip to Southern California to see my family for the Fourth of July weekend before coming back to Portland.

I sat down on a bench and people-watched, enjoying the cooler air and sunshine. A familiar figure emerged from behind the coffee stand twenty feet from where I sat. My skin prickled and my stomach twisted as Carson came into view. He was laughing with a friend. His blond hair was shorter than when I last saw him, but still plenty long enough to run your fingers through, and his blue eyes were covered by aviator sunglasses. His jeans hung off his hips, and his black T-shirt showcased all the right muscles. God, he looked good.

Desire rushed through my veins at the sight of him. I smiled and shook my head. Even after all this time, he still affected me. My heart swelled as I studied him.

He looked my way, turned around, and then did a double take, lifting his sunglasses to get a better view. He smiled at me, put his sunglasses back on, and turned back to his friend.

I looked away, disappointment seeping through me as I studied a fruit stand to my left. *You basically told him you didn't want him, so what did you expect Chloe?*

"Well, aren't you a sight for sore eyes?" I jumped and looked up to see Carson standing right in front of me.

"Hi, Carson," I said.

"How long have you been back?" He sat down next to me, his friend still standing nearby, watching our every move. Cason waved at him to go, before turning back to me.

"Just a few days," I said. "I needed a break from unpacking."

"So you're back to stay?"

"They just put me in charge of the Oregon account so I would say yes." I smiled.

"Holy shit, that's amazing! Does that mean you get free tickets?"

"Of course, all boys care about is tickets." I rolled my eyes at him. He put his hand on my knee, his touch sending a spark of electricity through me.

"It's so good to see you," he said. The undeniable chemistry between us was still there. I took a sip of my coffee, our gaze never breaking.

"Are you seeing anyone?" I croaked out. I had to know. I tapped my fingers on my coffee cup nervously, while I waited for his answer.

"I don't know," he answered, and I looked at him, perplexed. "I started something with this girl a while back, but then she moved and left me hanging. I don't know if she's still interested." He winked at me. A huge grin spread across his face as comprehension dawned on me, and I laughed.

I leaned over and whispered in his ear, "She's definitely still interested."

Acknowledgements

I know many people have strong feelings about cheating and when I started this book I didn't imagine it going in the direction it did. I struggled with trying to give Chloe a "happy ending", even with Carson, because I didn't feel like she deserved one. What she did to Quinn was awful and unforgivable and she deserved to suffer the consequences. I know many people will hate Chloe and Carson, and maybe even hate this book, but I've come to peace with that. I've struggled for months with the idea of my first novel being one that I'm sure many people will have strong negative reactions to but it was a story I couldn't ignore.

I wrote this book based on ideas I think a lot of married people have, the what ifs, the fantasies. Everyone has fantasies, they don't all look the same, but what would happen if you got a chance to bring your fantasy to life? For Chloe it spiraled out of control and cost her everything. I know she isn't the most lovable character, but she's human and I hope a lot of people can connect with the emotions she feels; the good, the bad and the ugly.

Now onto the thank you's.

I never thought this day would come. I've dreamed of writing and publishing a novel since I was a little girl but for a long time didn't believe it could happen. It just goes to show anything can happen if you put your mind to it.

This book never would have happened without the love, support and encouragement of so many people. First, my husband John, thank you for giving me the time, space and support to follow my dream. I spent hundreds of hours hunched over my laptop, headphones on, completely ignoring you and you never complained once. Your silent support means the world to me and I'll never be able to thank you enough.

To my family, who have always been my biggest supporters, thank you for giving me the love and courage to always follow my dreams. Thank you for asking questions, encouraging me and continuing to support my dream to be an author. I love you all.

To Emily and Nicole, thank you for the thousands of text messages brainstorming ideas with me. Thank you for listening to my random musings and letting me ask you 8,000 questions. I couldn't have done it without either of you.

To Christina, Marissa and Shelby, thank you for being my original beta-readers and pushing me to finally write a book. You encouraged me to take that leap of faith and I'm thankful everyday that you did.

To my beta-readers, thank you for letting me pick your brains and for offering you honest opinions on the very rough beginnings of this book. Your thoughts and comments made it everything it is today.

To every person who has ever asked questions about this journey, been excited or interested in me writing a book thank you. Knowing that there is a whole community of people supporting me has made this scary journey a little more doable.

Last but certainly not least, thank you to the professionals (editors, cover designers, fellow authors, etc.) who allowed me to ask a million question and helped me get to the point I am at today. It is kind people like you who are willing to share their knowledge and skills that helped me make my dream of publishing a novel reality.

About the Author

Paige Fieldsted lives in Utah with her husband, son Mason and Willy the pug. She has been writing for as long as she can remember and eventually pursued a career in journalism before leaving her job as a reporter for a job in communications, where the hours aren't as long and the stress isn't as high. When she's not writing or working, Paige loves watching sports, especially football, cooking, having impromptu dance parties in the kitchen with her toddler, singing loudly in the car and reading.

Find Paige on Social Media

Website- paigefieldsted.com
Twitter- @paigefieldsted
Instagram- @paigefieldsted
Facebook- @paigefieldstedauthor
Email- paigefieldsted@gmail.com

Manufactured by Amazon.ca
Bolton, ON

30752666R00150